PLEASE **WRITE IN BOOK**

W9-AAX-594

John A.

Due 3.29

10   12   04

11   01

02   18
08   18

04
05   03

15   11

13
09

16

Freeport Public Library

314 W. Stephenson
Freeport, IL 61032
815-233-3000

The
Lost Bird

G·K
Hall
&Cº.

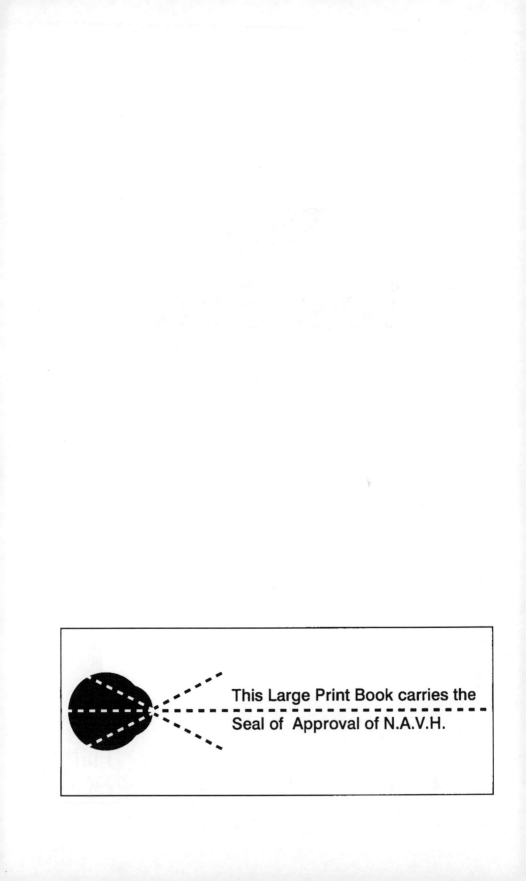

This Large Print Book carries the
Seal of Approval of N.A.V.H.

The
Lost Bird

Margaret Coel

G.K. Hall & Co. • **Thorndike, Maine**

Published in 2000 by arrangement with The Berkley Publishing Group, a division of Penguin Putnam Inc.

G.K. Hall Large Print Core Series.

The text of this Large Print edition is unabridged.
Other aspects of the book may vary from the original edition.

Set in 16 pt. Plantin by Al Chase.

Printed in the United States on permanent paper.

Library of Congress Cataloging-in-Publication Data

Coel, Margaret, 1937–
    The lost bird / Margaret Coel.
      p.   cm.
    ISBN 0-7838-8958-5 (lg. print : hc : alk. paper)
    1. O'Malley, John (Fictitious character) — Fiction. 2. Holden, Vicky (Fictitious character) — Fiction. 3. Indians of North America — Wyoming — Fiction. 4. Wind River Indian Reservation (Wyo.) — Fiction. 5. Arapaho Indians — Fiction. 6. Large type books.
I. Title.
PS3553.O347 L67 2000
813′.54—dc21   99-059552

For Bill, who should have been here

ACKNOWLEDGMENTS

The author wishes to thank the following people: Richard Frisque, professor of molecular virology, Penn State University; Bill Rankin, adoption consultant, Department of Family Services, State of Wyoming; Gary Beach, administrator, Water Quality, State of Wyoming; Lonnie Cox, FBI agent, Riverton, Wyoming; Tom Pruett, MD, Lander, Wyoming; and Sid Vinall, MD, Joan Reid, adoption attorney, Judge Sheila Carrigan, and Phil Miller, assistant district attorney, all of Boulder, Colorado; Dr. Virginia Sutter, member of the Arapaho tribe; Anthony Short, S.J.; Beverly Carrigan; George and Kristin Coel; and authors Ann Ripley, Sybil Downing, and Karen Gilleland.

Listen . . .
All you creatures
  under the ground,
All you creatures
  above the ground
  and in the waters.
May our boys and girls,
  our children of all ages . . .
May they increase
  and be strengthened.

Arapaho prayer

1

He was late.

Father John Aloysius O'Malley stopped the Toyota pickup behind the yellow school bus. The red lights flashed into the afternoon sun. A glance at his watch confirmed what he already knew. It was nearly half-past three, and twenty Arapaho kids would be in Eagle Hall waiting for confirmation class to begin. He should have gotten back to St. Francis Mission thirty minutes ago. The quiet melody of "Si, Mi chiamano Mimi" rose from the tape player on the seat beside him, punctuating his growing impatience as he watched the red lights. *Blink. Blink. Blink.*

Ahead the road butted into Circle Drive, which curved around the mission grounds, past the red-brick residence, the old school, the white church with the steeple framed against the sky, the yellow administration building, and, almost out of view behind the building, Eagle Hall. Beyond the grounds the flat, open plains of the Wind River Reservation stretched like sheets of burnished copper under the clear-rinsed blue sky. It was the last Monday in September, the Moon of the Drying Grasses, in the Arapaho way of marking time.

Shouts of laughter broke the quiet as kids jammed together to board the bus. Other kids were still straggling out of the red-brick Bureau of Indian Affairs school building with the white stucco entrance shaped like a tepee. A group of boys about thirteen years old started for the pickup. "You're late, Father," one called.

"Where ya been, Father?" Another voice. Brown faces pressed through the open windows.

Father John gave them a wave. He'd been at Riverton Memorial Hospital visiting Cyrus Elk. He'd anointed the old man last week, after doctors had informed the family that he was dying. But Cyrus was still hanging on. There was a day to die, Arapahos believed, and Cyrus's day had not yet come. This afternoon, as Father John sat at Cyrus's bedside and listened to the labored breaths and unintelligible sounds that burst forth, like forgotten, half-formed thoughts, he'd had the sense that the man was trying to tell him something, and that if he could only form the words, his spirit could depart.

At one point Cyrus had looked at him out of milky-brown eyes and called him Father Joseph, the only distinct words he had spoken. Father John had made a mental note to ask his temporary assistant, Father Joseph Keenan, to stop by the hospital. The seventy-two-year-old priest had been at St. Francis only two weeks, but, for a short while in the 1960s, Father Joseph had been the pastor here. He and Cyrus could have known each other. Maybe seeing an old friend would help the Indian unlock the words binding his spirit to the earth.

By the time Father John drove out of the hospital parking lot, he knew that even if he ran every red light on Riverton's main street, he would be late for confirmation class. He'd been teaching the class since mid-August, scheduling it around the games and practices of the Eagles, the baseball team he had started for the Arapaho kids during his first summer at St. Francis seven years ago. In less than two weeks the bishop would arrive for confirmation. He would question every candidate. And no matter what fastballs he might throw — What are the sacraments? What is the Eucharist? — Father John was determined his kids were going to hit home runs.

"You gonna cancel class today, Father?" the first boy asked. A wide smile exposed teeth too large for his face.

"Tell you what," Father John said, "if you guys beat me to Eagle Hall, I'm going to let the class out on time." The red lights flashed off; the bus started to pull into the road.

"All right!" the boy shouted. He and the others broke into a run through the cottonwoods that bordered the road, scooping up piles of leaves and tossing them into the air as they ran. The crackle of leaves mingled with the sounds of laughter.

Father John inched the pickup alongside a group of girls walking ahead. He tapped on the horn. Heads swung around, hands shot out as the girls pulled one another to the side of the road. "Hurry up, girls," he called. "You're late."

11

"You're the one that's late, Father!" they shouted. Laughter rippled over the sound of tires scrunching gravel. As he turned onto Circle Drive, he spotted the blue Escort parked at the far side of the administration building. Father Joseph was back. He had left early that morning to visit parishioners, but nothing was close on the reservation. Homes of parishioners stood thirty, forty miles apart. Father John was glad the older priest had finished the visits before the warm, sunny day had drifted into the biting coolness of an autumn evening.

He left the Toyota alongside the Escort and bounded up the concrete steps to the front entrance. The jangling sounds of a phone filtered from inside. By the time he'd flung open the heavy wood door and crossed the corridor to his office on the right, the ringing had stopped. He rifled hurriedly through the papers on his desk, half aware of Father Joseph's low, cultured voice in the next office: "Yes, yes, of course." A long pause, followed by a reassuring, "I'll come right away."

Father John slipped his class notes into a folder and lifted his Bible from the bookshelves behind the desk. The kids were probably tearing through Eagle Hall by now. It would take fifteen minutes of class time to settle them down. He started across the office just as the older priest appeared in the doorway. A slight man, half a head shorter than Father John's almost six feet, four inches, he had an angular, intelligent face

12

and a forehead that rose into thin, sand-colored hair. He wore thick, steel-rimmed glasses that gave him the owlish look of a philosophy professor accustomed to peering at scholarly texts in university libraries, which is what he had been doing until a heart attack last spring had forced him into retirement.

Three weeks ago, the Jesuit Provincial had called to say he'd found someone to help out temporarily at St. Francis. "You've heard of Joseph Keenan?" he'd asked, a tone that suggested he didn't expect an answer.

Father John had heard of the man: scholar and philosopher; on the faculty at various times at Marquette and Georgetown and Boston College, even at the Gregorian University in Rome. Author of a number of weighty philosophical treatises that Father John knew he would never get around to reading. But lately he hadn't seen anything about Joseph Keenan in the Jesuit newspapers.

"What's he been doing?"

"Some health problems." The Provincial had hurried on. "Look, John, it's Joe Keenan or nobody. Could be a while before I find a permanent man."

Could be never, Father John had thought. There weren't a lot of priests clamoring for an assignment on an Indian reservation in the middle of Wyoming. It was the last place he had expected to find himself, back when he was teaching American history at a Jesuit prep school

13

in Boston and dreaming of teaching at a university himself someday. But something had intervened, canceled his plans. He thought of that time in terms of a fall — his fall into alcoholism. After spending the best part of a year in treatment at Grace House, he'd been eager to return to work, but no Jesuit superior had returned his calls. A recovering alcoholic? Always a worry. You never knew when . . .

And then the call had come from Father Peter, the pastor at St. Francis Mission. A mission to the Arapahos. Father John knew little about the tribe. A name in history books. One of the Plains Indian tribes? On a reservation where? And he'd never imagined himself doing mission work. But it was a job. A temporary job. Until he could prove himself, redeem himself in the eyes of his superiors. He had boarded a plane and flown to Wyoming, staring for the last hour of the trip at the endless expanse of plains below. Three years later Father Peter had retired, and he'd become the pastor.

Now, with religious and adult education classes, Alcoholics Anonymous and counseling groups, and dozens of other programs under way for the fall, he was in the same position Father Peter had been in. He needed help.

But when Joseph Keenan had stepped out of the blue Escort, Father John had wondered how much help the retired scholar would be. He seemed robust — firm handshake, purposeful stride — but a deep tiredness shadowed his eyes, as if he had long labored under a crushing weight: the academic meetings attended and books written, the thousands of student projects evaluated. That first evening over dinner at the round oak table in the kitchen at the residence, he had mentioned his brush with death, his bypass surgery. "Guess the good Lord doesn't need another windbag philosophy professor," he said, throwing back his head and giving a brittle laugh, as if, by the choice of his profession, he'd played a clever joke on death.

When he reminisced about St. Francis Mission, a faraway look had come into his eyes. So many changes in the last thirty-five years: new people, more traffic. Hardly the quiet backwater he remembered. He was eager to take on his share of the work now, he'd said. He was as good as new — "surgeons work miracles these days."

Father John worried about the man. He'd tried to give him the least tiring jobs — visiting with the elders at the senior center, saying the Saturday-evening Mass, the shortest Mass. Still, Joseph Keenan spent most days driving around the reservation. Renewing acquaintances, rekindling friendships, Father John had assumed. The tiredness had taken up permanent residence in the old man's eyes.

It was there now as Father Joseph stepped into the office. "I just received an emergency call." A note of sympathy rang in his voice. "Annie Lewis is dying."

Father John stared at the other priest. "Who?"

15

"Surely no one expects the pastor to know all of his parishioners." Father Joseph waved a thin hand, as if to dismiss an impertinent question. "The poor woman's son called. Says the cancer will most likely take her tonight, and she's anxious to receive the last sacrament. They live on Thunder Lane. I'm going over there." He turned into the corridor.

Father John followed. Thunder Lane was a deserted stretch of road that snaked along the foothills of the Wind River mountains at the far western edge of the reservation. Only a few families lived out there; he knew them all. No one by the name of Lewis.

"What's the son's name?" he asked.

Father Joseph glanced over one shoulder. "I don't believe he gave a name, poor man. His only concern is his mother."

But if she's dying, Father John thought, *why did he wait until the last minute to call a priest?* He held the door and waited until the older man stepped onto the stoop before following. "It's an hour's drive," he said.

"It must be done." Father Joseph started down the steps.

Father John hurried after him. "I'll drive over to Thunder Lane after class." The old priest had probably covered a couple of hundred miles today. Often in the afternoons, he disappeared for an hour or so — a much-needed nap in the residence, Father John suspected. But there probably hadn't been time to rest this afternoon,

16

and Father John could see the exhaustion in the slump of the other man's shoulders, the flat-footed, deliberate way in which he moved past the red Toyota pickup toward the Escort.

Suddenly Father Joseph turned toward him. "Perhaps you believe I'm too infirm to take this call. Perhaps you believe I'm the one on the deathbed."

"Of course not. But surely the woman will live a few hours."

"Suppose she doesn't? Would you forgive yourself? A dying woman longing for the last comforts of the Church?"

Father John drew in a long breath. "You've been out most of the day, Joseph. Let me take the call. You can teach the confirmation class." He held out the folder and Bible. "My notes are here. I've marked the Bible passages I want to discuss with the kids."

A startled look came into the other priest's eyes. Hands rose in protest, lips moved word-lessly. Before he could speak, Father John thrust the folder and book at him. "Take the class, Joseph. I'll go."

17

2

Vicky Holden hurried up the outside stairs that led from the parking lot to her second-floor law office on Lander's main street. She let herself through the back door, dropped her briefcase onto her desk, and crossed to the window. Jiggling the frame until it clicked into track, she tugged the window open several inches. A hot, dry breeze flapped at the papers on the desk and on the filing cabinet, chasing the afternoon stuffiness from the small office.

Slipping into her chair, she snapped open the briefcase and extracted a legal pad. She had spent the last three hours taking depositions at another lawyer's office a few blocks away. Her client, Sam Eagle Hawk, alleged that the Custom Garage had fired him — the garage body man for twenty-five years — because he was Indian. She had wanted to believe her client, but something nagged at her. If Sam was fired because he was Indian, why hadn't he been fired years ago?

Then, in the deposition, the owner had mentioned something about Sam not relating to younger customers with new, expensive cars.

"Could you explain?" Vicky had kept her voice steady — a simple request for clarification.

"Well, it's no secret, Sam's a lot older."

"A lot older?" She had jumped on the statement. "And eligible for retirement benefits in a couple of years, isn't that a fact?"

The man's eyes went dull with discomfort. There were several rapid blinks, nervous snorts of laughter.

"Isn't that a fact?"

Looking down, studying his boots, the garage owner had conceded that yes, that was a fact.

It was then she delivered the lethal thrust: "Which is why you fired him. Isn't that a fact?"

The owner had sputtered and hedged, attempting to recall his own words. But they had been spoken; they existed. Truth had a way of bursting forth, and now it was on the record.

She expected to receive a settlement offer tomorrow. Before she left the office that afternoon, she intended to go over the numbers: what constituted a fair settlement for a twenty-five-year employee, unjustly fired and deprived of retirement benefits?

As she flipped through her notes, she heard a small scuffling noise, like a chair scraping the floor in the outer office. She glanced at her watch. Five-thirty. She'd assumed that Laola White Plume, her secretary, had already left. She should have locked the front door.

Vicky got to her feet as the door to the outer office flung open. Laola slipped inside. Pushing the door behind her, she leaned against the panels. Little beads of perspiration sprinkled her nose, as if she'd just come in from the rain. Her dark eyes were blazing. "You're not gonna believe who's out there," she said in a whisper of excitement.

Ben, Vicky thought. She could feel her stomach muscles tighten. There was always excitement in the secretary's voice when she passed on a message that Vicky's ex-husband had called. But women always found Ben exciting. He'd called several times last week, and Vicky had managed to put him off: So much work staring at her. A full schedule. Clients to meet. All true. She put in long days at the office. She was grateful for an occasional quiet evening at home. And she didn't want Ben back in her life.

"Who is it?" she asked matter-of-factly.

Laola started toward the desk. Dressed in a sleeveless blouse and short, too tight skirt that revealed her long, brown legs, she looked like the new high-school graduate she'd been last spring when Vicky hired her. Leaning over the desk, as if to confide a secret to her best friend, she whispered, "Sharon David."

"Who?" Vicky searched for a face to fill out the name.

"*The Sky People. The Cowgirls. Ranger Woman.*" Laola emphasized each syllable. "She got the nomination for an Academy Award for *Ranger Woman.* Should have gotten the Oscar, too."

Vicky held the secretary's eyes. "Are you sure it's Sharon David?"

Laola nodded so hard, her shoulders shook.

"Can you believe it? A movie star! Waiting to see you." She flung one arm toward the closed door.

Silently Vicky ticked off the possible scenarios that might bring a Hollywood star to a one-woman law office in Lander, Wyoming. Purchase some real estate in the area, perhaps a ranch. Scout the location for a movie. Neither explanation made sense. Sharon David would have her own lawyers and a phalanx of other people to handle such matters. She said, "Ask her to come in."

Laola swung around and let herself through the door. In an instant she returned, ushering in a tall, striking-looking woman. Vicky realized the billboards and movie screens didn't do Sharon David justice. She crossed the office with the grace and self-possession of a star moving onto center stage. Pale blue dress flowing about the straps of her high-heeled sandals, suede bag the color of honey draping from one shoulder. Tied around her head was a dark blue scarf that held her black hair back from her face, emphasizing the prominent cheekbones, the dark, almond-shaped eyes, and the golden brown cast of her skin. Her nose was small and came to a perfect point; the lips surprisingly full and a deep red color, like that of her square-tipped nails. She was in her mid-thirties, Vicky decided, only six or seven years younger than herself. She might be Asian or Middle Eastern. Yet there was something about her, some indescribable way of being. Sharon David was Indian.

21

Vicky reached across the desk and shook the movie star's hand. Her grip was firm and determined. "What brings you to Lander, Miss David?" She motioned the actress to one of the twin barrel-shaped chairs arranged in front of the desk.

"Will you need me for anything?" Laola sounded hopeful.

"I don't believe so." Vicky took her own chair, aware of Sharon David's eyes watching her, taking her measure. There was a tenseness about the woman.

At the sound of the door closing, the actress seemed to relax. "Call me Sharon," she said. "I'd like to call you Vicky. I hope we're going to be friends." She paused, then hurried on: "I feel that I've come home." The words were barely a whisper, but so clear, Vicky thought, that patrons in the last row of a theater could have caught the line.

Vicky sat back against the leather cushion of her chair and studied the woman across from her. This was not home. The newspapers and television would never have stopped reminding people that a local Indian girl had made good in Hollywood. There would have been stories about every movie, every appearance on *The Tonight Show*, every scandal. In the quiet that settled over the office, she realized the next line was hers. "How can I help you?"

The actress cleared her throat, a quick, impatient sound, as if the previous lines had been blown and it was necessary to begin again. "I want you to find my parents." A smile tinged with sadness started at the corners of the red lips. "Does that surprise you? A movie actress searching for her biological parents, trying to find where she belongs, who she really is?"

Vicky said nothing. She was struck by the irony: a woman known to millions, yet unknown to herself.

Suddenly Sharon propelled herself out of the chair and stepped over to the window. She stared outside a long moment then turned back. Every action, Vicky thought, calculated for dramatic effect.

"What about this?" Sharon David might have been pitching a script. "Parents claim child is their own. 'But why is my hair black?' child wants to know. 'Why do I have brown skin?'

" 'You're just like Great-uncle Al,' parents explain. 'Just like Aunt so-and-so or Cousin we-forgot-her-name. They had black hair and dark skin, like you. You're our only child, and we love you just as you are. So don't ask any more questions.' "

Sharon let out a long sigh as she strolled across the room and sank into the chair. "No child could have asked for a better home," she said. "But at night, before I went to bed, I used to stare at the brown face and dark eyes in the mirror. I knew the home wasn't mine. My home was somewhere else . . ."

The actress's voice trailed off, and her gaze

shifted to some point beyond Vicky's shoulder. After a moment she said, "I had decided long ago not to try to find my birth parents as long as my adoptive parents were alive. I didn't want to hurt them. Besides" — a quick shrug — "I was caught up in my career, which took off like a hot air balloon and surprised everybody, me most of all. So I rode with it. Why not? I told myself it didn't matter who I really was or where I came from because I had everything — money, fame, more men than I needed."

She gave a little laugh and raised one hand. The red-tipped fingers smoothed back the blue scarf. "I was kidding myself. There wasn't enough money or fame, not even enough men, to fill up the emptiness or drive away the sense of abandonment. I knew someday I would have to find the truth." Drawing in a long breath, she seemed to consider the next line. Then she said, "My father died five years ago. Last spring, when my mother died, I knew the time had come to find my real home, so I sat down and had a long heart-to-heart with my aunt. She was reluctant to tell me the truth at first. But she understood I wasn't going to give up, and eventually she admitted my parents had been unable to have a child. I was adopted from the Loving Care Adoption Agency."

Vicky was quiet a moment, allowing the sacred information the woman had just divulged — the most important fact of her life — to settle in the air. Finally she said, "What makes you think you came from here?"

Sharon David lifted the flap on the suede bag and extracted a small, brown envelope, which she handed across the desk. "I found this in my parents' safety-deposit box."

Vicky took the envelope and shook out two papers. One was a folded, cream-colored sheet of stationery. The other, a birth certificate for Sharon Marie David. An amended certificate, Vicky realized, issued by the court that had granted the adoption. It constituted a new identity, new parents. Mother: Isabel Mackey David. Father: Robert David. Date of birth: December 24, 1964. Place: San Diego Hospital. Race: Caucasian. An undecipherable signature scrawled over the words *attending physician*. Vicky glanced up.

"It's not true." Sharon spoke hurriedly, as if to forestall any objection. "None of it is true. I'm not white. They aren't my biological parents. And that isn't my birthday. The real information is there." She nodded toward the cream-colored sheet.

Vicky pulled the sheet toward her. It felt fragile in her hands, as if it might break along the creases. Carefully she began unfolding it. There was a small line of writing: *91464 WRR Maisie*. Beside it was the figure of a bird, wings poised in flight.

"The numbers could be my birth date, September fourteenth, 1964," the actress said. "I always believed I was born the day before

Christmas. 'You were our best gift,' my parents told me. But my aunt told me the truth. My parents had gotten me from the Loving Care Adoption Agency on Christmas Eve. I was three months old."

She squared her shoulders and tilted her head thoughtfully. "I'm certain the rest also refers to my birth. WRR stands for Wind River Reservation. Maisie could be my mother's name. Maybe she had something to do with birds."

Vicky glanced again at the notation. "WRR could stand for Women Reach for Recovery. Wyoming Research and Reclamation. Probably a dozen other organizations." She slipped the paper and certificate into the envelope and pushed it across the desk.

The actress shook her head. "When I learned the initials could stand for the reservation, everything fell into place. The little girl with black hair and dark skin finally knew where her home was. Naturally I turned the matter over to my lawyers."

She set both hands on the armrests, rose out of the chair, and walked again to the window. She stared outside a moment, then turned slowly. The afternoon light blinked in the glass behind her. "Nothing but dead ends everywhere they turned. The San Diego Hospital has been closed for twenty years. And there are no records for a Loving Care Adoption Agency. Not unusual, my lawyers said. Some agencies at the time were nothing more than well-meaning individuals trying to find good homes for unwanted children. They stayed open awhile, then closed. Sometimes they weren't even licensed."

The actress drew in a long breath before going on: "They listed me with reunion registries throughout the country. Discreetly, of course. 'Woman born in Wyoming, September 14, 1964, possibly Native American, seeking biological parents.' That sort of thing. They ran ads in magazines and newspapers for searchers looking for their biological families. They tried the Bureau of Indian Affairs. Unfortunately the law that requires states to notify the bureau of any Native American children adopted to outsiders was passed long after I was adopted."

The woman strolled back to the chair and gripped the top. "Of course my lawyers tried the official channels in Wyoming. Adoption records are sealed here. I could be dying from some genetic disease, and the bureaucrats still couldn't release what they call 'identifying information.' And all the while the same bureaucrats are staring at my records." A mixture of discouragement and contempt came into her voice. "Complete strangers know the most personal details about me — the names of my parents. But I'm prohibited from knowing."

Vicky nodded. It was true, but there were reasons for such laws. Not every biological parent or every adopted child wanted to be found. It was a road of minefields that had to be carefully tread. She said, "Wyoming allows confidential intermediaries to search through sealed birth certificates and hospital and adoption-agency records."

Sharon David nodded. "The court in Cheyenne appointed an intermediary. Another stranger with the right to look into my life." The red nails tapped an impatient rhythm on top of the chair. "The intermediary couldn't find any records for an infant girl born September fourteenth, 1964, and placed for adoption. A year of searching, and absolutely nothing."

The actress moved around the barrel curve of the chair and sat down. Vicky drew in a long breath and leaned forward. "Sharon, what do you want from me?"

The other woman sat as motionless as a piece of sculpture, her gaze steady and hard. "I told you. I want you to find my parents."

"Your lawyers have already —"

"You're Arapaho," Sharon David said hurriedly. "You can talk to people on the reservation."

"I'm going to be perfectly frank," Vicky said. "It's highly unlikely you were adopted from this reservation. Arapaho people don't adopt children to outsiders."

"Some young woman, pregnant and alone . . ." A note of desperation crept into the woman's voice.

"Her own mother would care for the child," Vicky said. "Or a sister or aunt or cousin would adopt the child. No one would want to lose the child." Vicky clasped her hands on the desk. Keeping her voice soft, hoping to allay the woman's disappointment, she said, "You must understand. There were periods in the Old Time when we lost our children. They died of hunger and disease. They were killed by soldiers attacking the villages. Sometimes they were stolen and taken to white towns. They often died trying to find their way back to the people. When we went on the reservation, our children were taken from us and sent to government schools a thousand miles away. They got sick. Many died. Often those who survived were never able to return home. Their families never saw them again. We have always had to fight for our own children. No Arapaho family would give up a child."

Quiet seeped through the office, muffling the sounds of going-home traffic outside. After a moment Sharon said, "I might be Shoshone." Her gaze remained steady. Beneath the blank expression was a barely perceptible effort of control.

Vicky sat back, studying the woman. There was no hint of the soft, fleshy features, the light skin of the Shoshone people who lived in the northern part of the reservation. They were mountain people, sheepherders, not Plains Indians, who had followed the buffalo under the sun like the Arapahos. "It wouldn't matter," she said finally. "Indian people feel the same about adopting children to outsiders."

The actress leaned forward and slammed one fist against the edge of the desk. "Look at me, Vicky. I'm Indian like you. I could be your sister. You've got to help me find the people I belong to."

Vicky kept her eyes on the woman for a long moment, then glanced toward the window. Splotches of clouds clung to the sky, like globs of white paint flung onto a blue canvas. From the moment Sharon David had walked into her office, Vicky had sensed an inexplicable kinship, like an invisible cloud between them. Sharon David was Arapaho. She could feel the truth of it. Perhaps the unthinkable had occurred. Perhaps thirty-five years ago a young, pregnant woman on the reservation had believed she had nowhere to turn. She might have gone to Casper or Cheyenne to have her baby. She could have placed the child privately for adoption.

Bringing her gaze back to the woman across from her, Vicky said, "I'll make some inquiries."

The actress pulled back the flap of her bag and produced a gold pen and leather-sheathed checkbook. Snapping open the cover, she began writing. Then she got to her feet and laid a check on the desk.

"I knew you would help me," she said. "I don't want any publicity. You understand the public thinks it has a right to my business. I hope I can trust you to be discreet."

Vicky glanced at the amount on the check. The actress must have mistakenly added an extra zero. Then she realized the zeros were correct. She looked up. "I can't accept this."

"I'll pay whatever it takes to find my family," Sharon said. "You can reach me at the Hell's Corner Dude Ranch."

The afternoon was beginning to gather into dusk when Vicky left the office. Long, gray shadows swept down the brick building and chilled the parking lot, but the Bronco still held the day's warmth. She switched on the ignition, let the windows down, and tuned in her favorite country music station. Her thoughts were on the famous movie star who seemed so lost. Sharon David had hurried out of the office, past Laola bubbling about how great she was in *Ranger Woman*, how she should have won the Academy Award. The moment the actress was gone, Laola had stuck her head around the door to say she was also leaving.

"We'd better keep this quiet," Vicky told her.

The girl's face fell, and Vicky knew that ten minutes after Laola had walked out the door, the news would have been flashed over the moccasin telegraph to every house on the reservation: Sharon David here looking for her Arapaho family! Not news Vicky wanted bantered about; not if she wanted to keep her own inquiries discreet.

After Laola left, Vicky had spent the best part of an hour checking the figures for Sam's settlement and jotting down notes on the interview with Sharon David. The idea of an Arapaho woman giving up her child had begun to seem even more preposterous. She should have told the actress any further inquiries would be a waste of time. But she hadn't. The amount on the check had stopped her objections. An amount large enough to pay Laola's salary for several months with some left over for other office expenses. An amount large enough to calm her ongoing fears about keeping the office open. She was going to have to earn the retainer fee.

Now Reba McEntire's voice spilled through the Bronco as Vicky pulled out of the parking lot and joined the evening traffic moving past the flat-roofed, brick buildings on Main Street. The leaves on the aspen trees that dotted the sidewalk shimmered a deep amber color in the graying light.

She drew up at a stoplight, her mind still on the unexpected new client. Sharon David. Arapaho. What would the press make of it, if the news ever came out?

Suddenly the Reba McEntire song stopped. A man's voice came on: "We bring you this late-breaking story from our news bureau. A homicide has just been reported on the Wind River Reservation. A man was shot this afternoon as he emerged from a red Toyota pickup on Thunder Lane. The victim has not yet been identified, but a spokesman at the Wind River police headquarters confirms the victim was a priest at St. Francis Mission."

3

Vicky felt as if an unseen force had hurtled through the atmosphere and reconfigured the world. The stretch of asphalt ahead, the trucks and cars at the curb, the brick buildings beyond the sidewalk — everything melted into the shadows, into a gray blur. The radio voice droned on, background noise with no meaning. Somewhere a horn was honking. Tires squealed as a pickup jerked past, the driver shaking his fist and shouting through the open window. She struggled for her breath, a hard lump in her chest, unable to think where she had been going, what she had been doing when the earth had spun out of orbit.

Gradually the realization came over her, like a slow-burning fever, that the light had turned green. She sat holding on to the steering wheel, a frail grip on reality. Finally she managed to inch the Bronco around the corner and alongside the curb. The tears were coming now, warm on her cheek, salty on her lips. She continued to grip the wheel, trying to still her shaking, to stop the earth from rumbling beneath her. John O'Malley dead! "No!" she cried. Her voice sounded strange and disconnected over the growl of the engine, the music pouring from the radio. "It can't be!"

Memories flooded over her, a strong current that bore her along. She had no will to resist.

John O'Malley meeting her at the juvenile detention center to help some kid picked up for disturbing the peace or reckless driving; sitting across from her and discussing the best way to help some single mother keep her child; leading the prayers at a wake in Blue Sky Hall; striding across the grounds at St. Francis Mission, suddenly looking up as she stepped out of the Bronco. The familiar smile that broke across his face whenever his eyes fell on her.

She had met him nearly four years ago — yesterday, it seemed. She'd opened her law office two weeks before. No matter what advice she gave, her first clients had looked away, stared out the window, or studied their boots and wondered out loud what Father John would say. She'd decided to drive over to St. Francis Mission to meet the man who had woven such a spell over her people.

She'd arrived unannounced. The door to his office in the administration building stood open; he sat at a desk across the small room, head bent over a clutter of papers. At first she thought he was ignoring her. She rapped on the pebbly glass, a sound of impatience. He'd looked up instantly, then jackknifed to his feet. She was surprised at how tall he was — about six-feet-four, she guessed — but there was something graceful and well put together about him: broad shoulders that filled out the plaid shirt, whose sleeves were rolled up just below his elbows; muscular forearms sprinkled with freckles; large hands with long, slender fingers.

He was younger than she had expected, somewhere in his early forties, and handsome in a way that suggested he was unaware of the fact. His hair was red, fading into blond, with a few gray specks at the temples. He had light blue eyes that seemed to take her in at first glance. She was used to men looking at her; she was aware of the appraisals, the sly smiles. But she felt as if John O'Malley had seen into the lonely, private place inside her.

"You don't know me," she'd blurted, realizing it wasn't quite true.

"Come in." His smile was open and welcoming.

She had known as she walked across the office and extended her hand that they would be friends. His grip was warm and strong, and she had allowed her hand to stay in his a moment. Then he had stepped around the desk and, with one hand, swung a straight-backed chair close to the corner. He waited until she sat down before returning to his own chair. They had talked for the best part of an hour. At one point he'd stepped over to the coffeepot on a metal table near the door, filled two mugs, and handed her one. Then he'd sat down again, sipping at his coffee, listening as she babbled on. She had done most of the talking, she had realized even then, although she couldn't remember now what she had talked about. Only that she could talk to this man, that he was listening.

Now she realized that she had been drawn to him at that first meeting. Her feelings had been sudden and sure, like a thunderstorm rising over the mountains. Not, as she'd always thought, a gradual unfolding in the hours and days they had spent together helping people through divorces and deaths, even trying to prove a young man innocent of murdering his uncle and stopping the construction of a nuclear waste facility on the reservation. John O'Malley was the man she had turned to when she had to rescue Susan, her twenty-one-year-old daughter, from drug dealers.

Lawyer. Counselor. They made a good team. But he was a priest, a fact she respected and never forgot. She'd tried to hide her feelings and ignore the growing sense he was doing the same. They had arrived at a mutual, unstated resolve: they never called each other, they never met, unless there was a legitimate reason — someone who needed their help. Months had passed when they hadn't seen each other.

Months, she thought now, sobbing silently. Precious lost time they might have been together. She should have told him how she felt, that he was the man who filled her thoughts. But she had never told him. And now . . . now he was dead. She dug through the black bag on the seat beside her until her fingers closed over a wad of tissues, which she dabbed at her eyes. The blur beyond the windshield gave way to the shapes of passing cars and trucks, the dim glow of headlights. Pulling on the wheel, she made a sharp U-turn and slid back into the traffic heading north, her reflexes on automatic.

She caught Highway 789 and drove on, slowing through Hudson, speeding up as the restaurants and small houses dropped behind. Automatic. Automatic. Soon she was plunging through the graying dusk. Headlights swept over the asphalt ahead and, all around, the sky dipped into the earth, like an inverted bowl of blue-black glass. On she drove, ignoring the passing trucks and cars, the pickup that swung around her, tires squealing, her entire being collapsed into a pinprick of necessity. She had to go to him.

She took a left at Arapaho Crossing, accelerating in front of an oncoming semi, its horn bellowing like the cry of a mad bull. On Seventeen-Mile Road, she passed the mission cemetery sprawled on top of a dark bluff and began sobbing again, wiping at her eyes with one hand, steering the Bronco down the narrow road with the other. A line of pickups and cars were stopped ahead, waiting to turn in to the mission, and Vicky slowed behind them. With a fist at her mouth to quiet the sobs, she followed the red taillights onto the narrow, straight road lined with cottonwoods. Branches arched across the asphalt, forming a tunnel of darkening gold.

In the headlights Vicky could make out the forms of cars and pickups parked around the mission grounds, the groups of people hovering in front of the church and walking toward the residence. She parked in front, next to a brown pickup, and hurried up the sidewalk, passing several grandmothers — a parade of mourners — carrying casserole dishes and platters of cakes. Lying next to the sidewalk was Walks-On, the golden retriever Father John had found in a ditch and rushed to the vet. The dog had lost a hind leg, but he could run and fetch and snatch a disk from the air. Now the red disk lay beside him.

The front door stood open as she came up the cement steps. People drifted past the shadows of the entry, moving through a hushed murmur of grief. As Vicky stepped inside, she saw Elena talking to a group of elders in the living room that opened on the right. Catching her eye, the housekeeper came toward her. In the dim light, the woman looked older than her seventy years, her face creased in shock and confusion. Strands of gray hair sprang from a series of bobby pins, as if she'd forgotten to smooth them into place.

The irony swept over Vicky like a cold wind. Elena never forgot anything that had to do with taking care of the priests at St. Francis Mission, which she had done for more years than anyone could remember. So many priests through the years to cook and clean for, look after, mother. They had come and gone, but she had remained, taking in the next priest the Provincial sent, training him in the routine: breakfast at eight, lunch at noon, dinner at six. There was a day for everything — laundry on Mondays, cleaning on

Tuesdays. Everyone on the reservation knew that Elena expected the priests to stay in step and that John O'Malley was almost never in step.

She put her arms around the housekeeper, trying to comfort herself by holding the old woman who had known him so well, had spent every day in his house, had loved him like a son.

"Oh, Vicky." Elena pulled back and swiped at her eyes with a thick wad of tissues. "He was a good man. He didn't deserve to die out in the road like a dog."

"Where is he?" Vicky heard her own voice, distant and disembodied against the sounds of grandmothers coming through the door, the hushed conversations in the living room, and people shuffling through the hall to the kitchen.

Elena nodded toward the closed door on the other side of the entry. "You'll wanna go in the study," she said. "Chief Banner and that fed, what's his name, Ted Gianelli, are gonna want to see you."

Vicky gave the door a soft knock before pushing it open. As she stepped inside, the room seemed to fall away: the desk with papers and books tumbling over the surface and the Bureau of Indian Affairs police chief perched at one corner; the bookcases stuffed with books and folders; the pair of blue wingback chairs with the FBI agent sitting in one, a polished black boot swinging into space. She shut the door and leaned back, holding on to the knob to keep from sliding to the floor, her eyes locked on the man across the room, the light from the lamp shining in his reddish-blond hair. John O'Malley.

4

Father John crossed the study and grabbed Vicky by the shoulders, fearing she would crumble to the floor. She was in shock. He knew the signs from too many trips to emergency rooms: face leached of color, eyes shiny with pain.

She stepped into his arms and buried her face against his chest. He was dimly aware of Gianelli and Banner on their feet beside them as he ran one hand over the silk of her hair, the curve of her head, his own breath mingling with the smell of her — the faint smell of sage.

"I'm sorry," he whispered into her hair, struck by the inadequacy of the words. He led her over to the nearest wingback and eased her down onto the cushion.

"I'll get some water." Banner's voice sounded behind them, followed by the click of the door opening, closing.

Father John perched on the armrest, one hand on Vicky's shoulder, aware of the rapid pace of her breathing — in-out, in-out. He was stunned by her grief. He'd had no idea she was close to Father Joseph. She must have known the priest when he was here before. She couldn't have been more than seven or eight years old, a second-grader in the mission school. But her family might have adopted the young priest. It often happened. An Arapaho family taking pity on a man stationed far from his own people, inviting him to dinner and birthday parties, making him part of their family. There was so much he didn't know about her, he thought, a lifetime of people she had loved.

The door creaked open. At the periphery of his vision, Father John saw the bulky frame of the police chief: the dark blue uniform trousers and dark blue shirt, the outstretched hand holding a glass of water. Vicky took the glass and raised it slowly to her lips. Banner stepped back toward the agent, who stood at the side of the desk, both hands stuffed into the pockets of his suit pants, red tie hanging limply down the center of his starched white shirt. The other men were like him, Father John thought, helpless at the sight of grief.

Vicky tilted her head and looked up at him with an intensity that brought the warmth into his face. She said, "I thought it was you."

The words hit him like the sting of buckshot. He got to his feet and walked back to the window. Outside a band of light lingered over the mountains, and faint streaks of yellow and red traced the dark sky. He tried to steady himself, regain his equilibrium. The pain and grief he'd seen in her eyes were for him! He had never imagined, never intended . . . *I have done this all wrong,* he thought. They could be friends, that was all. He knew his own weaknesses. He had never wanted to snare anyone else in them, and the knowledge that he had done so compounded his guilt. A woman in love with him; a murdered priest. Both should have been avoided.

He forced himself to turn back to the room. Banner was half sitting on the edge of the desk; Gianelli had dropped into the other wingback chair. They were watching him — Vicky, the two men. "It should have been me," he said.

"Don't say that!" Vicky jumped to her feet. Water spilled from the glass over her hand. "Don't ever say that."

"She's right, John." Banner swung around the desk and sat down in the leather chair behind it. Fingers curled over the armrests. "You're surmisin', John," he said. "Until we find the guy who pulled the trigger, we don't know what happened out there."

"Joseph was driving the Toyota pickup," Father John said, the words an angry staccato. "Everybody on this reservation knows I drive that Toyota. The minute Joseph stepped out, he was shot."

"Okay, okay." Gianelli scooted his bulky frame toward the front of the wingback. From his coat pocket, he pulled out the small pad he'd been writing on earlier. Then he produced a pen. "Let's stay with the facts," he said, flipping through the pad. "Father Joseph took the call around three-thirty. Right?"

"We've been over this," Father John said. He felt choked with impatience. The fed and the police chief had already knocked on the doors of the few houses out on Thunder Lane. No one

43

had seen anything. They'd gone through the mission: Father Joseph's bedroom and office, the Escort. Nothing. Gianelli had copied Joseph's computer files, which, Father John suspected, contained scholarly papers and letters and notes on mission programs. For the past forty minutes they had been in his study going over the same question: why would anyone want to kill a seventy-two-year-old priest?

"We're going over it again." Gianelli's voice was calm. The pen ran across the pad, like a mouse skittering over the floor.

Father John turned back to the window and stared at the purple shadows creeping over the grounds as the fed summarized what they'd been talking about: the caller said his mother was dying. He asked for a priest. Father Joseph agreed to go.

"That the story, John?"

Father John waited a moment before turning back. Vicky and the men were staring at him. They were his friends, the few close friends he had. An FBI agent who hailed from Quincy, next door to Boston, who knew more about opera than he did, who had four little girls and a wife who turned out steaming platters of spaghetti and ravioli; an Arapaho police chief who'd spent his life on the reservation, savvy and compassionate, with a son on the BIA police force; and Vicky. Since the first day she'd walked into his office, almost four years ago, he'd been struggling to contain his feelings for her, praying she

44

would never feel the same about him. Prayers that had gone unanswered.

He said: "The call came for me."

The fed started to protest, but Father John interrupted. "Classes and meetings start in the mid-afternoon. Anybody who knows this mission knows they can find me in the office then."

"You weren't there today." This from the police chief.

That was true. Father John glanced back at the window. "You're saying whoever made that call knows the mission routine?" Banner asked.

"I'm saying the caller thought he was talking to me."

Gianelli held up one hand. "Wait a minute . . ."

"I told you, I heard Joseph on the phone," Father John said. "He didn't give his name. The caller said what he had to say and hung up. It was a brief conversation. I shouldn't have let Joseph go."

"You're wrong, John." Vicky set the glass on the desk — a hard thump in the quiet. Then she walked across the office to him. The color had returned to her face, and her eyes were flashing. "Father Joseph answered an emergency call. He was a priest. You couldn't have stopped him."

A part of him — the logical part — knew she was right. The afternoon scene reeled across his mind, like a black-and-white film in slow motion. The incredulous look on the old man's face. *"Teach confirmation class?"* *The quick shake*

45

of the sandy-haired head. *"Surely you're not serious. I'm afraid my teaching experience is severely limited to graduate students in philosophy. What in the name of all that is good and holy would I say to a roomful of adolescents?"* The Escort door opening, the old man sliding behind the wheel. *"I shall return in time for dinner."*

Father John had started to walk away when a loud, thumping noise, like pieces of metal clanking together, erupted from the Escort. He'd turned back. The other priest was already out of the car. "It would appear my means of transportation does not wish to move from this spot," he'd said, and Father John had tucked the folder and Bible under one arm and dug the Toyota key from the pocket of his blue jeans. He'd tossed the key to Father Joseph, who reached across the hood and grabbed it out of the air. *A good catch,* Father John remembered thinking at the time. Oddly it had made him feel easier about the long drive Father Joseph had ahead of him.

He'd spent the next hour explaining the sacraments to twenty kids who probably wished they were somewhere else. He hadn't given Father Joseph another thought. Not until after class. He was heading home, and Elena was coming toward him, hands thrust forward as if to ward off some terrible evil. A chill had run through him. "What is it?" he'd called.

"Oh, Father," Elena blurted out when he reached her. Lifting her apron, she crumbled it in front of her mouth. It was difficult to understand what she was saying.

"Take a deep breath," he'd instructed, setting one hand on her shoulder. "Tell me."

And she had told him: she, kneading bread and the phone ringing. Leaving the dough on the counter and walking into the hall to pick up the phone. Chief Banner saying two patrolmen out on Thunder Lane had found Father Joseph's body next to the Toyota. Saying the old priest had been shot.

Now, in the quiet of the study, Father John realized Gianelli had asked a question and was waiting for a reply.

"I'm sorry," he said, switching his thoughts to the present.

"Father Joseph," Gianelli said. "What day did he arrive?"

Father John glanced about the room. Two weeks ago Friday? Saturday? "I don't know," he said. "He's been here about two weeks. Not long enough to make an enemy who would want to kill him." He was quiet a moment. "Father Joseph had been the pastor here in the 1960s."

"Maybe somebody's been harboring a grudge," the agent said.

"For thirty-five years? Come on, Ted." The notion seemed preposterous, beyond the bounds of logic and understanding.

"Everybody liked Father Joseph back then." The police chief tilted back in the chair and laced his fingers over his blue uniform shirt.

"I've got good memories of the man. I was just a loudmouthed, know-it-all teenage kid with long braids and a bad case of acne, but he always had time for the likes of me. Steered me and my buddies on the right road. I wouldn't be sittin' here right now, weren't for that priest."

Gianelli jotted something onto the pad. "Let's say you're right, John. Somebody intended to shoot you. Anybody real mad at you lately?"

Father John exhaled a long breath. Here it was, the question he'd been asking himself: who wanted to kill him? The drunk he'd asked to leave a meeting in Eagle Hall a couple of weeks ago? The kid he'd dressed down for bringing a joint to the teen dance last Friday? Somebody he'd counseled? He'd been striking out lately with marital counseling. Four couples had decided on divorce. Did they blame him? One of the husbands? One of the wives? He didn't have the answer.

"Any more trouble with Sonny Red Wolf?" Banner asked.

Vicky wheeled around. "What trouble?"

"Red Wolf and some of his followers held a demonstration at the mission last spring," Father John said. "They chanted and marched around with some signs."

"I can guess what the signs said." Vicky kept her eyes on his. " 'White man must go. White man off reservation. White man not wanted here.' "

Father John gave a little shrug. "Something to that effect."

The police chief got to his feet and walked around the desk. Leveling his gaze on Vicky, he said, "Red Wolf and some of his gang blocked the mission entrance out on Seventeen-Mile Road. Had to send a couple of my boys over to remind them we got trespassin' laws on the res. Ordered 'em to get their tails out of here."

"Why didn't you tell me about this, John?" Vicky asked.

"It was over in a few hours."

"It's never over with Red Wolf," Gianelli said. "It could be important. The man hates whites. All kinds and shapes. Thinks whites don't have the right to live here or anywhere else, for that matter. Wants Indians to take back the land. He and his followers stay holed up in that compound out in the foothills, stewing in their own hate."

The agent raised himself out of the wingback and stepped over to the police chief. "Red Wolf's already spent ten years at Leavenworth on a manslaughter conviction for beating a guy to death in a fight. No telling what he might have taken it into his head to do next."

Banner let out a long sigh. "My boys would've arrested him for trespassin' if John here had agreed to press charges."

"Look," Father John said. "Red Wolf held a demonstration. It doesn't mean he decided to —" He stopped. The notion seemed impossible, incomprehensible.

"Assassinate you," Vicky said, the hint of a

tremor working through her voice. The room was quiet a moment before she continued: "You're the most visible white man here, John. Killing you would make quite a statement."

Father John stared at her. It was hard to imagine that kind of hate. "Red Wolf knows he'd be a suspect. Why would he take the risk?"

"Red Wolf likes to take risks," Gianelli said. "I'll have a talk with him. Find out how he spent the afternoon."

"Hold on." Banner faced the agent. "You go walkin' into Red Wolf's compound and start askin' questions, you might want some of my boys along."

Father John understood. Homicide on a reservation was a federal matter; Gianelli was in charge. But the police chief didn't like staying in the background, not with a killer loose in his territory.

Gianelli nodded and started for the door. Then he turned back. "I want a list of names, John. Anybody else who might have a beef with you." Another start. Another halt. "One more thing. Stay out of this investigation. Keep your head down. Keep a low profile. Stay close to the mission. If the killer got the wrong priest, more than likely he'll try again. And next time . . ." He gave his head a slow shake, yanked open the door, and walked out.

The chief followed. As he closed the door, he said, "Be careful, John."

"You have no intention of doing what they

say, do you?" Vicky stood close to him, and as he turned toward her, he saw their reflections in the window — two shadowy figures against the blue gray evening outside.

"How do I know who wants me dead?"

"I mean, you're not going to stay out of the investigation."

Father John took a moment before he said, "What do you expect me to do? Wait until Joseph's murderer shows up at the mission?"

"Let me help you."

"No, Vicky," he said, surprised at the harshness in his voice. Then, a softer tone: "Stay out of this."

She said: "When I came here this afternoon, I thought you were dead. I felt as if . . ." She hesitated, then, her voice low: "I don't ever want to feel that kind of pain again." She held his eyes, and in that moment Father John had the sense that something was changing between them, that she would not return to the mission, that he might never see her again.

"I don't want to see you dead," she said, in the same hushed voice. Abruptly she turned and walked across the study. Pausing at the door, she glanced back. "Somebody on the res knows what happened this afternoon and why. I'm going to get the answers."

Before he could say anything, the door opened. The buzz of voices in the entry slipped through the opening, and she was gone, closing the door behind her. The study seemed empty, the trace of sage lingering in the air.

He drew in a long breath, trying to contain the anger and worry rising inside him. He was thirsty, and his tongue felt as dry as a piece of cracked leather in his mouth. He wanted a shot of whiskey. One shot, and he could walk into the living room whole and confident, visit with the mourners, bluff his way past the guilt that pressed down on him like hundred-pound weights.

An innocent man had died in his place. He owed the man something. He had to find out why somebody had wanted to kill him and had shot Joseph instead. Before another innocent person died.

5

The living room was filled with people: grand-mothers on the sofa, gray heads bobbing in the circle of light cast by the table lamp; elders on straight-back chairs somebody had brought from the kitchen and lined up in front of the television across the room; groups of young men standing around, black braids dangling beneath baseball caps; and two women in upholstered chairs, jostling babies on their laps. A microcosm of the reservation, Father John thought as he came through the archway. Here to mourn the death of a priest.

Several people held paper plates covered with half-eaten sandwiches, potato chips. Stacks of empty plates lay scattered over the coffee table among the books and magazines. Almost everyone had a foam cup in hand; the aroma of coffee filled the room.

One of the young men broke from the others and stepped toward him, hand outstretched. His grip was firm. "Sorry to hear about Father Joseph," he said, disbelief in his voice. The others joined in. "Sorry. Sure too bad. Real good heart, Father Joseph." A litany of condolences.

Father John made his way around the room, greeting the elders and grandmothers, shaking hands, thanking people for coming, the words like dry leaves in his mouth, his own burden of guilt heavy inside him.

One of the grandmothers, Esther Tallman, inched forward on the sofa, balancing a foam cup and a plate with remnants of crusts and chips. "I won't ever forget Father Joseph," she said, moisture pooling in her eyes.

Father John nodded.

" 'Cause he never forgot about me and Thomas. Sure, he might've gone away, but that don't mean he forgot us. Soon's he got back, he drove over to see how me and the kids was doin' now Thomas is gone. I was glad to tell him everybody's doin' okay." The woman let her eyes roam the room, remembering. "Father Joseph was real young when he first come here. Wouldn't've thought he'd spent enough time on earth to have any sense. But he helped us through hard times. So Thomas give him an Arapaho name. *Ni'ho:no'oyeihi.* Means Red Hawk. He was a good man."

Father John gave the woman a nod of understanding. Few men could be considered good in the Arapaho Way. Those who were humble and generous, who placed others before themselves.

The woman talked on. Father John hardly listened. He was thinking that for two weeks he'd lived under the same roof with a man he didn't know at all. There had been so many assistants — a parade of priests marking time, passing through on the way to more interesting and prestigious assignments. The faces blurred in his memory.

Another man passing through, Father John remembered thinking as he'd helped Joseph Keenan unload two suitcases and a couple of cardboard boxes from the Escort — the total of the man's worldly possessions. They'd talked on several occasions in the last two weeks. On a warm evening last week they had sat on the patio after dinner drinking coffee. Father John had asked about St. Francis Mission thirty-five years ago. Had Joseph's responses been noncommittal and abrupt, as he'd thought, or had he simply not taken the trouble to draw out the other priest? Had he not wanted to get to know someone who would soon be saying good-bye? There had been so many good-byes. Was that why he'd stopped asking questions? They'd spent the rest of the evening talking about the World Series, for God's sake. The memory stung. He blinked it back and, excusing himself, made his way through the crowded room.

He found Elena in the kitchen ladling a casserole onto paper plates. Spread across the oak table were half-empty casserole dishes and platters piled with sandwiches and brownies. He knew she was preparing plates of food for the elders and grandmothers to take home. The rest she would send to the shut-ins, the sick, people out of work. It was no secret who could use extra food. The moccasin telegraph kept everyone up on the news.

"You should eat something, Father," Elena said, the familiar scolding tone laced with undisguised concern. So like his mother, the way she tried to stuff food down his skinny frame when he was a kid.

"Maybe later," he said, pulling a foam cup from the stack on the counter next to the coffeemaker. He poured himself some coffee. It was the thirst he wanted to satisfy.

Leaning back against the counter, he wondered how he would tell the woman that he didn't want her at the mission for a while. Everything had changed. If the killer had intended to kill him, and not Father Joseph, everyone at the mission could be in danger.

The housekeeper was snapping sheets of plastic wrap over bowls and plates as if the task might fill up her thoughts. For the first time he saw the pinched look of grief in the woman's round, flat face.

"Did you know Father Joseph in the 1960s?" he asked. He wasn't sure how long Elena had been the housekeeper at St. Francis, only that it was an indeterminate length of time. "Long as I can remember," was the way she'd put it whenever he'd asked. And when she disapproved of something he planned to do, she would remind him she had been here long enough to know that it would never work.

Now she raised her eyes to his and shook her head. "Alvin and me wasn't even livin' on the res then." Reluctance seeped into the words, as if she didn't like admitting to a time when she was not the housekeeper at St. Francis.

Father John gestured toward the casseroles

and sandwiches. "People thought a lot of Father Joseph," he said, still absorbing the fact that his temporary assistant had once been a much-loved pastor here.

She gave a little nod, and he saw that she was fighting back tears. "All he was doin' was tryin' to help somebody. He was a real good priest." She lifted the corner of her white apron and began dabbing at her eyes. "If you'd been the one that got the call, you would've been shot. Then what would we've done?"

Her words stung him; he hadn't expected them. She was grieving for *him,* the man the murderer had intended to kill. "Oh, Elena," he said, setting down the mug and placing his arm around her.

She huddled next to him, trembling. "I don't want nothin' to happen to you." Her voice sounded thick and muffled against his shirt. "You're like my own son, John O'Malley." Suddenly she pushed him away and lifted her head. A little smile played at her mouth. "Big, tall, red-headed, Irish son. Imagine the Lord givin' me such a boy! So stubborn, too. And such a worry. What was He thinkin'?"

From outside came the crack of boots on the back steps. Another instant and the door swung open. Leonard Bizzel stepped inside, trailed by Walks-On, who loped over to the corner and stared forlornly into an empty bowl.

"You doin' okay, Father?" the caretaker asked. He was in his late forties, close to Father

57

John's age. A big man, with the narrow, finely chiseled face of the Arapahos, and kind eyes. Like most men on the reservation, he wore blue jeans and a plaid shirt, the rolled back cuffs exposing thick, brown forearms and wide, capable hands.

Father John nodded. He waited until Leonard shook some dry food out of a bag into the dog's bowl. Then he said, "I'd like you both to take a few days off."

"What?" Elena reared back from the table, eyes shiny with surprise. "Leave you here all alone? You'd never eat a bite. You'd starve to death."

"What're you sayin', Father?" This from Leonard.

Father John cleared his throat and began again. "It's possible that whoever murdered Father Joseph had intended to shoot me." He spoke calmly. He didn't want to frighten them.

The words hung in the space between him and the two Arapahos. He saw by the tight clamp of Leonard's mouth, the steadiness in Elena's eyes, that they had reached the same conclusion. He hurried on: "Until Father Joseph's murderer is found, we have to be careful."

Suddenly the housekeeper slapped a paper plate onto the table. "So the devil that killed poor Father Joseph is gonna tell us how we gotta live? Well, I don't care what you say. I ain't leavin' you alone here."

Leonard came around the table and planted

himself next to the housekeeper. "I figure the more people at the mission, the safer you're gonna be, Father. I'm plannin' on bein' here like usual."

Father John drew in a long breath. "It's been a long, hard day," he said, a new tack. "At least take tomorrow off. Gianelli and Banner will probably be back. Whoever killed Father Joseph isn't going to show up at the mission tomorrow."

Both Arapahos were quiet, eyes steady, faces unreadable. He refilled his coffee mug and started down the hallway, wondering if he'd won the argument.

A group of grandmothers were letting themselves out the front door; the cool evening air drifted down the hallway and bit at his face and hands. He turned in to the study, avoiding the prolonged good-byes, the reiteration of grief and condolences that fed his own guilt. The front door thudded shut as he sank into the leather chair at his desk. The study was dark. Obelisks of moonlight crisscrossed the carpet and speckled the papers in front of him.

He heard the shuffle of footsteps in the hall, the front door opening and closing several more times. Gradually the quiet of death began to settle over the house. He knew it well. So many houses where he had sat with bereaved families, engulfed in the quiet. Now it was here. He dropped his head into his hands and prayed silently for the soul of Father Joseph. He prayed for himself, for the strength to deal with his guilt.

And he prayed that — someday, someday — he would conquer the terrible thirst that was turning his throat and mouth into dust.

Finally he flipped on the desk lamp and pulled the phone into the puddle of light, dreading the call he had to make. He lifted the receiver and punched in the Provincial's number.

6

The metallic voice of an answering machine sounded on the line. "You have reached the Wisconsin Province of the Society of Jesus. Our office hours are . . ." Father John hit the pound button to fast-forward the message. "If this is an emergency, please stay on the line."

The bland, irritating sounds of canned music replaced the voice. Father John took a draw of coffee and stared at the piles of paper awaiting his attention: letters to answer, thank-you notes to send to strangers who kept St. Francis operating with a few dollars stuffed into envelopes and mailed off to Indian Country, a place they'd never seen, phone messages to return. He shuffled through the top of a pile. Elena had taken several phone messages this afternoon. Most from parishioners. One caught his eye: *Mary James called. Wants you to call back. Important.* Below the message was a number. He tossed the paper aside. He did not know anyone named Mary James. It would have to wait.

There was the sound of footsteps in the hall followed by a rap on the door. Elena peered around the edge. "Leonard and me are gonna be leavin' now," she said.

He thanked her for everything she'd done.

"Your dinner's in the fridge."

Another thank you.

"You sure you gonna be all right?"

"I'll be fine."

"See you first thing tomorrow," she said, backing into the hall, pulling the door toward her. The hinges squealed like a small, frightened animal.

"Elena . . ."

The slammed door sent a little ripple through the floor. He heard the receding footsteps, the thud of the front door, and he knew that it didn't matter if a crazed gunman was on the loose. Elena would come to the mission anyway. She would block the door herself if she thought someone meant to harm him. Tomorrow Leonard would also be here, and the volunteers who worked at the museum in the old school. He could order them to stay away, and still they would come. He felt humbled by the loyalty and love he had found here.

As for Vicky — he exhaled a long breath. She would ask questions around the reservation, and somewhere there was a killer who would learn of her interest. With a sickening clarity he understood there was nothing he could do. He couldn't protect her. He couldn't protect the people at the mission.

A tinny melody, irritating in its familiarity, burst over the line. It struck him he had spent his entire life among stubborn people who dug their heels into the ground and held on to their position, no matter how foolish it might be. Who better than his own people, the Irish? He was a bit like that himself, he knew. Contrary, his father had called him when he'd announced he was going into the priesthood. "Why be so contrary, Johnnie? You got a great future ahead of you. A couple years in the minors, you'll be pitchin' at Fenway Park, and that will be grand. The whole family'll be there to cheer you on. Eileen, too. The girl loves you to distraction."

"I want to be a priest, Dad."

"And would you tell me something, boy? How you gonna pitch fastballs from a pulpit? The Lord give you this talent. He'll be wantin' you to use it. And what about Eileen? You wanna break the girl's heart?"

"A priest, Dad."

"God almighty, the Lord put breath into a contrary lad."

Father John closed his eyes against the bittersweet memory, the irritating melody jangling in his ear. He had loved Eileen, and he'd been good at baseball. He might have made a different life, but something had intervened. A vocation, the Church termed it. A calling. It had come in the spring of his senior year at Boston College, with the scouts taking him to dinner and visiting his family. It was as if he had been struck to the ground by the force of it, like St. Paul struck down on the road to Damascus. He had understood he was to be a priest, a Jesuit. He would teach history at Georgetown or Fordham or Marquette. His would be a quiet, scholarly life, writing papers and books, influencing students.

That wasn't how it had gone, not how it had gone at all. He'd spent most of a year in Grace House trying to parse out what had happened, how he had become an alcoholic priest who had let down his family, his superiors, and everyone who had believed in him. When he came to St. Francis, he had welcomed the emptiness of the reservation, as if the great open spaces could cover his shame. Gradually he'd been drawn in by the people until, instead of losing himself, he felt he had begun to know himself. Now this: someone here wanted him dead.

"Wisconsin Province." The man's voice startled him out of his thoughts.

"This is Father O'Malley." He gripped the receiver tightly against his ear and added: "At St. Francis Mission."

He could hear the quiet intake of breath on the other end, the unspoken thoughts: Who? Where?

"In Wyoming."

"Oh, yes, Father O'Malley. The Provincial is in the office between eight and five. You can reach him tomorrow."

"I have to talk to him now." Father John heard the stubbornness in his tone. "Put him on."

There was a short silence, a muffled cough. The voice said, "Is this some type of emergency?"

"Father Joseph Keenan is dead."

Another silence. "I see. Well, that's very unfortunate."

"He was murdered."

A gasp, like that of a small bellows, sounded through the line. "Please hold."

The canned music returned. The imitation of a waltz, light and merry, the strains of an imaginary ballroom: ladies in gowns swishing across the floor, gentlemen in tuxedos. Hardly appropriate for the news he had just delivered. He drained the remainder of the coffee. It was cold and thick as syrup. Then he picked up a pen and began tapping the edge of the desk, a crescendo of impatience.

"John, what's this all about?" Father William Rutherford's tone was peremptory, annoyed, the tone Father John remembered from their days in the seminary together. Television noise sounded in the background.

Father John explained. Father Joseph had taken a call to an isolated part of the reservation. Someone had shot him.

"Good Lord." Shock and disbelief sounded in the Provincial's tone. "What's going on out there?"

Father John was quiet. He didn't know the answer.

"Some kind of drive-by shooting? Are there gangs on the reservation?"

Father John said he didn't believe so.

"A random shooting? A lunatic?"

"The FBI is investigating."

"The FBI! My God."

"They handle homicide cases on reservations."

"Oh, yes," the Provincial said, as if he'd momentarily forgotten some important piece of information that it was his job to remember. "Well, Joseph Keenan dead," he mused. "I believe he was prepared. Yes, I believe he went there to die."

"What?" Father John tossed the pencil across the desk. The Provincial had a doctorate in psychology, he knew, but he was in no mood for psychological babble. Nobody went someplace to be shot.

"Joseph's prognosis was not good," the Provincial was saying. "His heart disease was quite advanced. You knew that, of course."

"No, I didn't know that," Father John said. He was thinking that had the Provincial mentioned the fact, he would have suggested that, perhaps, a mission on an Indian reservation might not be the best place for a man with advanced heart disease.

"He was fully aware his time was limited," Father Rutherford said, a steady, matter-of-fact tone. "Joseph Keenan was not a man content to await his death in a retirement home. When he heard I was looking for an assistant priest at St. Francis, he came to the office and insisted on taking the job. I turned him down, of course. Frankly, I didn't think a man in such poor health should be sent back into the field."

Father John could feel the guilt curling inside him like a snake gathering its deadly strength. An old man with advanced heart disease, who'd spent the day driving across the reservation — that was the man he'd allowed to take an emergency call miles away.

Father John picked up the coffee mug. Empty. It didn't matter. Coffee was a poor substitute. Slamming down the mug, he struggled to follow what the Provincial was saying: Father Joseph had kept coming back, determined to return to St. Francis Mission.

The Provincial hesitated, as if searching for the argument he'd used to convince himself when he'd given in to the old priest's entreaties. "Frankly, John," he said finally, "I wasn't having much luck finding anyone else, so I agreed to send him there on temporary assignment. Just until I found a permanent man. Joseph had very fond memories of St. Francis Mission." A pause, then: "Yes, I believe he went there to die. Of course, he couldn't have known anything like this would happen. But he knew his time was approaching. He chose the place, and left the rest in the hands of God."

Father John pushed back in the leather chair, tilting the front legs off the carpet, trying to make sense of what the Provincial said. Something was missing, the logic skewed. Even if Father Joseph had been a popular pastor and people still remembered him, he hadn't been on the reservation in thirty-five years. He'd had a distinguished career, other assignments. Why would he choose to spend his last days here? Unless the man had nowhere else to go, no one he wanted to be with.

This new thought filled Father John with sadness. Was this the culmination of a priest's career? In the end there was no one? Suddenly he realized Father Rutherford was talking about the funeral arrangements, saying he would contact Joseph's family.

"He had a family?" Father John heard the surprise in his voice. A family made the man's decision to come to St. Francis all the more perplexing.

"A couple of nephews, I believe," the Provincial said. "I'll have to notify them. In the meantime . . ." Another hesitation. "We must take the necessary precautions, John. We don't know what Father Joseph's murder is all about, do we?"

Father John admitted that was true. He had a theory, which he realized he hadn't mentioned to his superior. What was there to say? Someone had shot the wrong priest?

"We don't know how far this may go," Father Rutherford went on. "This could be a hate crime against the Church."

"I don't think so."

"Well, we don't know. I want you to take a leave of absence until this is settled. Go to Boston. Visit your family."

Father John set the front legs down hard and stared at the lamplight flickering against the blackness of the window across the study. He'd gone to Boston in the spring. The last thing he wanted was another awkward visit with his brother, Mike. It was as if, after twenty-five years, Eileen still stood between them. His brother's wife. The woman he would have married had he not gone into the seminary. That was the reason he hadn't mentioned his theory about Joseph's murder: the Provincial would send him somewhere he didn't want to go.

"I can't leave St. Francis," he said, his tone firm. "There wouldn't be anyone to say Mass. The fall classes and programs are already —"

The Provincial cut in: "I can't have another priest killed. There are fewer and fewer of us, you know. I can't take any chances."

"Look, Bill," Father John began, marshaling his argument into what he hoped would have the force of logic. "I know the FBI agent and the police chief here. They're first-rate. They have some strong leads." A bit of a stretch. Gianelli and Banner were groping in the dark. He hurried on: "They'll have Joseph's murder solved in a couple of days. There's no sense in closing down the mission."

The Provincial was quiet a moment. Then: "Do you have a gun?"

"Of course I don't have a gun."

"A rifle or something. Don't you go hunting? Isn't that what the Arapahos do?"

Father John wondered how far out in the wilderness the Provincial thought he lived. Did he think the Arapahos still hunted buffalo? He said, "I don't hunt."

"Let me make certain I understand. Should whoever murdered Joseph show up at the mission, you have no way to protect yourself. Is that true?"

Father John glanced at the lights dancing in the window, the blackness beyond. "Give me a couple days, Bill," he said.

There was a long, considered pause on the other end of the line. "I don't like it."

"A couple days."

The Provincial was quiet. "All right," he said finally. "You've got two days and then —"

"Good." Father John interrupted. He didn't want to receive an order he would find painful to obey. "Let me know about the funeral arrangements."

He hung up quickly and made his way down the darkened hall into the kitchen. The light above the stove cast a thin yellow glow over half of the room, leaving the other half in shadow. A soft snoring noise came from the corner where Walks-On lay on his blanket, his hind leg stretched back at an angle, as if to make room for the missing leg.

Father John lifted the coffeepot. It felt light in his hand. He slammed it down and whirled about, his gaze on the gray-shadowed cabinets, the counters. There was no alcohol at the mission. That was the first rule he set for every new assistant, even an eminent scholar like Joseph Keenan. No alcohol! What he didn't explain was the fear behind the rule — his fear that he would be the one to consume any alcohol brought on the premises.

Now he wished a bottle were here, hidden in a cabinet behind the canned goods, wedged behind boxes of rice and pasta, stashed under the sink with the can of cleaner and bottle of dishwashing liquid. But there were no whiskey bottles in the kitchen. None at the mission.

Unless — the thought came like a light streaking through the night sky — Father Joseph had brought a bottle with him. Why not? A man used to faculty cocktail parties and dinners, conference banquets. Joseph had nodded when he'd mentioned the rule, but the bottle might have been packed in one of the suitcases or cardboard boxes. It could still be here.

Father John hurried down the hall and up the dark stairs. Moonlight slanted through the small window over the landing and bathed the upstairs hall in a soft white light. He strode to the closed door halfway down the hall and pushed it open, flipping on the light as he stepped inside. Gianelli and Banner had left the room tidy: bed made up like an army cot, blankets tucked at the corners; books neatly arranged on the small bookcase; magazines stacked on the desk; shaving kit on the bureau. He flung open the closet door and swept one hand across the shelves above the hanging clothes, pushing aside a couple of sweaters, an umbrella. Nothing. He checked under the bed, behind the drapes, the usual hiding places. He knew them well. He pulled open the bureau drawers, lifting out the clean shirts and underwear. Then the desk drawer, rummaging through the folders. Still nothing.

He slammed the drawer shut and sank onto the edge of the bed. *My God,* he thought. What was he doing? Desecrating a dead man's things, and for what? A drink. An almighty, all-powerful drink.

He switched off the light, closed the door, and made his way back downstairs to the kitchen. After brewing another pot of coffee, he sat at the table a long while, sipping on the steaming, black liquid. A calmness gradually came over him and with it the understanding that he could not wait for Joseph's murderer to try again. On edge, riven with guilt and thirst. Like a fly pinned to a board, awaiting the merciful blow. There would be no more murders. He understood what he had to do.

7

Vicky pointed the Bronco west on Ethete Road, darting in and out of the pale bands of moonlight. Clouds had rolled eastward to reveal a clear sky and a sea of stars. A rim of light outlined the high peaks in the distance, and flat, violet shadows drifted down the foothills like smoke.

She drove on automatic, her thoughts on John O'Malley. The killer had missed him this afternoon, but he would try again. After the mourners and well-wishers had driven out of the mission grounds, after Elena had finished tidying up and said good night, after Leonard Bizzel had checked the buildings and gone home, the killer would return. In the blackness of the night, when John O'Malley was alone.

Or would the killer wait for him to dash across the grounds to a meeting, or walk to the altar for Mass? Is that when it would happen? Or would there be another dying woman begging for the last sacrament? Vicky felt her whole body grow tense, her heart thump with the certainty that, if an emergency call came, he would go.

She peered into the darkness beyond the sweep of headlights, pulling her thoughts back to the moment, surprised that she could have missed the narrow sign for Stewart Road. She knew the geography of the reservation — the swells and dips of the earth — as well as she knew the contours of her own body. She searched the shadows for a familiar landmark.

Suddenly she spotted the thin silver pole glinting at the edge of the moonlight. She tapped on the brake and turned onto the gravel road. Another half mile, and she was parking in front of a frame house that rose like a small butte out of the dirt yard.

She rapped at the door, hugging her black bag to her chest against the cold snap of the wind. "It's Vicky," she called, knowing Aunt Rose would have heard the scrunch of gravel, the hum of the engine in the night.

The door slid inward and an elderly woman with a round, fleshy face and narrow, dark eyes stood in the flickering light of a television. Two fleshy arms reached out for her. Vicky could sense her own thinness in the older woman's embrace. Then she felt herself being pulled inside, as if her aunt wanted to protect her from the cold wind, or whatever had brought her to the door.

Vicky clung to the older woman. Everything about her was familiar: the blue-print housedress, the black hair streaked with gray, smelling of wildflowers and wind. Her mother's sister, which, in the Arapaho Way, meant Rose was also her mother. When her own mother had died three years ago, leaving her stumbling in space, unable to get a foothold, it was Aunt Rose who had led her back to herself.

"You had your supper?" The woman stepped back, assessing her with narrowed eyes.

She gave her head a little shake, and Aunt Rose took her hand and led her through the living room, past the television propped in front of a plaid-upholstered recliner, past a little table covered with family photos and into the kitchen.

They sat at the wood table pushed against the window next to the counter. Vicky nibbled at the cold fried chicken and buttered bread Aunt Rose had extracted from the refrigerator while the older woman sipped at a cup of tea and talked about the weather: winter was coming, but, oh, September was beautiful. The teakettle made a small hissing sound over the laughter bursting from the television. She went on: the wild grasses so pretty, all golds and coppers. The sky turning softer blue every day.

"Real sad about Father Joseph," Aunt Rose said, finally turning the conversation to the matter that they both knew had brought Vicky to her door.

Vicky was quiet. She sipped at the hot tea, wondering at the cold fear still inside her, like a chunk of ice in her heart. "What if the killer made a mistake?" she said, finally giving voice to the fear. "What if he shot the wrong priest?"

A look of comprehension crept into the older woman's expression, followed by shock and disbelief. "You sayin' the killer was after Father John?"

"He drives the Toyota."

"Nobody wants to hurt Father John." Aunt

Rose shook her head, as if to banish an intolerable idea.

"Father Joseph had been at the mission only two weeks. Why would anyone want him dead?"

"He used to be here."

"Thirty-five years ago." Vicky got to her feet and began to circle the small space that divided the refrigerator and stove from a bank of cabinets. "I remember. I was in the second grade. He used to visit the classroom and tell us to be good students, a credit to our families. Do our people proud."

"He was a nice man."

"Well, he didn't know anything about kids." Vicky slapped the palm of her hand on the counter. "He was arrogant and —" She swallowed, surprised at the idea that had come to mind. "A little scary."

"Scary?" Aunt Rose threw her head back and gave a little laugh. "He was real shy, that's a fact. Used to talk in big words. Half the time nobody knew what he was talkin' about. I heard he went away to become a professor in some university. Maybe they understood him there." She reached out and grabbed Vicky's hand. "He had a good heart, Vicky. Used to drive all over the res, just like Father John, checkin' on people, seeing who might need help. Soon's he come back, he went out visitin' people, just like before."

Vicky exhaled a long breath and nodded toward the phone on the counter. "What have you heard?"

76

Aunt Rose shook her head again. "Moccasin telegraph's so loaded, it's likely to fall down. But nobody knows anything. Nobody can figure it out. An old man like that. Who'd want to kill him?"

Exactly, Vicky thought, withdrawing her hand and starting to circle the kitchen again. The cold knot of fear tightened within her. It wasn't Father Joseph the murderer was after. She swung around and faced the older woman. "Maybe it was Sonny Red Wolf who tried to kill Father John," she said.

"What makes you think so?"

Vicky stared at the older woman. *She hadn't disagreed.* "Sonny wants whites off the reservation. St. Francis Mission has been here more than a hundred years. It's a symbol of white presence. Father John is a symbol. Last summer Sonny blockaded the mission. Banner had to run him off. That must've made him angry — the Arapaho police chief helping the white mission." She smiled to herself at the irony.

Aunt Rose got to her feet, picked up the teakettle, and filled both of their cups. Little curls of steam rose in the air. After setting the kettle back on the stove, she pulled two tea bags from a box on the counter and dropped them into the cups. Sliding back onto her chair, she said, "Sonny Red Wolf don't speak for folks around here. He had his way, we'd all be livin' in the Old Time, out huntin' buffalo. Well, I don't wanna spend all day butcherin' buffalo meat and tannin' hides, thank you very much. I like my modern-day comforts." She tilted her head toward the television noise in the living room. "Besides, there ain't enough buffalo left."

Vicky felt the conversation lurching into small talk. "Have you heard any talk about Sonny?" she asked.

"Talk? Sure. There's always talk about Sonny. He's so full of hate, only natural his name comes up."

"Tell me what you've heard."

The older woman studied the steaming liquid in her cup. "Somebody might've seen Sonny's white truck ridin' up in the air on those big, fat tires out on Thunder Lane this afternoon."

"Who, Aunt? Who saw the truck?" Vicky felt her heart turn over. The demonstration last spring, the truck in the vicinity of the murder. It was adding up to what Gianelli liked to call a preponderance of evidence.

"Don't know any names. Just somebody lives out that way." The older woman raised her eyes; there was fear in them. "Sonny Red Wolf's real mean, Vicky. He killed a man once. You gotta stay out of this."

Vicky drew in a long breath, fighting back the panic rising inside her. "Whoever saw the truck is probably scared. The only witness could disappear."

"You gotta get hold of yourself, Vicky." Aunt Rose fixed her with a stern gaze. "You got yourself so worked up about Father John, you're half-sick. You got that peaked look about you, like white blood was flowing in your veins. You gotta put that man out of your mind. He's a priest."

Vicky took her eyes away. It was true, all true. She still felt limp from the waves of pain that had crashed over her when she thought he was dead. She had seen the people streaming into the mission that afternoon, the grief and fear in their faces mirroring her own. How many had come, as she had, believing John O'Malley had been killed? He belonged to them; he was their pastor.

Suddenly the phone screeched, like an alien presence in the kitchen. Aunt Rose turned toward the counter and lifted the receiver. "Hello," she snapped. Then: "Vicky's here now. Call me later."

Vicky laid a hand on the other woman's arm. "Can you get a name?"

Aunt Rose drew in a long breath, then lowered her eyes to the receiver. "Guess somebody seen Sonny Red Wolf's truck on Thunder Lane," she said. "You hear about that?"

A burst of television laughter spilled through the kitchen. Vicky held her breath.

"Yeah, that's right." Aunt Rose glanced up. "Lucy Travise? Don't know as I know her. She live out there? I see. Near the big bend on Thunder Lane."

Vicky dug through her bag hanging from the back of the chair and pulled out a pen and notebook. She flipped to a clear page and wrote: *Lucy Travise. Big bend. Thunder Lane.*

The minute Aunt Rose hung up, Vicky picked up the receiver. It was still warm and moist. She punched in Gianelli's number. An answering machine interrupted the rings. "You have reached the local offices of the Federal Bureau of Investigation. Leave your name and number . . ."

"I've got something," Vicky said when the machine voice stopped. Hurriedly she gave the information: the name, the location of the house — a lifeline for John O'Malley. Her whole being surged with hope.

"You oughta be thinkin' about Ben," Aunt Rose said as she replaced the receiver.

"Ben!" Vicky swung around. Struggling for a calm tone, she said, "Ben and I have been divorced thirteen years."

"He still loves you."

"That can't be true."

"He was your husband."

"That was a long time ago," she managed.

"You think Ben's still drinking, but you're wrong," Aunt Rose persisted. "I see his mom over at the senior citizens' center on Thursdays. Rayleen says Ben helps her out all the time, now she's been sick. He's a good son. Sober as the day he come into the world. Hasn't had a drink since the drunk he went on last winter, Rayleen says. After you turned him down again."

Vicky glanced toward the doorway to the living room: the TV sounds of brakes squealing, men shouting. Was it always her fault? Her fault when Ben had gotten drunk and hit her?

Bringing her gaze back to Aunt Rose, she said, "Ben and I are no longer married. I've made a different life."

"Some life, longin' for a priest."

Vicky closed her eyes a moment against the sharp sting of the words. There was no response to the truth. Slowly she got to her feet, lifted her bag, and started through the living room, aware of the soft padding of footsteps behind her. At the door she remembered Sharon David. The earlier part of the day, her own work, she realized, had been swept from her mind.

She turned toward the woman behind her. "Something else, Aunt. A woman came to see me today." She paused. She did not want to mention the woman's name. She did not want the news flashed over the moccasin telegraph. "The woman seems to think she was adopted from this reservation in 1964."

"We don't let our babies get adopted out of the tribe," Aunt Rose said.

"I told her that. But maybe there was a girl who thought she had nowhere to turn. Did you hear of anyone like that back then?"

In the pale white light of the television, Vicky saw the other woman's expression change as she clicked back the years, searching her memory. She shook her head. "No girl would've done that. Not then. Not with all those babies dying. We was goin' to funerals and prayin' over those little caskets every few weeks. It was terrible,

81

losin' the future generation all because of bad water."

A thin memory stirred in Vicky's mind: her mother boiling pans of water on the stove — the only water she was allowed to drink or use to brush her teeth or wash her face. "What was wrong with the water?"

"There was lots of talk." Aunt Rose shrugged. "Health-department people comin' on the res and givin' opinions. Said those old gold mines in the mountains was poisoning the water. You ask me, it was that uranium processing mill that used to be on the res. Whatever it was, a lot of people was sick with bad stomachaches, and a lot of new babies died."

The older woman gazed across the small living room, into the shadows. "Rayleen lost a boy. Lots of families lost babies, even though most of the women went to that fancy clinic in Lander 'cause they was so worried. That doctor that went off and got famous ran the clinic. You know, Jeremiah Markham."

Vicky nodded. It was a source of local pride that Jeremiah Markham, the baby doctor, had gotten his start in Lander. Was there a book rack in any store, any airport, that didn't stock the books he'd written — *Let's Deliver Healthy Babies* or *Your Infant's Health* or *The First Weeks of Your Infant's Life*? A new mother who didn't keep a Markham book on her bed table? Only a few weeks ago she had seen Dr. Markham interviewed on television. A stately, grandfatherly man with wavy white hair and a commanding voice, exuding the wisdom and kindness that had made his books so popular. Markham had left Lander years ago, but the clinic he'd started was still open. She had met the director, Dr. Roland Grace, on several occasions.

"With all that sickness goin' around, people was in a panic," Aunt Rose was saying. "Everybody wanted to make sure the pregnant women got the best care possible. So anybody had insurance went over to the Markham Clinic. There was some families didn't have insurance, I remember. We took up a collection so they could go to the clinic and not have to stick with the Public Health Service doctors. We wanted to make sure they got real good care. That's why I know, any girl got pregnant, the people did everything for her and that baby. No way did we let any babies go."

Vicky thanked the old woman. What Aunt Rose said had only confirmed what she knew, what she had told Sharon David. She let herself through the door with the usual good-byes, the promises to come again soon, the promises to take care of herself.

"You promise to think about what I told you about Ben," Aunt Rose said.

Vicky gave her aunt a smile and pulled the door closed behind her. Then she hunched her shoulders against the wind as she made her way across the dirt yard in the darkness to the Bronco. The last was a promise she had not made. She would not think about Ben. She had other matters to fill her mind. Tomorrow she would call Sharon David and suggest she take her search to another reservation. She would have to return the movie star's check. Tonight, she wanted to talk to a woman named Lucy Travise.

8

The bi-level house hugged the ground, like a shadow splayed on the earth. As Vicky turned into the dirt yard, her headlights shone on the pale green siding, the cement steps, the little stoop. A faint light filtered through the curtains in the front windows. Red reflectors of a truck gleamed in the darkness at the side of the house. She parked behind the truck and slid out into a gust of wind that felt as if it had swooped down off a glacier. The clack of her heels on the steps mingled with the staccato thumps of rap music coming from inside.

Just as she was about to knock, the door swung open. A young man in his twenties stood in the slant of light. Arapaho, by the narrow face, the finely honed cheekbones, the little crook in the nose. There was a familiar look about him. She tried to place him in one of the clans, but she couldn't find the right one.

She said, "Is Lucy Travise here?"

"Who wants to know?" The tone was insolent, challenging. The music pounded behind him.

"My name is Vicky Holden. I'm a lawyer. I have to talk to Lucy."

The young man's eyes bored into her. "I know you. You used to be married to my uncle."

Oh, God, Vicky thought. He had probably eaten at her table when he was a kid, played with

Susan and Lucas. The clan she'd been searching for was her ex-husband's. She forced a smile. "Which nephew are you?"

"James."

The nephew she'd once forbidden her kids to play with, he was so mean. The nephew always in trouble. The last she'd heard of James Holden, he was in jail in Denver.

"I want to see Lucy." Vicky raised her voice over the pounding music. The woman was probably somewhere inside.

"Sorry, Aunt Vicky." The tone was harsh. "Lucy ain't here, so you better be runnin' along."

"That your aunt, James?" A woman's voice, small and childlike, came from behind the door.

"Lucy, it's important I talk to you." Vicky moved sideways, attempting to see around the man blocking the door. She caught a glimpse of the room: green sofa, crumpled cushions; small table littered with foam food boxes; rap sounds filling the air like a physical presence.

Suddenly a girl came into view. A white girl, not much more than a teenager, with pale skin and long blond hair that hung in clumps down the front of her black T-shirt. She had on blue jeans that hugged her thin hips and exposed a slip of white midriff. Her feet were bare. Laying a hand on James's arm, she tilted her face toward him. "Can't she come in a minute?" she asked, a pleading voice.

James jerked backward, bringing the girl with

him in a kind of dance, and Vicky stepped into the room. Reaching around, he gave the door a shove. The *thwack* punctuated the monotony of rhythms coming from speakers on either side of the sofa. A stereo stood against the right wall, next to a couple of webbed metal chairs, and the black halogen lamp between the chairs splashed light over the ceiling.

"Are you Lucy?" Vicky locked eyes with the girl a moment.

"Yeah, that's me." The girl glanced hurriedly at James, then stepped over to the stereo and turned one of the knobs. The music receded to a buzz, like the noise of a chain saw in a distant field. "You here about that shooting up the road?" she asked, tucking her hands into the back pockets of her blue jeans.

"I told you to shut up about that." James whirled toward her. "It's none of our business."

Lucy's gaze shifted uneasily around the room. "Well, that's what everybody's been callin' about." Her voice was tentative. "Everybody's wantin' to know where the old man got shot."

"I told you, I'm gonna rip that phone out, you don't do what I say."

Vicky stepped toward the girl. "A priest was murdered this afternoon, Lucy. If the killer isn't found soon, another priest might also die."

"White men," James said, a kind of snort. "Let white people take care of it. What do we care if they kill one another off?"

Your girlfriend's white, Vicky thought. She said,

87

"Tell me what you saw."

"I'm tellin' you, she didn't see nothin'." James moved to the girl's side and slipped an arm around her, pulling her toward him. "So, Aunt Vicky, why don't you just get outta here?"

Vicky didn't take her eyes from the girl. "Why didn't you tell the FBI agent you saw a white truck this afternoon? You could be in a lot of trouble for withholding information about a murder."

"You gotta leave," James said. There was a crack of fear and uncertainty in his voice. He started pulling the girl toward the shadows of a hallway.

Vicky ignored him. "A man's life depends on you telling the truth, Lucy. I know the FBI agent. His name is Ted Gianelli. He's going to come back here tonight. I'm a lawyer and I can stay with you while you talk to him."

"She ain't talkin' to nobody." James pushed the girl into the hall. His face grew darker, his eyes squinted with intensity. "Lucy tells the fed she seen Sonny Red Wolf's truck out here this afternoon, you know what Sonny'll do to her? He's been givin' us enough grief, drivin' by, shouting 'white whore' and a lot of other stuff. Last week he drives by and fires off a round of buckshot. We was just lucky Lucy and me didn't get killed. Most likely he come out here today to keep on harassin' us 'cause he wants Lucy outta here."

"Have you reported this?" Vicky knew the answer even as she framed the question.

"Yeah, right. I'm gonna report Sonny to the police 'cause I'm real tired of livin'."

"Listen to me, James." Vicky moved toward him. "If Sonny killed Father Joseph, he'll kill again."

"Well, it ain't gonna be Lucy gets killed, and it ain't gonna be me. So I don't care what you heard. Lucy didn't see nothin', and she ain't sayin' nothin'."

Abruptly he let go of the girl, crossed the room, and yanked open the front door. "Get outta here."

Vicky held her place, her gaze on the girl hovering in the shadows at the end of the hall. "Sonny will keep making your life hell." She spoke slowly, deliberately. "You can put a stop to it by telling the truth."

Out of the corner of her eye, Vicky saw James reach for her. She slid sideways, dodging his grasp. "My office is on Main Street in Lander," she said as the young man's hand came down hard on her arm, propelling her backward. She jerked herself free, swung around, and walked out the door.

Vicky gripped the steering wheel as the Bronco fishtailed over the gravel road. Warm air poured out of the vents, but she was still cold with worry. She'd wanted to convince Lucy Travise to tell the truth. She'd believed — mistakenly, naively — that if she, a lawyer, stayed at her side, the girl would talk to Gianelli. Instead she'd given James the excuse he'd probably been looking for. She knew what they would do: pack some things, leave the house, lose themselves in the clan, who, they believed, would protect them from Sonny Red Wolf. She had to reach Gianelli or Banner before that happened.

As she came over a rise, she saw the lights of Ethete blinking in the darkness ahead. Within a few minutes she was slowing past the small houses lining the road, past the Sun Dance grounds lost in the darkness. At the intersection, she swung onto the cement apron in front of the café and filling station. Her headlights played over the white letters on the plate-glass window: BETTY'S PLACE. Behind the window was blackness.

She drove around the gas pumps and braked in front of the telephone mounted on the brick a few feet from the door. Leaving the engine running and headlights on, she dragged her bag across the seat and hurried toward the phone, digging through her bag for coins as she went. The wind plucked at her face and hands and whipped her suit coat back as she slipped a quarter into the slot and punched in Gianelli's number.

The same message as before: You have reached . . . She hit the pound button and spoke into the hollowness of the machine, elaborating on the message she'd left earlier. Now she'd talked to Lucy Travise and her boyfriend, James Holden. Now she knew for certain they were scared of Sonny Red Wolf. Gianelli had to get to them before they disappeared.

She pulled down the disconnect lever, slipped another quarter into the slot, and tapped the numbers for the BIA police. Her fingers felt numb with cold. A woman's voice answered. Vicky gave her name and asked to speak to Chief Banner.

"What is this about?" A calm, just-doing-my-job tone.

"Tell him I'm on the line."

"Well, there's lots of people wantin' to talk to the chief. He can't take everybody's call."

"This is Vicky Holden." She identified herself again. "I'm an attorney, and this is an emergency."

"Hold on." The woman might have been stifling a yawn. "Maybe I can patch you through."

The line went quiet. Vicky huddled against the phone box, shivering in the wind that sent little eddies of dust swirling about her. There was the sound of tires screaming out on the road. Then the ragged thump of a truck careening over pavement. Lights flared around her. She whirled about, squinting into the brightness of a spotlight mounted on a white truck that was swerving past the gas pumps and heading toward her. She jumped sideways, gripping the receiver, stretching the metal cord around the edge of the box.

The truck squealed to a stop about ten feet away. The spotlight switched off, leaving pinpricks of red lights dancing in front of her eyes. She blinked frantically, trying to see in the dim light of her own headlights.

"Vicky, that you?" The chief's voice burst over the receiver.

"I'm in front of Betty's Place at Ethete." Vicky struggled to keep her voice calm. "I think Sonny Red Wolf just drove up."

"You alone?"

"I'm alone."

"Jesus, Vicky." She heard the chief take a gulp of air. "I'll get a car there as fast as possible. Stay on the line, you hear?" A click, and the hollowness returned.

Vicky gripped the receiver tight. She could see now: the truck door swinging open, the massive figure of Sonny Red Wolf sliding out. The man gave the door a gentle push with one leg, as if there was all the time in the world, as if there was nothing she could do, nowhere she could run. Even if she bolted for the Bronco, he could grab her before she got inside. Slowly he started toward her.

The headlights cast an eerie yellow glow over the chiseled face and long black hair, the dark leather jacket and blue jeans. With her free hand, Vicky groped inside her bag for some kind of weapon. Her keys! Where were her keys? Panic rose in her throat, a stifled cry. She'd left the keys in the ignition. She felt as if the air had been sucked from the earth and she couldn't breathe. She backed into the edge of the phone box.

92

"Chief Banner." Her voice was loud. It echoed into the receiver, a cold, dead thing in her hand. Sonny stopped, and she hurried on, repeating what she'd said a moment ago. She could feel the Indian's eyes on her. From the distance, across the sounds of the wind, came the howl of a police siren.

"Vicky!" Banner's voice again. "One of my boys is on the way. You all right?"

She saw Sonny throw a backward glance toward Ethete Road. The siren grew louder. Abruptly he stepped back, pulled open the truck door, and ducked inside. In a half second the engine growled into life. The truck started across the cement apron and shot out onto the road just as a white BIA police car rolled under the street-light at the corner.

"Vicky?" Banner's voice boomed in her ear.

"I'm okay." She was shivering. "He's gone."

"Wait till the patrol car gets there."

"I'll wait," she said, before setting the receiver in its cradle.

The patrol car had turned onto the pavement and was coming to a stop where the white truck had stood a moment before. A patrolman lifted himself out as she walked over. The wind snapped at her suit coat and flattened her skirt around her legs. She felt chilled to the bone.

"What's going on?" the patrolman asked.

She told him about Sonny Red Wolf driving up, fixing her with a spotlight, approaching her.

"He do anything else?"

93

Vicky shook her head. Sonny Red Wolf had not done anything else.

"Say anything?"

"No."

"Threaten you?"

"Scared me," she said.

"Well, no crime turnin' in here. Maybe he was waitin' for you to get off the phone."

"I don't think so." Vicky pulled her jacket tight around her. She couldn't stop shivering.

There was a burst of static from the radio inside the car, followed by the bark of the chief's voice: "Put Vicky on."

The patrolman opened the rear door and nodded. Vicky slipped inside, taking the small black microphone he handed over the seat. Warm air flowed around her, but she was numb with cold.

"Everything okay?" the chief asked.

"For the time being."

"So what did you do to get Sonny's interest?"

Vicky drew in a long breath, then explained that a white girl named Lucy Travise had seen Sonny's truck on Thunder Lane about the time Father Joseph was killed.

"You sure? We canvassed the houses out there, talked to that white girl. Said she didn't see anything."

"She's scared, Banner. I've been leaving messages for Gianelli."

"Okay." The chief's voice sounded fainter. "You take yourself home, you hear? And Vicky, stay out of this investigation. I don't want to have to worry about you. Bad enough I gotta worry about Father John gettin' himself involved. At least we got his Toyota locked up. Should keep him close to the mission, but you're just gonna have to promise me you'll tend to your own business. Red Wolf's not somebody you wanna get real mad at you. You don't want any more run-ins with that Indian."

Vicky handed the microphone back to the patrolman and got out of the car. The chief was half-right. She didn't want another run-in with Sonny Red Wolf. She wanted the man behind bars.

9

The Escort's steering wheel felt strange in his grip. The plush seat and hum of the engine — strange and annoying as Father John drove west on Seventeen-Mile Road. Flat, gray wind clouds stretched over the mountains, but the afternoon sun glinted off the asphalt and warmed the car. The plains crept into the far distances, the only signs of human habitation an occasional dirt road, a frame house hugging the earth. The wind battered the sides of the car and echoed the dull pounding in his head.

He'd slept badly, waiting for morning, half-aware of the shadows flitting across the bedroom, the light growing around the curtains. He'd awakened feeling stiff and sore, his temples throbbing. After a quick shower and shave, he'd pulled on a clean pair of blue jeans and flannel shirt. Downstairs he'd coaxed Walks-On off his rug and out into the cool morning air, then headed for the church. The sky was ablaze in purples, reds, and golds as the sun lifted itself over the horizon. A line of trucks and pickups stood in front of the church — he could not stop people from coming. Not unless he closed the mission. He didn't want to close the mission.

There was a scattering of people in the church. Leonard moved about the sanctuary, setting the Mass books into place on the altar. Seated in the pews were the faithful elders who came to Mass every day to pray for the people. The Creator would listen to their prayers. They had reached the fourth hill of life, close to the Creator, a sacred place. Those who dwelled there were also sacred. Father John knew that today the elders would ask the Creator to remember Father Joseph. He offered the Mass for the murdered priest. *Requiescat in pace.*

In the sacristy following Mass, he had reminded Leonard he wanted him to take the day off.

"Lotta work around here." The Arapaho puttered about the small room, setting the Mass books on the shelves, placing the chalice inside the cabinet. "Dead cottonwood branches gotta be hauled off today. All them tumbleweeds that blew in front of Eagle Hall gotta be cleaned out."

"It'll wait, Leonard."

The man had stopped puttering and locked eyes with him. "We been talkin' " — a little wave toward the church and, Father John knew, the parishioners — "and we decided we ain't leavin' here, Father. We gotta keep things runnin' like normal. People comin' and goin' — that'll keep the murderer from comin' round."

Father John had exhaled a deep breath. He was up against stubborn people. He could order them off the grounds, but he wasn't sure they would go. St. Francis Mission belonged to them. It was a sacred place. They would not relinquish it to a murderer. Besides, he had no intention of waiting for the murderer to return. He would draw him out, put him on notice, perhaps stop him from trying again.

He'd asked Leonard if he could get Father Joseph's car running.

The Indian had stared at him a long moment, wariness creeping into his expression. "Dunno," he said finally.

"I need the car."

Leonard began running a cloth over the counter. "That a good idea, Father? Chief Banner said yesterday it's best you stay close to the mission."

"I'd appreciate your help, Leonard," Father John had told the man.

It was noon before he heard the engine rattle into life outside his office. He glanced out the window as a plume of blue-gray smoke burst from the Escort's tailpipe. Leonard was bent under the hood.

Now Father John guided the car through a gust of wind and punched the radio scanner. Nothing but twangy western music and talk-show hosts shouting and screaming about government, taxes, schools, roads, and life's unfairness. He switched off the radio. He missed his opera tapes. When he'd called Banner that morning to see when the Toyota would be returned, the line had gone quiet. Then the chief had told him: "Bad news, John. The killer cleaned out the glove compartment."

Father John had thrown his head back and

stared at the ceiling. That's where he kept his favorite tapes. *La Bohème*, *Tosca*, *La Traviata* — all gone.

"What else was in the glove compartment?"

"Flashlight." Father John thought a moment. "Tire gauge." That was all he could think of. "Why would the killer want a bunch of opera tapes?"

"My guess is he grabbed whatever was there. Flashlight and gauge are gone, too. Maybe he thought some of the tapes might be to his liking. Must've gotten a shock when he found out all he had was opera. Lab boys are still checkin' the pickup," the chief went on. Father John heard the hedging. "Wanna make sure we get every trace of fingerprints and hair. It'll be a while before I can release the pickup. Anyway, it's best you stay close to the mission until we get the killer."

Well, he was miles from the mission. He turned north on Highway 132 and angled west through Fort Washakie. And then he was climbing into the foothills alongside the Little Wind River. As he rounded a wide curve, Sonny Red Wolf's compound came into view: a cube of a house set among the pines and boulders, gray boards visible through the white paint. Beyond the house, a cluster of unpainted outbuildings and trucks parked at indiscriminate angles, as if they'd been dropped from the sky. A slight distance upslope in a stand of pines, a white truck sat high on fat tires beside the rectangular-shaped brush shade.

Father John turned into the dirt yard and drove past the house and buildings. The Escort bounced over washboard ruts, gravel pinging against the undercarriage. He stopped in front of the brush shade, got out, and pulled down his cowboy hat against the glare of the sun. A warm wind hissed through the pines and rustled the willow branches that formed the roof and three sides of the shade. An opening faced the east.

Just as he started toward the opening, Sonny Red Wolf stepped outside. A big man, close to six feet, with rounded shoulders and broad chest that sloped into a slightly protruding middle. He wore a black leather jacket over a dark shirt and blue jeans. His long black hair was brushed straight back, exposing the high forehead, the eyes set wide apart over fleshy cheekbones, the determined jaw. "What d'ya want?" he said.

"A friend of mine was murdered yesterday." Father John heard the barely controlled rage in his voice. "He was an innocent man. A priest just trying to do his job." It was an opening. Father John held his breath, waiting for the man to say something he hadn't intended to say. Truth had a way of slipping past barriers, demanding to be told.

The Indian shrugged and walked over to the white truck. "What's that got to do with me?" he said, lifting two dead rabbits out of the bed. Locked in a frame across the rear window was a shotgun, and Father John wondered where the man kept his rifle.

Red Wolf walked back into the brush shade, dangling the rabbits by the hind legs. Father John followed. Daylight flitted past the willow branches and dappled the hard-packed dirt floor. A metal table stood against the leafy wall. There was another table, a scattering of webbed chairs. In the shadows in back, he could make out several cots and boxes heaped with clothing. This was home, he thought. Just like in the Old Time. Except that in the Old Time, Sonny and his followers would have moved their cots into buffalo-skin lodges for the winter, not into a frame house with fading paint.

"You're the guy who wants the mission closed," Father John said. "You blocked the road last spring."

The Indian slung the carcasses across the metal table and turned around. "Sendin' you a message, was all. We don't want you people here. We don't need white government people and white priests tellin' us how to think, how to talk, how to pray. We can run this res the Indian way. Follow our own traditions. We know how to live off the land." He nodded toward the dead rabbits on the table behind him. "So take your white road right on out of here and leave us be."

"I'll leave when the people tell me to go." Father John kept his eyes locked on the Indian's.

Sonny Red Wolf folded his arms and leaned back against the table. "There's gonna be a new council election this winter, and I'm gonna get myself elected, along with some other real Indians. Soon's that happens, we're gonna invite you and a lot of other whites to go home where you belong."

"And if we don't go?"

"We've got ways to make it real uncomfortable. You white people . . ." A sneer. "You like your comforts."

"How about murder, Sonny? Is that one of your ways? Did you kill Father Joseph? Was he the man you were after, or am I the man you wanted?" Father John kept his eyes on the other man, watching for the flickering eyelids, the twitching muscles — the faintest sign that he had hit upon the truth.

"You're a brave man, O'Malley." Red Wolf was shaking his head. "I gotta hand it to you, coming out here to my compound and accusing me of killing some white man."

"I came out here looking for answers." Father John struggled to control his own fury.

"I was born a warrior, O'Malley." The Indian's gaze was steady. " 'Nam gave me some modern training, that's all. If I wanted you dead, you'd be dead. You wouldn't see me coming. Just like those jacks . . ." A backward nod. "They never heard me sneaking up on them. All of a sudden they were looking down the barrel of my shotgun, eyes as big as saucers."

Father John didn't say anything. Silence settled between them, except for the shush of the wind in the willow branches. He had a sense that

102

the man was telling the truth. Sonny Red Wolf was the kind of warrior who didn't make mistakes.

And yet, and yet . . . A man who hated whites. Who wanted the mission closed. That man might have come after him and shot his assistant who happened to be driving the Toyota. He said, "The FBI agent is going to want to know where you were yesterday afternoon."

Red Wolf gave a little snort and shifted his weight against the table. "So I got you to thank for siccin' the FBI on me this morning. Too bad you didn't get here sooner. Could've seen the look on that fed's white face when he couldn't find anything in this compound to tie me to the murder. Went scurrying out of here with his tail between his legs."

Suddenly the Indian pushed himself away from the table and stepped closer. Father John could see the tiny specks of dried blood, like red gnats splattered on his leather jacket. The faint odor of blood wafted through the air.

"Why don't you do the same, O'Malley? Get on outta here. I know what you white folks are up to. You and that fed and that lawyer lady that hangs around with you, a white wannabe. You'd like to pin this murder on me and get me out of the way before I take over the res. It's not going to work. I've got a lot of people with me." He shot a glance around the brush shade. "I'm not getting mixed up in your white fight."

Father John kept his eyes on the Indian's.

"What do you mean, white fight?"

Sonny Red Wolf lifted his chin and stared. A look of disbelief flashed in his eyes. "Listen in on the moccasin telegraph once in a while, why don't you? There isn't an Arapaho on the res that's got a clue why that old man was shot. You're a Jesuit. Figure it out. The people don't know anything because nobody had anything to do with it. Some white guy had it in for that priest and went out to Thunder Lane and killed him."

Father John glanced through the opening at the sun slanting gold across the hood of the Escort. It wasn't Father Joseph the killer had been after. The old priest had been here only two weeks. Yes, he'd been at St. Francis before. But the possibility that someone had been biding his time for thirty-five years, waiting for Father Joseph to return so he could kill him, didn't make sense. No one could have expected Joseph Keenan to return to St. Francis. Father John hadn't even known the man was coming until a few days before he arrived. Yesterday, both Gianelli and Banner had dismissed the possibility, and in their expressions Father John had seen the reflection of his own skepticism. The fact was, Joseph Keenan had been driving *his* red Toyota pickup.

There was another possibility, he realized now. One not so easily dismissed. Maybe Joseph Keenan had been the intended victim. Maybe the killer wasn't someone Joseph had known on

104

the reservation. Maybe he had followed the priest here. What better place than the open spaces of the reservation to commit a cold-blooded, anonymous murder? A white fight, Sonny Red Wolf called it.

Father John brought his eyes back to the Indian's. "If you've got a beef with me, Sonny, take it up with me. I don't want any innocent people hurt." He swung around and walked through the opening.

"Tell that to your white friends," the Indian called after him.

The Escort's engine growled into the mountain quiet as Father John drove downslope past the buildings and the house. He turned onto the road. A dark truck was hurtling toward him, dust rising from the tires like a swarm of mosquitoes. He hit the brake pedal, and the Escort skidded to a stop at the edge of the barrow ditch. The truck screeched to a halt, and a small, wiry man jumped out. Robert Cutting Horse, one of Red Wolf's followers. Father John recognized him from the demonstration last spring.

The Indian started toward the Escort, bobbing and weaving around the hood. Even before he thrust a brown face into the opened window, Father John could smell the whiskey. Instinctively he leaned away.

The Indian blinked, comprehension working slowly into his expression. "I gotta talk to you, Father," he said.

"Is this about Father Joseph's murder?" Father John asked.

"Murder? I don't know about no murder." Another blink. "I gotta get my life turned around. I hear you run some AA meetings."

Father John sighed. The man had probably been at a drinking house and hadn't heard about the murder. "Come see me at the mission when you're sober, Robert," he said.

"I wanna stop this drinkin' shit."

"Come to the mission, and we'll talk." Father John eased up on the brake, and the Escort started to creep forward. The Indian stepped back. As he wheeled around the truck and started down the road, Father John saw the man blinking after him in the rearview mirror, hands jammed into the pockets of his jeans. The odor of whiskey drifted in the air, as clear and strong as a memory.

He drove forty miles across the reservation, the sun fracturing the rear window into a kaleidoscope of colors, his thoughts on Sonny Red Wolf. A clever man. Deflecting suspicion from himself by suggesting someone else was to blame was the oldest ruse of a guilty man. But truth rang in what he said, like the faint, distant clang of a bell. Father John had often heard the sound in the confessional, in counseling sessions: the irrelevant, offhand remark that caused everything to click into focus, as if the binoculars had been adjusted and what was once hidden and obscure had suddenly snapped into view.

Father John stared at the empty stretch of road ahead, searching for the logical connections. A white fight, Sonny had called it. What was it the Provincial had said? Joseph Keenan had *insisted* upon coming back to St. Francis Mission. Why had he wanted to return to a place he hadn't seen in thirty-five years? What had he been running from? What had followed him here?

He slowed for the turn into the mission. Cottonwood branches swayed overhead, leaves shimmering gold in the last flare of sunlight. As he banked around Circle Drive, he saw that the grounds were empty, except for Elena's old Chevy parked next to the residence. Like Leonard, the housekeeper had come to work today, despite the fact that a killer could show up at any moment looking for him, if his own theory was correct.

What proof did he have otherwise? The remarks of a man who might be guilty of murder? Who had killed a man in the past? Who had every reason to send the investigation in another direction — away from himself? Still . . .

He thought about the papers and books in Joseph's room. Gianelli and Banner could have missed something. The image of himself raging through the man's possessions brought a stab of pain. He hadn't found anything unusual, but he'd been looking for a bottle of whiskey, not something to explain a murder. He decided to have another look.

The unmistakable odor of beef stew floated into the dim hallway as he let himself through the front door of the residence. From the kitchen came the sounds of metal scraping metal, tap water gushing. He tossed his cowboy hat onto the bench in the entry and started up the stairs.

"That you, Father?" Elena appeared below, dabbing her hands onto the apron. "We been waitin' for you."

"We?" He stopped halfway up the stairs and leaned over the banister.

"You got a visitor. Been here most the afternoon. I was startin' to get worried, you bein' so late."

Father John turned and came back down the stairs. "Who is it?" he asked, heading toward the closed door of the study.

"She's waitin' out on the patio."

Vicky, Father John thought. She'd talked to somebody, learned something. He'd been worrying all day about what she might do, the danger she might put herself into. It was the worry about the people around him — the people he loved — that had made him decide to pay a visit to Sonny Red Wolf.

He brushed past the housekeeper and walked through the kitchen to the small utility room that opened onto the outside stairway. Footsteps trailed behind.

"You're gonna be real surprised," Elena said.

108

He opened the back door and stared down the short flight of stairs at the redheaded woman seated in one of the patio chairs, Walks-On curled at her feet.

10

The woman lifted herself out of the webbed chair, a graceful, confident unfolding of her slim, attractive figure. She tilted her face and fixed him with the bluest eyes he'd seen in a long while. Intelligence and defiance mingled in her expression and enhanced her beauty. A mass of copper-colored hair caught the light of the sun dropping behind the mountains. Freckles sprinkled her nose and cheeks. Her lips were touched with red. She stood at the edge of the table, a small purse tossed on the top, the breeze plucking at her silver-colored blouse and black slacks. For an instant he felt as if two planes had collided — past and present — and he had been transported back twenty-five years, so strong was her resemblance to Eileen.

"Megan O'Malley," he said, hurrying down the stairs. Walks-On raised his head and eyed him sleepily as he placed his arms around the girl.

She stepped out of his arms and fastened her eyes on his. "Hello, Uncle John," she said. There was a hint of anger in her voice, or had he imagined it?

He kept one hand on her shoulder, scarcely believing she was here. No one in his family had visited in the seven years he'd been at St. Francis. But who would come? Not his brother Mike. Certainly not Eileen, or any of their six kids — he still thought of them as kids. Yet Megan, the oldest, had to be about twenty-five, hardly the gangly sprite of a girl he remembered in his early visits to his brother's home, before the visits had become so uncomfortable he'd decided to curtail them.

His visit last spring had been cordial. Perfectly cordial and formal. The youngest kids had trailed into the house — quick hellos, disinterested exchanges. He'd had to shake himself into the realization they were already in high school. The others were away: one in law school, another at Boston College. And Megan, an architect living in New York, engaged to be married.

"You look fantastic," he said.

She gave him a mirthless smile. "Is that because I have red hair and freckles like you?"

His own laugh sounded forced and uncertain in his ears. "What brought you all the way to Wyoming?"

"Just a visit." He caught the false note. Something was wrong. And she had come at the worst possible time.

As if she'd read his thoughts, she said, "Oh, I know about the murdered priest. Elena told me that it could have been you. Shouldn't you close the mission and go away?"

"You sound like my boss," he said, trying for a lighter tone.

"You have a boss?" The blue eyes widened in mock surprise. "I never thought of you as having a boss."

"I have a lot of them, I'm afraid." Father John shrugged.

"So you ignore them?"

"I do my best. Look, Megan," he hurried on, "the mission might not be the safest place right now —"

"Something told me I had to come," she interrupted. "Now I understand why I was drawn here. Elena said I could stay at the guest house."

That explained why he hadn't seen her car on the grounds. It was parked at the guest house behind Eagle Hall, and she was already settled in. He sighed. "Promise me you'll be careful," he said. "Don't walk around the grounds by yourself at night."

"Don't worry about me," she shot back. "I've been living in New York City for three years. I can take care of myself." He saw by the way she pulled her gaze toward the dark ridge of mountains in the distance that there was something else on her mind.

The door squeaked above them, and he glanced around. Elena stood on the landing. "Dinner's on," she called. "Come eat while it's hot."

Megan scooped the purse from the table and, brushing past him, started up the stairs. The sun had disappeared, leaving an electric sky of reds and purples and oranges. Shadows had started to gather at the perimeters of the mission grounds, like animals stalking their prey.

He started after his niece. Walks-On trailed

alongside, an easy lope up the stairs on three legs. In the kitchen, the dog headed for his rug. Elena led the way to the dining room. Sometimes he forgot about the hollow, dark space between the kitchen and living room. The last time he'd eaten there was two years ago, when the bishop had come for dinner. Elena had gotten out the mismatched china and yellowed tablecloths, the candles and brass candlestick holders, and transformed the room into a place of warmth and comfort, like a real home, he had thought.

He saw that the housekeeper had worked the same magic this evening. Candlelight flickered over the tablecloth and licked at the white plates with tiny tongues of fire. He held a side chair for Megan before taking the end chair close to her. Within a moment Elena set bowls of hot stew in front of them.

"Please join us, Elena," he said as she started toward the kitchen.

The housekeeper stopped. Leaning toward him, she sent him an accusatory glare. "My grandbaby's birthday party's tonight. Remember? I told you all about it." The whisper of a memory came to him. Breakfast a couple of mornings ago. Elena stirring oatmeal at the stove and prattling on about an upcoming party. And he — he grimaced at the thought — half listening, sipping at his coffee, perusing the morning paper. "Besides," the housekeeper was saying, "you need to have a good chat together, just the two of you. Don't need no outsiders listenin' in.'"

"I wouldn't call you an outsider."

"Don't see me with red hair, do you?" Slowly she ran a brown hand over the clumps of Megan's red hair, as if to feel the color. Then, giving the young woman's shoulder a little pat, she whirled around and slipped past the door.

Father John bowed his head over the stew, drawing in the hot, pungent odor as he said the grace out loud. *Bless us, O Lord, for these thy gifts* . . . The words familiar, ingrained in his heart. Then he added, "Thank you, O Lord, for bringing Megan here today, and keep her and all of the people at St. Francis Mission safely in your care."

Megan said nothing, eyes cast downward, like those of a convent girl whose thoughts were elsewhere. Wisps of steam lapped at the sprinkle of freckles on her face. He kept his gaze on her as he took a bite of the stew. It was delicious, a sharp reminder of the hunger he'd tried to ignore as he'd driven across the reservation this afternoon. She was poking her fork into her bowl, absent-mindedly stirring the thick brown gravy and chunks of beef, carrots, and potatoes, eyes still cast down. Finally she raised her fork and nibbled at a chunk of potato.

From the kitchen came a scuffling sound, the rattle of keys. Elena stuck her head through the doorway. "I'll be goin' now," she said. "Leave the dishes. I'll tidy up tomorrow." An announcement, he realized, that she *would* return tomorrow. And then she was gone, footsteps clacking in the hall, front door shutting.

Father John turned his attention to the young woman beside him. "What brought you here, Megan?"

"Didn't I tell you? I wanted to see you." There was a hard edge to her tone.

Father John took another bite of stew and waited for her to go on. When she didn't he said, "Is everything okay between you and your fiancé?"

"Jay? This has nothing to do with Jay." A mixture of amusement and anger flashed in the blue eyes. "He insisted I come. He's been very supportive, even when I quit my job."

"Quit your job?" Father John set his fork down and stared at her. Whatever lay beneath the confident exterior was darker and more troubling than he'd guessed.

"My boss said I could take two weeks." A defensive tone. "What if I needed more time? I wasn't sure how long I'd want to stay."

"What's troubling you?" His voice was soft. "What's going on?"

Tears had begun to pool in her eyes and trickle along her cheeks, blurring the freckles. She raised a hand and wiped at the tears, leaving a sheen of moisture that caught the candlelight. Finally she said, "You really don't know, do you? You don't have a clue. All these years you've been busy being a priest, teaching and working at a mission . . ." She stopped and looked away. He realized he was holding his breath, waiting for the rest: drinking, trying to recover in Grace House.

She brought her gaze back to his. "You've gone on with your life," she said. He felt a rush of gratitude she hadn't completed the litany of his life. "Didn't you wonder? Didn't you ask yourself any questions?"

He had a sense of floundering, as if he were lost in the expanse of the plains, where everything looked the same, and he couldn't spot a point of reckoning. "What is it I should understand? What is it I should know?"

She threw her napkin into the center of the table, pushed the chair back, and jumped to her feet. "That you have a daughter," she said. "You should know that."

Father John felt his mouth go dry, the air he was breathing turn to dust. He sat stunned, unable to make his legs lift his weight out of the chair. After a long moment he forced himself to his feet and, stumbling against the table, went after her. He caught her in the entry at the door.

"Coming here was stupid." She yanked open the door. He took hold of her arm, but she wrenched away and slipped outside, breaking into a run down the sidewalk. He sprinted after her and, catching her by the arm again, pulled her to a stop. He clasped her shoulders, holding her tight.

"Don't go, Megan. We've got to talk about

this." In the dim light slipping past the windows, he could see the tears flowing down her cheeks — a river. She was trembling in his arms, crying silently. "Please," he said.

He felt her shoulders sinking, her muscles relaxing. With one hand lightly on her shoulder, he guided her back into the house. In the living room, he flipped on the lamp, his eyes never leaving hers as she sank into a corner of the sofa. The confidence and determination had evaporated. She looked like a scared child: the tears, the shaking hands.

He pulled a side chair over to the coffee table in front of the sofa and sat down across from her. In the glow of the lamplight, she seemed paler, her hair a burnished bronze. "There's some terrible mistake, Megan," he said, the counseling tone. "I'm your uncle. Your parents are my brother and his wife."

She gave a startled laugh and turned her face away. "I know about you and my mother. I found the diary she kept when you were both at Boston College."

Father John felt his heart turn over; he fought to catch his breath. *Eileen kept a diary.*

"It was so . . ." She hesitated, still looking away, as if she could summon the memory from the shadows in the entry. "Weird, the way I stumbled onto it. Mom said I could take some old furniture from the attic. There was a bureau that I wanted behind some boxes. I started pulling the boxes away when I saw the small books stacked in one of them. Old photo albums, I thought, so I decided to take a look. But they weren't albums. They were diaries that Mom kept through high school and college. The last one was for 1974, the year I was born. I wondered what the year had been like for Mom, so I started reading."

Slowly she brought her eyes back. The blue had deepened to the darkness of a thundercloud. Her world, he realized, had tilted on its axis; everything she had believed to be true dissolved into some formless mass. She threw her head back and laughed. It was the sound of hysteria. "What a joke! I'd idolized you all my life. My favorite uncle. A priest!"

Father John said nothing for a moment. Then, a whisper: "I don't deny I once loved your mother very much."

The lamplight flickered, as if a gust of wind had blown through the room. Megan's eyes locked on his. "You abandoned her." She spit out the words. "She was pregnant, and you abandoned her."

"No," he said. *He would never have abandoned her.* Silence dropped like a heavy curtain over the room. After a moment he asked if that was what Eileen had written in the diary.

"Not in so many words. But I can read between the lines. She married my . . ." A hesitation. "Mom married your brother three months after you went into the seminary, and I was born five months later. Figure it out."

This cannot be, he thought, slumping back against the hard chair knobs. Eileen had never said, had never told him . . . There must be some other explanation. He said: "Have you talked to your mother about this?"

Megan drew one hand slowly across her cheekbones. Moisture ran along the edge of her index finger. "I could see from the diaries that my mother has been in denial since the day you left her. She would never admit the truth. That's why I came here. I hoped you would tell me the truth."

The truth? he thought. *What was the truth?* The quick, spastic sounds of her breathing invaded the space between them. He looked past her toward the window. The lights around Circle Drive shimmered in the black glass. His mind searched for the words to calm her suspicions, set his own mind at rest. This was not the past he remembered; this was not what he wanted. She was his brother's child.

Finally he leaned across the coffee table and took her hand. "You are going to have to talk to your mom, Megan. Tell her what you've told me. Surely she'll be able to explain . . ."

She yanked her hand away and propelled herself to her feet. "I'm wasting your time," she said, starting for the entry. "I'll be out of here first thing in the morning."

He rose and followed. She already had the front door open. "I want to know the truth, too, Megan," he said.

She swung around and fixed him with a long, questioning look. There was the smallest softening in her expression, or did he imagine it? "Come on." He took her arm. "I'll walk you to the guest house."

The night was cool. Strips of white clouds floated like contrails across the sky. He guided her on the path through the wild grasses in the field and out along Center Drive, past the old school, the church, down the narrow alley between the administration building and Eagle Hall, in and out of circles of light. At the guest house, he fumbled with the key, unlocked the door, and pushed it open. Megan slid past. He waited as she switched on the inside light. It sparkled in her hair. Her face was in shadows.

"Don't leave tomorrow, Megan." He placed his hand flat against the door to stop it from closing. "Stay for a while."

"No thanks."

"We'll talk some more."

When she didn't reply, he said, "We could get to know each other. And I could use some help in the office." It was an excuse, a lousy excuse but the best he could come up with at the moment. He couldn't bear to let her go. Not yet, not with this matter unsettled between them. One extra day would give them a chance to talk. Even if a killer was about, Gianelli and Banner would also be about. Megan would be safe for one day.

He felt the sting of her gaze on him. After a moment she said, "I'll think about it."

11

Father John walked back across the grounds, scarcely aware of the slumbering buildings, the breeze nipping at his hands and face, the distant whir of a truck on Seventeen-Mile Road. *It cannot be,* he said to himself over and over. *Dear Lord, this must not be true.*

He let himself into the residence and stopped in the hall. The creak of a floorboard, the smallest squeal of a closing door? — he couldn't identify the sound. He waited, muscles tensing in his shoulders, hands balled into fists. Someone was here; he could sense the presence, the faintest whiff of perspiration.

He stepped into the living room. It was as they had left it: the straight-back chair pulled to the coffee table, the indentations in the soft cushions of the sofa. On he walked through the dining room, cupping the candles and blowing them out as he passed. In the kitchen, he saw Megan's small black purse on the counter where she'd left it. A few feet away was the automatic coffeemaker, a couple of mugs, and a platter with two slices of cake. They hadn't gotten to the coffee and cake before the world had imploded.

From his corner, Walks-On lifted his head and gave him a half-lidded glance before snuggling back onto the rug. The kind of greeting the dog would have given an intruder, Father John knew.

Walks-On was used to strangers, people passing through. He ran to visitors outside, red disk clenched in his jaws, hope in his eyes. What did the dog know of a killer?

Suddenly Father John saw the door. It was slightly ajar. He walked over, flung it open, and stepped out into the utility room. The back door hung open, swaying in the breeze. Down the stairs, the patio was dark and deserted, and beyond, the mission grounds lost in shadows.

He shut the outside door and threw the lock, then stepped back into the kitchen and locked that door. The tension began to dissolve in his muscles. He was the last one into the house earlier; perhaps he hadn't closed the doors. The noise he'd heard could have been the wind catching at the back door and whistling into the kitchen. And yet . . . There was something in the air, the musty odor of perspiration.

Still feeling uneasy, he poured a mug of coffee, carried it down the hall into the study, and sank into the contours of the leather chair. Fatigue weighed on him like a heavy cloak. He reached for the lamp switch, then withdrew his hand, preferring to sip at the hot coffee and watch the moonlight angling through the window, forming patterns on the carpet, lapping at the papers on his desk. After a moment Walks-On wandered down the hallway, nails *tick-tick-tick*ing on the hard floor. He flopped next to the chair and set a cold nose into the palm of his hand, as if to remind him he was not alone.

He was not alone! A young woman had wandered into his life. How could such a thing be possible — that he could have a child and, all these years, not have known? It couldn't be true.

The memories crowded in on him, like the black shadows shrinking the room. Their senior year together at Boston College, he and Eileen, and the slow unfolding in his mind, the gradual understanding of what he must do, how he was meant to live his life. Finally, the certainty of it. He had struggled against the certainty, like a bull ramming a stone wall. He had not asked to be called out from other men, from an ordinary life, like Abraham called to a new land and knowing he must go, regardless of what he may have wanted to do. He had loved her; he had wanted to be with her.

Three months after he'd entered the seminary, she had married his brother. The news had hit him like a punch in the stomach, a sickening thud that still reverberated inside him. She had forgotten him so easily, when he had known it would take years, a lifetime perhaps, to forget her. Had she hurried to marry Mike because she was pregnant? And did his brother know? Did that explain the years of polite coldness?

She had never let on . . . He'd had no idea. Had she told him, it would have ended his struggle. They would have been married, their lives different. It was hard to imagine: he, a family man, probably teaching history in some small college in New England today. If she had told him . . .

That was what bothered him, her silence. It was unlike her. What had attracted him to Eileen from the beginning was her forthrightness and honesty. Whatever she happened to feel or believe, she blurted out. It had led to many an argument, shouting matches at times. She was his equal in stubbornness, but there had been no periods of brooding silence, no imaginary wrongs looming between them. They had been honest with each other. He had told her from the beginning he felt called to be a priest. He had struggled against the calling, and she had known he was struggling. Surely she would have told him?

The red numerals on the clock at the corner of his desk glowed 10:42. He got to his feet and walked into the hall. Removing the phone from the table at the foot of the stairs, he started up to bed, trailing the cord behind him, an old habit. He always brought the phone to the top landing at night in case someone needed a priest. It never left his mind that he was a priest. His legs were slow moving, the climb up the stairs an effort. He flipped the switch at the top. A white light shone down the narrow hall, past the closed doors to the bedrooms and bathroom. He started toward his room at the far end, then stopped at Father Joseph's door. He'd been on his way to take a closer look at Joseph's things when Elena had stopped him on the stairs. You've got a visitor, she'd said. *You've got a daughter.*

He pushed open the door and found the switch. A dim light splashed over the room. He grimaced at the neatness. Elena had put everything back together after his rampage last night: she knew what he had been looking for. Instinctively, he started to back away. Gianelli had already searched the room. What could he hope to find?

His mind rephrased the question: what did he hope to avoid? His own room and the assault of memories, old emotions? Despite the tiredness that dragged at him like a heavy chain, sleep would be a long time coming, if it came at all, and while he waited, the thirst would come, invisible shackles slipping over him.

He walked over to the desk and began thumbing through the papers: Sunday bulletins, a syllabus for the class Father Joseph had scheduled on the meaning of the Christian message, various magazines. He jerked open the drawer and lifted out a writing tablet. A quick flip through the pages. Blank.

Slowly he looked around the room, surprised for a moment at his own reflection in the mirror above the bureau: pale face shadowed with fatigue, shoulders hunched in exhaustion. Perching on the bed, he began pulling books from the bookcase a couple of feet away. He turned each one over in his hand, examining the titles. A compilation of philosophy. Works of philosophers from Aristotle to Kierkegaard. What had he expected? Joseph Keenan was a renowned philosopher. His own bookcases were filled with history books, and he was hardly a renowned historian.

He picked up the large, red leather book on the top shelf. On the front, embossed in gold, was the word Bible. It was surprisingly heavy, the leather soft and nubby. He opened the cover and began gently turning the tissue-thin pages. A small bulge protruded into the center. Holding the book over the bed, he gently winnowed the pages until a newspaper clipping folded into a small square dropped onto the bedspread.

He set the Bible down and unfolded the clipping, the paper brittle in his hands, the edges ragged with age. The date in small black print at the top was September 26, 1964. In the center, a gray-smudged photo of a young woman smiling into the camera, chin tilted in a haughty challenge, a white nurse's cap topping the long dark hair. A two-column headline in large black letters ran above the photo: LOCAL NURSE FOUND DEAD. Below, in smaller letters: *Body Discovered on Banks of Wind River. Police Call Death Suicide.*

He read quickly through the article: Dawn James, twenty-four-year-old Lander resident, graduate of Lander High School and Casper College. Nurse at Markham Clinic. Survived by sister, Mary James of Riverton.

Father John stared at the name, trying to place the woman. Had he met her at some point in Riverton? Been introduced after Mass one

126

Sunday? Suddenly it hit him. Mary James had called the mission yesterday, and Elena had taken the message. He'd pushed the message aside, not recognizing the name, thinking he would return the call later.

He refolded the clipping and walked down the hall to his own room, where he laid it inside the top drawer of his bureau — a flat packet of yellowing newspaper on a stack of white T-shirts. A clipping that Father Joseph had kept for thirty-five years. It came to his mind that perhaps he was not the only priest who had spent years praying for forgiveness. But whatever had been between the twenty-four-year-old nurse who had shot herself and Joseph Keenan no longer mattered. They were both dead. *May their souls rest in peace.*

He slammed the bureau drawer shut, consigning the clipping to its own privacy. His thoughts turned to Mary James. What painful memories had crashed over her at the news of Joseph Keenan's murder? He would call the woman first thing in the morning.

12

Vicky saw the newspaper headline as she pulled into the curb. A stack of newspapers slumped inside a white metal box on the sidewalk in front of her office building. She hurried over, one hand on her briefcase, the other digging through her bag for change, her eyes riveted on the large black type: MOVIE STAR SEARCHES FOR FAMILY.

She managed to extract a coin and feed it into the slot. A quick pull on the glass door and she had the newspaper in hand. Splashed below the headline was a photo of Sharon David striding along Main Street, past the hardware store, the café. There was the flash of long, dark legs in the slit of her skirt. Snapping the paper into a fold, Vicky hurried up the stairs and along the outside corridor. Her heels made a hollow, thumping sound on the wood. She pushed through her office door and crossed the small waiting room, throwing a little nod to Laola, who sat at the desk in the far corner, tapping the keyboard and cradling the phone against one shoulder.

In her private office, Vicky dropped the briefcase and bag on the desk and, sinking into her swivel chair, opened the newspaper. Her eyes moved quickly down the column of print. A familiar story: girl staring in the mirror, wondering why she was different, longing for her real home. How moving when Sharon David had delivered the lines in her office. Vicky had wanted to cry.

She tossed the paper across the desk, sending the ball-shaped pen holder skittering to the floor. What a fool she was! Duped by a publicity stunt concocted in some Hollywood studio. Sharon David stars as Indian woman in *The Sky People*. Sharon David searches for real Indian family.

"A discreet inquiry!" Vicky said to the empty room, mimicking the movie star's confidential tone. "None of the public's business."

"Who you talkin' to?"

Vicky swung her chair around. Laola stood in the doorway, her expression shaded in bewilderment and curiosity. She glanced about the room as if she expected someone to pop up from one of the barrel-shaped chairs.

"We've been taken for a ride on a bucking bronco," Vicky said, picking up the newspaper and waving it toward the young woman.

Laola walked over and set a small stack of papers on the desk. "Phone's been ringing all morning. Reporters from Cheyenne, Casper, Denver. Some guy from CNN. You really think CNN . . . ?" The words trailed into a question.

"Sharon's publicity people have obviously notified everybody," Vicky said. A mixture of rage and helplessness surged through her. The article asked anyone with information about Sharon David's natural parents to contact Vicky Holden, attorney-at-law. She pulled her briefcase over the newspaper, blocking out the smiling, striding actress. A symbolic gesture that brought a small measure of satisfaction: she may have been played for a fool, but Sharon David would soon be out of her life.

The phone emitted an abrupt, jangling noise, and Laola turned and disappeared through the doorway. Vicky opened the desk drawer and withdrew the legal pad on which she had jotted down the telephone number of the dude ranch where the actress was staying. A simple phone call, and she could sever ties with her newest client. She would return the retainer fee.

She picked up the receiver, then hesitated, holding it in midair. Her practice had been busy lately, but fees came in slowly, usually on the installment plan, a few dollars every payday. She expected a settlement in Sam Eagle Hawk's case, which would give her own accounts a much-needed infusion, but the agreement hadn't been signed. It would be a while before she received her fee. She needed Sharon David's check.

But so far she hadn't earned it. She had Aunt Rose's opinion and her own, but that was hardly enough to justify keeping the money. She would have to make a few more inquiries.

Slamming down the receiver, she turned her attention to the paper-clipped pages Laola had delivered. The settlement she intended to demand from the Custom Garage for Sam Eagle Hawk. She could imagine the opposing lawyers' outrage: the garage would be bankrupt, forced to close its fifty-year-old doors. She knew the dance, had participated in the steps on behalf of her own clients. In less than an hour she had a meeting with the attorneys.

Just as she set the pages in her briefcase and snapped it shut, Laola reappeared in the doorway. "That anchorwoman from Channel Two keeps calling." The breathless voice again. "You know, Sue Causeman. She wants to know where she can find Sharon David. What am I s'pposed to tell all these reporters?"

Vicky got to her feet, swung her bag over one shoulder, and picked up the briefcase. "Tell them 'no comment,' " she said, brushing past the secretary. In the outer office, she stopped and turned back. "Oh, and Laola, call the Grace Clinic. See if the director has a few minutes to see me this afternoon. Then call Luther Benson and ask him to meet me later."

It was mid-afternoon when Vicky turned in to the parking lot of the Grace Clinic, a tan-brick building surrounded by a sweep of tree-studded, manicured lawn. Shadows lay over the walls, making the clinic seem cool and inviting after the heated meeting she'd just left. Lawyers for the garage owner had spent the night dreaming up new hoops for Sam Eagle Hawk to jump through, all unacceptable. She'd held firm for the settlement, and finally, reluctance seeping from them like blood from an opened wound, they'd agreed. In her briefcase on the seat beside her was the signed agreement.

Glancing in the rearview mirror, she patted her hair into place and touched up her lipstick. She'd called Laola from the lawyers' offices and learned that both Dr. Roland Grace and Luther Benson could see her. Dr. Grace was expecting her at two o'clock. Ten minutes ago.

She slid out of the Bronco and hurried up the brick-lined sidewalk bisecting the lawn. A warm gust of wind caught at her suit skirt, molding it around her legs. Overhead the sky stretched as far as she could see, a smooth blue satin. Clouds rose over the mountains like white smoke. A rush of cool air hit her as she opened the glass door and stepped into the clinic.

Rows of chairs in bright, cheery colors lined the waiting-room walls. There was only one patient: a woman seated in the middle of an empty row, looking as if she might deliver a baby at any moment. At her feet, a small boy was pushing a miniature truck across the carpet. An image flashed into Vicky's mind, like a photograph superimposed on the woman and the boy: she, with another baby on the way, Lucas playing at her feet.

How often the memories came, unbidden and unwelcome, triggered by some ordinary scene. And with the memories, a sharp stab of regret that somehow things had not gone as she'd planned, not as she'd planned at all.

She crossed the reception room to the counter on the opposite wall. Behind sliding glass panels sat an attractive woman in her forties, Vicky guessed, with stylishly cut blond hair and thin brown eyebrows penciled above eyes as green as the blouse she was wearing. She had a pale complexion, but her face took on a yellowish cast under the fluorescent lights, like a bleached canvas soaking up color.

"May I help you?" The receptionist leaned toward the small opening between the glass panels.

Vicky said, "I'm here to see Dr. Grace. My secretary called earlier."

"You're the attorney, then?" The eyebrows shot up in surprise.

"Please let the doctor know I'm here."

The woman was still staring. "I'm afraid Dr. Grace is with a patient. Perhaps I can be of help? I'm the business manager."

"I'll wait." Vicky gave the woman an assuring smile. As she started toward a chair, the door next to the counter swung open. A young woman with a small bulge at her waist stepped into the lobby. A glance back, a grateful smile: "Thank you, Doctor."

In the doorway behind her was a large man about fifty, wearing a white coat that hung loosely over his dark trousers and blue shirt. A red-printed tie was knotted sharply at the shirt collar. His forehead continued into a bald scalp that shone under the fluorescent light. His eyes seemed outsized and intense behind thick, pink-rimmed glasses. "Ms. Holden?" he said. Then, without waiting for a reply, "Do come in."

Vicky followed him down a narrow carpeted corridor past partially open doors. She caught a glimpse of white-sheeted examining tables, silver footrests, a nurse smoothing white paper over one table. The acrid odor of iodine hung in the air.

At the far door, before the corridor jutted into a north wing, the doctor halted and, stepping back, ushered her into a small office. Bookcases faced each other from opposite walls — the same-sized books stacked together, as if they had been arranged by height rather than subject. The rolltop desk across the room was open, exposing cubbyholes filled with envelopes that extended over papers and file folders arranged on the surface. Next to the desk, a narrow window covered with a blue semitransparent shade diffused the sunlight and gave the office a faint blue cast.

The doctor motioned her to a dark leather chair. He took the old-fashioned wood chair in front of the desk and, leaning toward her, said, "What can I help you with?" There was a veiled sharpness to the words, as if a visit from an attorney had put him on guard.

Vicky settled her bag on her lap. "One of my clients believes she may have been adopted from this area thirty-five years ago," she began. "She may have been placed through a private adoption, perhaps handled by a private clinic."

The doctor's face broke into a smile of undisguised relief. He shifted his bulky frame, leaned back, and crossed one thick thigh over the other.

"So Sharon David thinks she was adopted from the Grace Clinic!" He gave out a little guffaw. Then, in a low, confidential tone: "A beautiful woman. Tell me, what's she really like?"

Vicky ignored the question. "I know that women from the reservation came to the clinic for prenatal care in the 1960s."

"Still do," the doctor said.

Vicky went on: "Can you tell me whether the clinic ever handled private adoptions?"

Behind the pink-rimmed glasses, the doctor's eyes took on a harder look. He uncrossed his legs and sat up straight. "Not in the twenty years I've owned the clinic. What happened before that, well, I could hardly be responsible . . ." He raised both hands, palms up, as if appealing to some invisible authority. "Jeremiah Markham owned the clinic then. Got his start here, didn't you know?"

Vicky gave a little nod, and the doctor hurried on, undisguised pride working through his voice. "Founded the clinic. Delivered babies for about a year around 1964 before moving to Los Angeles. Started a large clinic there and . . ." He paused a moment. "The rest, as they say, is history."

Vicky found a pen and small pad in her bag. On a blank page she scrawled the name Jeremiah Markham. Glancing up, she said, "Wasn't that the year many Indian babies died?"

Dr. Grace shifted his weight sideways against one armrest. "I believe that year determined his

135

career. He has never said so, of course, but" —
he raised both hands again — "losing one baby
after the other. Not knowing the cause. Waking
up in the middle of the night asking yourself
what you might have done differently." The
doctor glanced away a moment, as if to bring the
enormity of what had happened into focus.
"Jerry understood there was nothing he could
have done. The water was seriously contaminated. But I believe the infant deaths at the clinic
led him to devote his life to ensuring that every
baby would have the chance of arriving safely in
this world."

"Are you saying babies were delivered here, at
the clinic?" Vicky had assumed the women delivered at one of the local hospitals, as she had.

The doctor gave her a tolerant smile. "Jerry
was ahead of his time by a decade. He preached
natural childbirth before it was called natural
childbirth. Offered a comprehensive program of
nutrition, exercise, stress reduction, and mental
preparation. Highly revolutionary at the time.
Most hospitals didn't want any part of it. So he
opened his own hospital right here." He nodded
toward the north wing where the corridor had
taken a sharp jog. "Women came to the clinic for
classes during their pregnancies and delivered in
the birthing rooms. As soon as the health officials determined the water was polluted, Jerry
instructed patients to drink only bottled water.
Unfortunately some women didn't follow instructions."

The doctor exhaled a long breath. "I always believed Jerry felt he had to leave here. What he was doing was beneficial to mothers and babies. Yet, many babies died. There was a stigma, don't you see? A dark spell cast over his revolutionary theories. Jerry had to start anew somewhere else, which he did in Los Angeles."

Vicky was quiet. The doctor only confirmed what Aunt Rose had said about a time of lost babies and dashed hopes. A time when no Arapaho woman would have given up her child. Yet there could have been one lonely frightened woman who had decided to do just that. She said, "Do you know whether Dr. Markham ever arranged private adoptions?"

"For an Indian child?" The doctor's eyebrows rose above the steel rims of his glasses. "You would have to ask him. He may have records from that period." Reaching across the desk, he pushed a button on a small intercom. "Get me Jerry Markham's number," he barked. Still holding down the button, he brought his eyes back to Vicky's. "Jerry hasn't practiced in years. Too busy writing books and lecturing. But he still works as a consultant. We call him from time to time, when we have a difficult case."

Static sputtered over the intercom, followed by the business manager's eager voice reciting a telephone number. Vicky jotted it down, then slipped the pad and pen back into her bag and got to her feet. Dr. Grace stood up and extended a beefy hand.

137

"You've been very helpful," Vicky said, her hand lost in the folds of the man's palm.

"About Sharon David." The doctor was smiling. "Perhaps you could arrange a dinner party?" he said.

Quid pro quo, Vicky thought. "I'll let Sharon know how helpful you've been," she said, ignoring the request. She retrieved her hand and escaped into the corridor.

As she stepped into the waiting room, the business manager pushed aside one of the glass panels and leaned forward. "Dr. Markham can be very hard to reach," she said.

"Any suggestions?" Vicky walked over to the counter.

A look of exasperation came into the woman's eyes. "You have to keep calling. Over and over. Leaving messages on that infernal machine. Eventually Dr. Markham gets back to you." She gave a long sigh. "He's very busy, you know."

Vicky thanked her and started to walk away.

"Is this about Sharon David?" Eagerness leaked into the other woman's tone.

Vicky turned back. "I want to talk to him about the clinic."

"Well, if it has anything to do about business, you should talk to Joanne Garrow. She was his business manager, and business managers know a lot more than doctors about business matters." She straightened her shoulders and gave the files stacked along the counter a proprietary glance.

"Where would I find her?"

"Joanne? Still lives where she always did. About four blocks south of here. The big red-brick house on the corner. Can't miss it."

13

A glance at her silver watch told Vicky she was late for the meeting with Luther Benson. But Luther, she knew, would wait. Ensconced at his favorite table in the back of the Mountain Lounge, one hand wrapped around a sweating martini glass, the other poking at the swivel stick, bobbing the olive in the clear liquid, Luther would wait, glad for the excuse to order another martini. Since he'd retired from his law practice a few years ago, he had few demands on his time.

She let up on the accelerator, suddenly aware that the green sedan ahead was traveling about fifteen miles per hour. She tapped out an impatient rhythm on the wheel as she followed the sedan down the residential block and through the intersection. Suddenly the car swerved right and crawled up a long driveway that ran alongside a two-story, red-brick house.

Vicky swung next to the curb as an elderly woman emerged from the sedan, opened the rear door, and lifted out a brown bag of groceries. Then she pushed the door shut with one hip and started across the lawn.

"Ms. Garrow?" Vicky called, sliding out of the Bronco.

The woman whirled around, clutching the groceries against her chest like a shield. "Yes?" she called. It might have been the chirp of a small bird.

140

"I didn't mean to startle you." Vicky started up the sidewalk.

The woman was peering over glasses that slipped partway down her nose. A pink cord hung from the side pieces and dangled below her chin. She looked to be in her seventies — the small, birdlike frame hunched around the grocery bag, the tightly curled gray hair and the face furrowed with worry.

As she approached, Vicky gave her name and said she was an attorney. "Could I talk to you a moment?"

"I can't imagine what it could be about." The woman started across the lawn toward the porch steps.

"About the clinic Dr. Jeremiah Markham ran in town."

The woman was halfway up the steps. She stopped and, without looking back, called out, "I don't know anything."

For a moment Vicky wondered if she had stopped at the right house. "Weren't you Dr. Markham's business manager?"

"Go away!" she shouted. "I don't want to talk to you."

"Ms. Garrow" — Vicky walked to the bottom step — "I only want to ask you . . ."

The woman had reached the porch. She swung around, staring over the carton of eggs poking from the grocery bag. "You're Indian, aren't you?" She hurled the words like an accusation.

Vicky caught her breath. For a moment she couldn't speak. Then: "I'm a member of the Arapaho tribe. I have a few questions about the Markham Clinic."

"Get off my property, do you hear? Get off my property." She was backing across the porch, one arm slung around the sagging grocery bag, the other fumbling in a jacket pocket. Pulling out a key, she pointed it like a weapon. "I'll call the police if you don't leave immediately. You're trespassing."

"I don't understand . . ."

"Trespasser! Trespasser! Indian trespasser!" the woman shrieked as she turned and began jamming the key into the lock, ramming the grocery bag against the door, as if the egg carton and bulge of groceries might break through the wood.

Vicky started backing down the sidewalk, her legs trembling beneath her. She forced herself to turn around and walk confidently to the curb. The whack of the door slamming behind her broke the afternoon quiet of the neighborhood. As she slid inside the Bronco, she saw the lace curtain flutter at the front window of the house, as if a breeze had caught it for the briefest moment before dropping it back into place.

She switched on the ignition. The engine growled into life, echoing the fury surging inside her. Giving the wheel a sharp turn, she pulled into the street. She hadn't seen it coming, that was all. The woman's reaction had caught her off guard. She could usually read the questions in the eyes of strangers: Greek? Italian? Spanish? And then the dawning realization: Ah, Native American. But there had been no questions in the eyes of Joanne Garrow, only hatred as pure and sharp as broken glass.

She turned the corner and headed east toward Main Street, her mind replaying the scene: she, walking up the sidewalk — the dark, slanted eyes and black hair, the coppery skin. Joanne Garrow had seemed only startled. Then Vicky had said she was an attorney. She had mentioned the Markham Clinic.

Vicky felt her muscles begin to relax. An alien from outer space with green skin and purple hair could have walked up the sidewalk. It would not have mattered. The fact that she was Arapaho did not matter. It was a convenient excuse, words hurled like stones to make her run away. What mattered, what had ignited the hatred in Joanne Garrow's eyes, was the name of Dr. Jeremiah Markham.

Vicky still felt shaky as she made her way through the clouds of smoke in the Mountain Lounge, past the men perched on bar stools, turning, staring. She found Luther Benson seated at a small table in back. As she approached, he started to his feet, stumbling sideways, righting himself against the table. A half-empty martini glass scurried toward the edge. He grabbed it and set it solidly into place.

"Thanks for seeing me, Luther." Vicky sat down across from him. The lawyer waited a moment before folding himself into his own chair. He was in his seventies, but he might have been taken for a man ten years younger: the thick, iron-gray hair and bushy eyebrows, the deep-set eyes with a perpetual look of amusement, the ruddy features of a man accustomed to the outdoors.

"Never let it be said Luther Benson turned down a drink with a beautiful lady." He lifted the martini glass and gave her a mock toast before taking a long sip. From the bar came the soft buzz of conversation, the sound of ice cubes clinking against glass. "You'll join me, won't you?" He waved over the bartender.

"Just water," Vicky said after the man in blue jeans and T-shirt had sauntered over, a white towel slung across one shoulder. She never drank alcohol; she feared its magical powers. It could draw out the very soul, transform someone into something unrecognizable. Before her eyes, it had transformed Ben into a stranger.

"Guess I'll drink for both of us." Luther glanced up at the bartender. "Bring me another."

The moment the bartender moved away, Luther leaned toward her and, in a low, raspy voice said, "I forgot about you being Indian."

Vicky knew that wasn't true. She said nothing.

"Indians either stay fallin'-down drunk or don't touch the stuff."

"You think so?"

"Think so! I been around these parts a good long time." He winked at her.

Vicky gave a little shrug. "I'm not here to discuss the problems some Indian people have with alcohol," she said. *Not with a man who wanted to meet in a bar in the mid-afternoon. Who has already polished off at least one martini and is about to start on another.*

Holding her gaze, Luther drew his wallet from inside his light-colored, western-cut jacket and plucked out a few dollars, which he tossed on the tray as the bartender delivered another martini and a glass of ice water. "You wanted to see me about Sharon David, right?"

Vicky wasn't surprised. Luther had kept up with everything that went on in the area for the last fifty years. He knew everybody's business. She had turned to him in the past, trying to get a handle on some case she was working on. His information had always been reliable. She said, "Any chance Sharon David could have been adopted from the reservation in 1964?"

Luther cleared his throat. "Didn't happen, honey. I would've known about it. Benson and Benson knew everything goin' on in these parts." Glancing at some point beyond her, as if he were plucking a memory out of the smoke-filled air, he went on: "Dad started the firm seventy years ago, and I joined up soon's I got out of law school. Oh, a few young turks set up storefront offices from time to time, thinkin' they could challenge us, but we ran 'em off. There wasn't

145

much law business 'round these parts back then. We had to corral what was here."

"Did you handle private adoptions?"

" 'Course we handled private adoptions."

"For women from the reservation?"

"Indians?" He nodded. "Sure. We got kids adopted to aunts and uncles, grandmothers, older siblings. Not much money in it, that's for sure. A lot of work we did pro bono. But we didn't get any Indian babies adopted outside the tribe, that's what you gettin' at."

Vicky leaned into the hard back of the chair and sipped at the ice water. Every trail led in the same direction. The tribe did not let its children go. Unless, she realized, the tribe didn't know. Unless an adoption had been arranged secretly. She wondered if Joanne Garrow had also guessed that she'd come on behalf of Sharon David. Was that why she didn't want to talk about Dr. Markham?

"I went to see Joanne Garrow this afternoon," she said.

"How's Joanne doin'?" The lawyer's voice was tight and controlled.

Vicky felt something change in the atmosphere between them. The bar conversation seemed louder, the guffaws sharper. A phone was ringing somewhere. She hurried on. "Garrow once worked for Jeremiah Markham. Did you know him?"

" 'Course I knew him." The old friendliness was gone.

"I thought his business manager might tell me whether the doctor ever arranged private adoptions."

"And did she?" A cold, clipped tone. Luther Benson must have been a formidable adversary in the courtroom, Vicky thought.

She said, "Joanne Garrow threw me off her property."

The man's expression dissolved to a point somewhere between amusement and disdain. "Well, don't take it personally, Vicky." The old friendliness had returned. "Lawyer comes around askin' questions, the lady probably got nervous. You wanna know what she would have told you? Jerry Markham wasn't runnin' any adoption agency. He was runnin' a clinic."

"There might have been a desperate woman. He might have known of a couple who wanted to adopt —"

The lawyer cut in. "It didn't happen." He took another sip of martini. Then: "Take the advice of an old barrister, honey. Tell your fancy client there are five hundred and forty-five tribes in this country, and she picked the wrong one. Collect a nice big fee and take yourself a long vacation."

Vicky studied the man a moment. She had a hunch he was lying, and it surprised her. Luther had always been straight with her, his information reliable. When she'd opened her office, he'd assumed the role of the older, more experienced lawyer whose advice she could count on. She still counted on it, despite the martinis that, lately, he seemed to consume in ever-greater volume. Why would he want to throw her off track? Where could she have been headed? She decided to take a chance: "You know what I think, Luther? I think the famous Dr. Markham may have arranged private adoptions for Indian women. I think his business manager and lawyer don't want to talk about it."

The lawyer stared at her. The clink of glass, the squeal of bar stools and droning voices filled the air. Suddenly she was aware of the bartender standing behind her. "You Vicky Holden?"

She glanced up.

"Secretary called. Says you should get back to the office on the double quick."

Vicky caught her breath. What kind of emergency would make Laola call her here? Pushing back the chair, she started to her feet.

"You're wastin' your time, Vicky." Luther Benson lumbered alongside her, the stale odor of his breath engulfing her.

Vicky stepped back. Struggling for a calm tone, she said, "Did it happen, Luther? Did Dr. Markham help some Indian woman find a home for her baby?"

"Listen to me, Vicky. I've always given you the lowdown when you come askin'."

That was true, she thought.

"I'm tellin' you it never happened. So forget about it. Tell your client to go lookin' somewhere else." He wheeled around and started

148

through the smoke-filled lounge, a stiff, bow-legged walk, like that of a cowboy just thrown by a horse.

Vicky watched until he flung open the door and stepped outside. A column of sunlight slipped into the lounge and dissolved in the smoky air before he slammed the door. As she reached for her bag, she saw that Luther Benson had left a martini glass half-full.

Vicky eased down on the accelerator and pulled onto Main Street. All she had was a hunch. A hunch that Markham could have helped some Arapaho woman place her baby with outsiders, and Luther could have prepared the relinquishment papers. An independent adoption thirty-five years ago, and the elders never knew. But if she was right, why would Luther deny it? All she had wanted to know was *whether* such an adoption had occurred. If it had, then Sharon David's search here might have some hope of success.

She squinted into the sun bouncing off the bumper of the truck ahead. In her bag was the Los Angeles number for Jeremiah Markham, and she intended to call the famous doctor when she got back to the office, as soon as she dealt with whatever emergency had led Laola to track her down. She expected Markham would also deny involvement with the adoption of an Indian baby. It didn't matter. She would tell Sharon David about her hunch. Advise the actress to continue her search in the area. There was a chance she had been born at the Markham Clinic to an Arapaho woman.

A block from the office, Vicky spotted the crowd milling about the sidewalk. Traffic ahead was moving slowly. A line of paneled trucks stood at the curb. She parked behind one with CHANNEL 2 emblazoned in black on the rear doors.

"Vicky Holden!" Someone shouted as she let herself out. Then the crowd was surging toward her: men shouldering boxlike cameras, women with notepads in hand. A couple of microphone poles sprang overhead.

"Where can we find Sharon David?" a woman yelled.

"Who's her family?"

"Is it true her Indian parents gave her away?"

"No comment." Vicky pushed through the crowd, briefcase thrust ahead pointing the way. An attractive woman with wide, serious eyes and wavy blond hair brushing the collar of her red suit blocked the stairway. "Sue Causeman. Channel Two," the woman said, a hopeful note in the tone. "Can we speak in private?"

Vicky dodged past and hurried up the stairs. The woman's high heels clicked behind her as she walked along the corridor. "We're the local news!" the anchorwoman shouted. "We should break the stories about our Indian people, don't you agree? You're Arapaho. Surely you can understand the importance of

150

Channel Two covering the story."

Vicky reached her office door and grabbed the knob. It sat motionless in her hand. Laola must have locked the door. She set the briefcase on the floor and fumbled in her bag for the key, ignoring the pleas of the woman at her side: good human-interest story, movie star comes home.

Out of the corner of her eye, Vicky saw the other reporters moving down the corridor, like water flowing through a canal. She gripped the cold metal key and jabbed it into the lock as the door swung open.

"Vicky! Thank God you're back." Laola reached out one hand as if she might pull her inside.

Vicky slipped past the door, slammed it shut, and threw the bolt. Then she leaned against the wood panel. "How long have they been here?"

"All afternoon. Filled up the reception room." Laola swept the small room with her eyes. "I kept tellin' 'em 'no comment,' but they kept on askin' questions anyway. I didn't know what to do, so I called around to find you. Finally I told 'em they had to wait outside. I thought I was gonna have to throw them out of here. I mean, physically."

Vicky smiled at the image. Laola had thrown calves in rodeos; she could probably throw reporters out of the office.

"Sharon David's been callin' all afternoon," Laola went on, breathless. "Says she's got to talk

151

to you right away. You want me to get her on the phone?"

"In a moment." Vicky pushed away from the door and crossed into her own office. She tossed her briefcase onto the desk, then perched on her chair and pulled the notepad out of her bag. She flipped to the notes she'd scribbled at the Grace Clinic. Gripping the phone, she tapped out the Los Angeles number.

"Dr. Markham's office." A woman's voice, clipped and efficient.

Vicky introduced herself and said she was an attorney calling from Lander, Wyoming. She asked to speak with Dr. Markham.

"What is this about?" A friendlier note seeped into the voice, as if the woman was used to fielding calls from around the country, scheduling the doctor onto popular television shows, radio stations with the largest audience.

"This is a private matter," Vicky told her. "It's important that I speak to Dr. Markham personally."

There was a moment of hesitation before the woman said, "Dr. Markham is on vacation."

"Is there someplace where I can reach him?" Vicky persisted.

A light laugh floated over the line. "The doctor's idea of a vacation is a place where no one can reach him. He's bow-hunting for elk in the Wind River Mountains."

Vicky shifted forward in her chair, scarcely believing what she'd just heard. "He's here?"

"Oh?" Surprise registered in the voice. "The Wind River Mountains must be close to you."

"He checks with his office, doesn't he?"

There was a moment of silence on the line. Finally: "I suppose so."

"Please ask him to contact me."

A series of explanations sputtered over the line: the doctor didn't want his vacations disturbed, he didn't always call, she couldn't guarantee —

Vicky interrupted. "Tell him it is a serious legal matter." She gave the woman her telephone number and address.

The instant she hung up, the phone screeched. In another moment Laola was in the doorway. "It's Sharon again. She says she's got to talk to you right away."

Vicky waved an okay and picked up the receiver. It was still warm. "Sharon?"

"I've been trying to get you for hours!" The movie star's voice sounded clear and crisp, as if it were amplified by surround sound. "The most wonderful thing has happened."

Vicky waited, listening to the long, drawn-in breaths followed by the rush of words: "I've found my real parents!"

14

Father John listened to the electronic buzz of a phone ringing somewhere in Riverton. He had waited until almost nine o'clock, a decent time of the morning to return Mary James's call. Outside his window, light-filled clouds scuttled across the sky. From down the hall came the soft *tap-tap-tap* of computer keys. Megan had settled in Father Joseph's office an hour ago and, within minutes, it seemed, had taken over the task of planning the reception for the Bishop following the confirmation ceremony in two weeks.

The ringing stopped. A woman's voice, firm and commanding came on the line: "Mary James speaking."

For half a second Father John thought he'd reached another machine. He said, "This is Father John O'Malley from St. Francis —"

"Yes, Father," the voice cut in. "I've been awaiting your call. I'd like to meet with you."

"What is this about?" he asked, a gentle probing.

After a brief pause the woman said, "It's a personal matter, Father."

"I'll be in my office today."

"Could you come to my home?" An instruction, rather than a question. "We'll have a private conversation."

Father John was quiet, his eyes following the

slow advance of a pillowlike cloud over the distant peaks. "Is this about Father Joseph Keenan?"

The woman remained silent so long he wondered if they had been disconnected. Finally she said, "In a way, Father. I'd appreciate a few moments of your time. I'll leave the bank early and be home by five. I work two days a week," she added, a kind of explanation. Then she gave him her address.

He told her he'd be there and replaced the receiver. The tapping in Father Joseph's office formed a background rhythm to the questions tumbling through his mind. Why did the sister of a woman who had taken her own life thirty-five years ago want to talk to him about Joseph Keenan?

He exhaled a long breath and set to work on the papers tumbling over his desk. Classes and programs to plan; liturgies to schedule, volunteers to contact. He made notes for the final confirmation classes. At noon Megan appeared in his doorway. "Do you eat lunch?" she asked, as if last night's conversation had never taken place.

"You go on," he told her, not unkindly. Elena would have bologna sandwiches ready, and he'd been waiting for a moment alone. Through the window he watched Megan walk down the front steps — a slow, preoccupied motion. She cut across the field, the red hair glinting in the sunlight. She was like her mother. It surprised him, the image of Eileen still in his mind.

He picked up the phone and tapped out his brother's number. He knew it by heart. Odd, he thought, since he rarely used it. Mike's voice left him momentarily at a loss for words. He'd expected his brother to be at the office. He did not want to ask for Eileen, so he tried for small talk: relaxed greetings and catch-up questions. There was puzzlement in his brother's responses, an unasked question: why this call in the middle of the day?

He told his brother he was glad Megan had come for a visit. The line seemed heavy with the ensuing silence. Finally Mike said, "So she went running to you, did she? Well, she's been upset lately. Quit her job. Most likely some trouble with that fiancé of hers."

"Most likely," Father John heard himself saying.

"Maybe you can help her. You do a lot of that, don't you? Counsel people?"

He did a lot of that, he said.

"I don't have to tell you what the girl means to us." Father John thought he heard a softening in his brother's tone. "We want her to be happy, her mother and I. Help her, will you, John?"

Father John replaced the receiver. He felt infinitely sad. How could he help her? How could he convince her that he was not her father, when they both knew it was possible? He pushed himself out of the chair and walked over to the window. Across Circle Drive, Leonard and his son Arnold were loading branches into the back

156

of a pickup. He watched them a moment — father and son. He and Megan would have to get to the truth. And yet . . . the truth could alter reality. He wasn't sure he wanted to know the truth. *Dear Lord,* he prayed. *Help me. Help Megan.*

He walked back to the desk and forced himself to concentrate on plans for the final confirmation classes. Then he started on plans for the confirmation liturgy, working through the noon hour. He didn't want to sit across the table from Megan, eating a sandwich, sipping coffee. Uncle and niece, an ordinary day. When she returned, she deposited a sandwich and Coke on his desk in the middle of a stack of papers. Sensing her disappointment — why hadn't he stopped for lunch with her? — he smiled, nodded toward the papers and folders. So much work. A weak excuse, they both knew.

Between bites of bologna sandwich and sips of Coke, he finished the liturgy plans and began working his way through the unanswered mail and messages, jotting replies, making phone calls. Outside the wind had come up. A cottonwood branch clacked against the glass pane. He pushed the papers aside and leaned back, raising the legs of his chair. Something about Father Joseph's murder had been nagging him all day, like a cold wind at his back. *I believe he went there to die,* the Provincial had said.

He pitched forward. The chair legs slammed onto the carpet as he reached for the phone and punched in the Provincial's number. A man answered, probably a young priest. There was the familiar runaround before Father Rutherford's voice came on the line. "John? Have the FBI made an arrest?"

He had to say that wasn't the case.

"Joseph's murderer is still free," the Provincial said, a musing tone. "Well, I'm going to have to insist —"

Father John stopped him. "What are the funeral arrangements?"

He heard the long sigh at the other end of the line. "The funeral will be here, in the Jesuit cemetery. We were in touch with the Lander coroner. He expects the body to be released soon. With the case still unsolved, John, we have no choice except to close the mission. It's only temporary. As soon as the murderer —"

"Wait a minute, Bill. You gave me two days."

"Yes, well, I believe the time is about up."

Father John drew in a long breath. He picked up a pencil and began tapping it against the edge of the desk. "People here remember Father Joseph from before," he said, a different approach. The pencil made a sharp drumroll. "They'll expect a memorial Mass."

"Offer the Mass this afternoon. You can leave tomorrow."

"You can't rush something like this." The harshness in his tone caught Father John by surprise. "The Arapahos will expect a solemn, well-planned liturgy. The elders will want to speak, and they'll need time to prepare their remarks. We'll have to arrange for the singers and drummers."

"Are we talking about Mass?"

"Of course we're talking about Mass," Father John said. "The way the Arapahos expect the Mass to be said."

There was another long sigh. "You're stalling, John."

"Give me a few more days. The FBI will have the murderer by then." He wished he felt the confidence he heard in his voice.

The Provincial didn't reply for a moment. "You have until Saturday, John, at which time I will expect you to be on a plane for Boston."

Father John flipped the pencil across the desk. Three days! He exhaled a deep breath. "Look, Bill, I've been wondering about something. You said Joseph came here to die."

Another silence. Then: "A figure of speech. I believe Joseph was prepared to die."

"But why here? Did he tell you?"

"Not in so many words. He remembered the mission fondly. It was obvious by the way he spoke. Perhaps he regretted leaving so precipitously."

Father John set his elbows on the desk. "What are you saying?"

"Well, naturally, I took a look at the record of his previous assignment at St. Francis before sending him there again. An exemplary record, I might add. He started numerous programs, ran the school with an iron hand. Students turned in excellent scores on national tests. Even though Joseph's assignment was for the usual six years, he left quite suddenly after about a year."

"Was there an explanation?" Father John asked.

"A philosophy position became available at Marquette University. He was a philosopher, you know."

Father John was quiet, considering. Then he asked the date that Joseph had left.

"You want the exact date?" A note of exasperation crept into the Provincial's voice. "Is that important?"

"Possibly."

"Wait a moment. Joseph's file is here somewhere." In the background was the sound of a drawer squealing on its runners, the rustle of papers. Then the Provincial's voice: "Arrived at St. Francis Mission on the Wind River Reservation, October twelfth, 1963."

"When did he leave?"

Another rustle of papers. "Resigned December twentieth, 1964."

Father John lifted his hand and squeezed the bridge of his nose. What had he expected? That Father Joseph had resigned immediately after the suicide of Dawn James? That he had been mad with grief and guilt? False propositions yield false conclusions, and he had started with the proposition that there had been some kind of relationship between Joseph and the woman.

He dragged his thoughts back to what the Provincial was saying, something about December 20 being the official date. "He left a couple months earlier. Actually departed the mission on September twenty-six."

Father John thanked the Provincial and slowly replaced the receiver. His hunch was correct. Joseph Keenan had left the mission the day following Dawn James's suicide.

The gray light of evening crept over the north side of Riverton, broken by the occasional headlight of an oncoming car, a lamp flickering inside a house. Father John drove past rows of bungalows that duplicated one another, shadows crawling over the sidewalks and lawns. He parked in front of a tan-brick bungalow that sheltered under a giant oak. A porch light resembling a carriage lantern glowed at the door, and a thin light outlined the curtains at the front window.

The front door swung open as he came up the sidewalk, leaves crackling under his boots. Framed in a rectangle of light was a slim woman, with short, blond hair, wearing a silky, shimmering blouse and pleated skirt that revealed well-shaped legs. She kept one hand on the door and stretched the other toward him. "Father O'Malley. I've been waiting for you."

Her grip was surprisingly firm. He guessed her age at about sixty. An attractive woman with honey-colored hair, light eyes, and finely sculpted features that bore the faintest trace of makeup.

Abruptly she withdrew her hand and waved him into a cozy living room. A brick fireplace covered the opposite wall, flanked by a pair of upholstered chairs. In front of the window on the right was a tufted, low-slung sofa. A black cat curled on the middle cushion. Lamps sent a dim, suffused light throughout the room. On a table near the door was a cluster of photos: young girls on horses and bicycles, leaning against a fin-tailed car, clowning, laughing.

"My sister and I," the woman said, following his glance. Then, indicating one of the chairs by the fireplace, she said, "Please have a seat, Father. I've made fresh coffee."

The woman disappeared through the shadows of a small dining room that opened off the living room. In a moment she returned, carrying a silver tray that rattled with a coffee server, bowls, cups and saucers, spoons. She set the tray onto the small table in front of the sofa, poured two cups of coffee, and handed him one. A tiny spoon lay on the saucer. Wordlessly, she lifted a creamer and sugar. He shook his head.

"Ms. James," he began as she let herself down next to the cat.

"Mary." She lifted her cup and took a sip, her eyes on his. "You were correct in assuming I wanted to talk to you about the priest who was murdered. Shocking."

Father John took a drink of coffee. His finger

barely fit into the handle of the china cup. "Was Father Joseph a friend of your family's?" he prodded.

The woman shifted her gaze toward the shadows in the dining room. He could hear the cat purr in the silence. Looking back, she said, "My sister, Dawn" — a glance toward the photos — "used to like to go to Mass at the Indian church. She often spoke of Father Keenan. When I heard about his murder, well, I began thinking . . ." Her voice trailed off, and she stole another glance at the photos. "She was such a wonderful girl, my sister."

Father John saw that she was sliding toward the edge of tears. "Tell me about her," he said gently.

"She was brilliant and very ambitious." The woman stared at the photos. "I was the pretty one, but Dawn was the smart one." Bringing her eyes back to his, she said, "I was also three years older, so after Father died, I helped Mother raise Dawn. I got a job after school at the movie theater, which was quite wonderful because, you see, I saw all the movies, and I always wanted to be an actress. The moment I graduated from high school, I intended to go to Hollywood and become a movie star." She gave a little laugh that betrayed the faintest hint of regret. The cup rattled on the saucer in her lap.

Placing one hand over the cup to still it, she said, "Dawn always wanted to be a nurse, and Mother insisted we help her realize her dream.

She was so intelligent, you understand. So, when I graduated, I took a job at the bank and helped to earn Dawn's tuition. She graduated from Casper College and went on to nursing school. Well, she won every honor you can imagine. It was a decision I never regretted."

The woman gave him a frank, proud smile, then went on: "Dawn was determined to repay me. I told her I didn't expect anything, but —" She hesitated, smiling at the memory. "You had to know Dawn. She was very proud. She wanted to make her own way. Once she set her mind on something, there was no talking her out of it. She got a job at the Riverton hospital, and every month she wrote me out a check. But she was impatient to pay off the debt. Eventually she found a much-better-paying job at the Markham Clinic in Lander. You've heard of Jeremiah Markham, haven't you?"

The name sounded familiar. Author? Lecturer?

"The mother-and-baby doctor."

"Ah, yes." Father John had seen the man interviewed on television. "He practiced in Lander?"

Mary nodded. "His theories were quite unusual for the time. Dawn was thrilled to be working for him. She had the chance to travel quite frequently. Dr. Markham sent her to medical conferences in different cities. You see, he was determined to run the most modern, up-to-date clinic. Well" — the woman gave a little shrug — "all the traveling and long hours at the clinic made the job quite stressful. And then a number of babies died."

Father John took a sip of coffee. Something moved at the edge of his memory: comments he'd overheard about the terrible year when the babies had died. He'd once asked one of the grandmothers what had caused the deaths, and she had talked about how the water ran red and foamy out of the faucets, about how the birds had flown away. The sadness had been so palpable, he hadn't brought the matter up again.

"It must have been terrible for your sister," he said. What the woman told him collided with his own theory. He'd feared that Dawn James had gotten involved with Father Joseph and that, out of grief and despair, she'd taken her own life. He was wrong. The despair had come from something much more profound. And Joseph? The priest who held the funerals? Praying over the tiny caskets, one after another. Was that what had driven him away — the unrelenting sadness? Had he been counseling Dawn James when, perhaps, he had also been in need of counseling? Had he blamed himself for her suicide? All possible. But nothing explained why Joseph Keenan had returned.

"The FBI agent seized upon the deaths of the babies," Mary was saying. "What a handy excuse! Dawn was depressed. The coroner ruled her death a suicide. Case closed. Another violent death on the reservation." She thrust out a slim hand in a gesture of helplessness.

Father John set his cup and saucer on the table. "Are you saying your sister did not take her own life?"

"My sister," she said, leveling her gaze with his, "was murdered, just like Father Joseph. I always believed she was murdered because of something she knew. Now I'm certain of it. Whatever it was, Father Joseph also knew."

The quiet was broken by the soft purring of the cat, the ticking of a clock. "What makes you think so?" Father John asked after a moment.

The woman slid her own cup and saucer onto the tray and clasped her hands in her lap. "Dawn had fallen away from the church for a time, but in the last few weeks of her life, she'd found her faith again. She became a very devout Catholic, Father. She went to daily Mass at the mission. She would never have taken her life. She was very calm and optimistic about the future."

Father John made an effort to keep his face unreadable. He was thinking that suicidal people often became calm at the end. The decision made, they have only to await the opportune time.

Mary was shaking her head, as if she'd seen into his thoughts. "My sister had been depressed, I admit, but she had worked through her depression. She resigned from the clinic and was about to take her old job at the hospital. She stood in this very room and said, 'Mary, I'm okay now. I'm happy.' "

The woman stared into the dining room, remembering. "The FBI agent couldn't trace the pistol beside her body, so he concluded she'd bought it in a pawnshop. Imagine! A girl like Dawn wandering into some pawnshop and buying a pistol. Absurd!" She spit out the word. Little drops of moisture peppered the surface of the table.

Father John leaned toward her. "What makes you think your sister and Joseph both knew something?"

Mary James brought her eyes back to his. "I believe she confided in Father Joseph. I believe she'd been going to him for counseling. He was the one who helped her. That's why she was able to take positive steps forward. Right after her murder, he went away. I think he was frightened that he would also be murdered."

"Have you talked to Ted Gianelli, the FBI agent here now?" Father John asked.

The woman gave a brittle laugh. "For thirty-five years I have tried to get the FBI to investigate my sister's murder. But the case is closed unless some new evidence appears. That's why I called you, Father. Perhaps you can make the agent understand that new evidence has appeared. The man my sister confided in has been murdered."

15

Darkness settled over the earth like a thick buffalo robe. The sky had turned violet; the moon and stars hazy pinpricks of light. Father John gripped the steering wheel and stared into the headlights washing across Highway 789. The cubelike buildings of Riverton flashed by, a procession of shadowy hulks. He wished he had one of his opera tapes. Puccini, to sort his thoughts by.

Something about Mary James's story bothered him, like the wrong note in a perfect aria. A plausible story, except for the fact that her sister's death had been ruled a suicide. He wondered if the beautiful woman who had sacrificed her own dreams for a brilliant sister had simply never been able to accept the fact that, in the end, her sister had chosen suicide.

And Father Joseph? Why had he run away? If Dawn had told him something in a counseling session, why didn't he give the information to the federal agent after her death? It might have led to a different investigation, a different finding.

The Escort's engine hissed into the quiet. There was another explanation, he knew. One that would support the woman's theory. Dawn James hadn't confided in Father Joseph during a counseling session; she'd confessed to him whatever was bothering her. And he was bound by the seal of the confessional.

Father John saw the picture: a young priest, burdened by unwanted, unsolicited knowledge. How soon after he'd heard the woman's confession had he started placing calls at universities around the country? When did he pack his bags, purchase the one-way train or bus ticket? He must have been ready to go because the day after Dawn James's death, Joseph Keenan fled the area.

Father John's hands relaxed on the wheel. He was alone on the highway now. The town had given way to shadows of scrub brush along the road and dark, vacant spaces beyond. Far ahead was a tiny stream of headlights. The explanation seemed logical. Except for one thing. Joseph Keenan had returned.

Father John swung right onto Seventeen-Mile Road. In the distance rose the dark mass of the mountains, the peaks lost in steel-gray clouds. He could imagine Gianelli's reaction to this new theory: *You're stretching, John. When you gonna realize the world doesn't fit into some logical Jesuit order?* Or Banner: *Been my experience, John, things are usually what they seem. Some crazy guy's got it in for you and killed the wrong priest.*

But what if there was logic in the world? He found himself wishing Vicky were at the mission. Together they could examine Mary James's story, probe for weaknesses and inconsistencies. Together, he knew, they would arrive at a stronger theory, one that might convince

Gianelli and Banner that Joseph's murder was related to a mysterious death thirty-five years ago.

But Vicky would not be waiting. That was reality. Logical and necessary. He would not call her. The evening of Father Joseph's murder, he had glimpsed the depth of her feelings, and it had left him shaken. She had hidden her feelings well. He had never guessed they mirrored his own. He had understood with the force of certainty that she would not come to the mission again and that he could not call her.

Megan would be at the mission. He'd promised that, tonight, they would have dinner and a long talk. He had no intention of burdening the girl with theories about murder. More than likely there was no connection between Joseph's murder and the death of a young nurse more than three decades ago, except in the mind of Mary James. The killer might still show up at St. Francis Mission looking for him, and he didn't want Megan to relax her guard.

He turned into the mission grounds. They were silent and empty. There were no vehicles about. Elena and Leonard would have gone home by now. He felt a pang of worry that Megan was alone. He glanced at his watch in the dim glow of the dashboard lights. Five minutes to seven; still early.

As he came around Circle Drive, he saw that the overhead light in front of the administration building was out. He made a mental note to ask

170

Leonard to replace the bulb first thing in the morning. His headlights streamed over the concrete stairs and stoop, the black railing glistening like ice, the front door. Suddenly he realized it was ajar. Leonard must have forgotten to lock up.

He hit the brake pedal and jumped out. As he started up the steps, he sensed something wrong. He could smell it in the air, like drifting smoke. His heart lurched. Megan was alone.

He took the rest of the steps two at a time and flung the door wide open. As it swung toward him, he saw the splintered wood, the lopsided lock. Someone had forced the door.

"Megan!" he shouted, stepping inside. His hand found the switch, and light flooded the corridor, illuminating the framed photos lining the walls of the first pastors at St. Francis Mission, silent witnesses to his growing panic.

He hurried down the hall. "Where are you?" His voice sounded hollow and distant in the old building. He burst through the door to Joseph's office, flipped the switch, and stopped. He felt as if the world had lurched sideways into a direction he couldn't comprehend. Papers and folders littered the floor; file-cabinet drawers tilted precariously. The chair was overturned; the top of the desk swept clean. The computer was gone, and so was Megan.

He swung around, shouting her name toward the ceiling and the storerooms upstairs. He waited, listening. There were no sounds except the familiar creak of the building, the *drip-drip* of a leaky faucet, the thumping of his own heart. He forced himself to think logically. Someone had broken into the building, ransacked Joseph's office, and taken his computer. But it probably happened after Megan left. She could be at the guest house or the residence.

He ran down the corridor and outside. Dodging past the Escort, he sprinted through the shadows of the alley between the building and the church, his breath coming fast and hard, his heart beating in his ears. The guest house was dark, but Megan's car sat in front. The evening was quiet, except for the sound of the wind hissing through the branches of the cottonwoods.

"Megan!" he called, pounding against the door. He tried the knob; it sat cold and lifeless in his hand. Pulling a master key from the pocket of his jeans, he rammed it into the slot and pushed against the door, shouting her name at the shadows of the table and sofa bed inside. He stumbled over a chair, found the lamp, and turned it on. Light flooded the small room and eddied into the alcove that served as a kitchen. He took in the suitcase against one wall, the jacket slung over a chair, clothing piled on another chair. Megan wasn't there.

He retraced his steps down the alley, past the Escort, and ran across the field to the residence, all thoughts erased from his mind except the safety of the girl. Throwing open the front door, he burst inside. The momentum carried him down the hall toward the light shining in the kitchen. Shouting her name: "Megan, Megan!" The table was set for two: plates, glasses, forks and knives, napkins. A note in the center of the table: Elena's instructions, he knew, on whatever she had prepared for dinner and left in the refrigerator.

He whirled around and ran back down the hall. The door to his study was closed, and he slammed it open, knocking the side of his desk — a loud whack in the quiet. Still no sign of her. As he started up the stairs, a cold fear, like ice water, poured over him. The hall was dark, and he flipped the switch. Light bounced off the walls and ran along the carpet. He stopped at the first door — the guest bedroom. Pushing it open, flipping the switch, taking in the room at a glance. Bureau. Desk. Neatly made bed.

He moved to the next door — Father Joseph's room — his eyes on the pencil-thin light seeping underneath. Gripping the knob, he threw open the door and called her name softly. "Megan. Megan."

A part of his mind took in the spilled contents of drawers, the tangle of clothing and blankets, the books strewn about. What he saw was the slim figure on the floor: the long blue-jean-clad legs and white sneakers, the T-shirt, the mass of red-gold hair.

"No," he said out loud, dropping to his knees beside his niece and placing one hand on her hair. "Oh, God, no."

16

"Take it easy, John." Ted Gianelli's voice floated through the emptiness of the Riverton Memorial Hospital emergency waiting room. They stood together on the hard vinyl floor, like two men waiting for a bus, Father John thought. No one else was there. A few minutes earlier the agent had come up the sidewalk into the light filtering outside through the glass entrance.

Before Gianelli arrived, Father John had been pacing the room, marking off the space between the entrance and the door on the opposite wall through which Megan, bundled on a gurney, small and helpless as a child, had disappeared. The reception area behind a counter next to the door gaped like an empty cave under the bright light. A nurse had been there when he'd burst in, shouting that his niece was in the car and needed attention. The same nurse had summoned the gurney, then followed it into the warren of tiny rooms that, he knew, crept behind the closed door. He was left with the muffled sound of footsteps and swinging doors and garbled, distant voices.

He'd called the police from the residence and told the operator to notify both Chief Banner and the FBI agent. Megan had regained consciousness as he'd knelt over her. Eyes snapping open, as if she were awakening from a nightmare. He'd stroked her forehead and told her she was okay, praying it was true.

She was fine, she'd insisted. Just a knock on the head. She'd gotten worse as a kid playing volleyball and roughhousing with her brothers. No need for the hospital. He'd felt relieved that the blue eyes seemed normal, the dark pupils small circles. But when he'd helped her to her feet, she slumped in his arms. The walls were falling, she'd admitted. The floor was turning. He'd laid her on the bed and gone for the Escort.

All the way to Riverton, he'd leaned on the accelerator, fighting back the fury that rose inside him, choking him. Who could have done this to her? Hurt her? He did not want to meet whoever had done this. He could understand the blind instinct that would drive a man to lash out at another human being. He did not trust himself.

Megan was talking quietly, a disjointed rambling that he found hard to follow: She'd left the office after he did and gone to the guest house. At some point she must have gone to the residence. Yes, to have dinner with him. No one was there, and she was watching television in the living room. There must have been some kind of noise, she wasn't sure. She'd gone upstairs to see about the noise. Yes, that must have been it. She couldn't remember.

Father John had clenched his jaws. He wanted to scold her. Why didn't she leave the residence? Lock herself in the guest house? Hadn't she been listening to him? A killer was on the loose. He

175

thought: this was what it was like to have a child. Consumed with rage because someone had hurt her, because she had put herself in danger, and, at the same time, weak with relief that she was safe, that she was alive.

Now Father John started pacing the waiting room again. Gianelli lowered himself into one of the blue plastic chairs against the wall, produced a small pad and a pen from inside his suit coat, and began firing questions. Father John didn't know the answers, only that Megan had been struck on the head and knocked unconscious.

Suddenly the door through which she'd disappeared swung open. A dark-haired woman with half-moon glasses perched partway down her nose and wearing a white smock stepped into the waiting room, hands gripping a clipboard. "Father O'Malley?" she inquired, peering over the dip of the glasses.

Father John crossed the room. "How is she?"

"I'm Dr. Ericson," the woman said. "I believe your niece will be just fine."

"You believe?" A cold space opened inside him.

"We can never be sure with head trauma. We've run her through the CT scanner. There's no sign of a skull fracture or interior bleeding. There's a mild contusion in the cerebellum area." The doctor glanced at Gianelli, who had joined them. "In other words, she appears to have a concussion. I want to keep her here for observation tonight, in case of any problems, such as vomiting or seizure."

"Seizure!" Father John fought to control the rising panic.

"We want to take every precaution," the doctor said matter-of-factly. "If all goes well, you can take her home tomorrow morning. Now, if you'd like to see her . . ."

Gianelli interrupted. "I'd like to talk to her." He flipped open his identification case and introduced himself.

"Follow me, gentlemen," the doctor said, turning toward the door.

The gurney took up the center of the small examining room. Megan seemed to be half-asleep, a white blanket pulled around her shoulders, red hair fanned over the little pillow under her head. An arm almost as white as the blanket rested on her stomach.

"How are you?" Father John leaned over her.

She gave him a faint smile. "I'll live."

"I'm glad to hear it. I'll pick you up first thing in the morning, and then I think you should go home."

"Where's home?" The doctor threw a glance from the side counter where she was scribbling something onto paper attached to the clipboard.

"New York," Megan said, weariness in her voice.

"It's not a good idea to fly right away," the doctor said.

"I'm driving."

The white smock swung around. "You're suggesting, Father O'Malley, that your niece set off tomorrow on a drive across the country?" She gave the pen a sharp snap against the counter. "She's likely to have spells of dizziness, disorientation, and nausea. She needs to rest for several days. I suggest you get used to the idea of having a houseguest." Another snap of the pen.

Father John brought his eyes back to Megan's. She was paler than he remembered.

"You want me to leave?" she asked. It was a whisper.

"I want you to stay." He smiled at her. Then, a nod toward the agent just inside the door: "This is Ted Gianelli, an FBI agent. He wants to ask you some questions."

Megan rolled her head toward the large, dark-suited man moving toward the gurney.

"Tell me what happened tonight," Gianelli said in a patient tone. He might have been speaking to one of his own daughters.

As Megan repeated the story, Father John struggled again to swallow back his own anger. She might have been killed! He reached over and took her hand. He wasn't sure whether the trembling was in her hand or his own.

"Did you see who attacked you?" Gianelli asked.

Megan shook her head. Strands of red hair squiggled over the pillow.

"Did you see anyone in the room?"

"I can't remember."

"Temporary amnesia," the doctor interrupted. She was leaning against the counter, the clipboard clenched to her chest. "I'm sorry, gentlemen. She's had enough for one night."

"So far as you know, the intruder took only Father Joseph's computer. That right?" Gianelli asked.

Father John stared at the man seated in the wingback chair, scribbling in a notebook. He felt as if he were watching an old movie. Three nights ago the agent had sat in the same chair, asking questions about Father Joseph, writing in the same pad. He had stood in the same place in front of the window, and the same shadowy darkness stretched beyond the black glass. They were no closer to finding Father Joseph's murderer.

Outside, Chief Banner and several of his men were combing the grounds, checking the buildings. They'd been here when he'd gotten back from the hospital — two white police cars parked in front of the residence, red and blue lights on the roof streaming into the darkness. He'd parked the Escort behind them. The headlights of Gianelli's Jeep turning around Circle Drive had flashed in his rearview mirror.

Now the agent closed the notebook and shifted in the chair. "I've gone through Father Joseph's files. A number of papers on various philosophical topics. Hard to understand." He shrugged. "Some letters to colleagues around the world. I doubt whoever broke into his office was looking for any of it. There was also a long list of names and addresses. Professors at various universities, Jesuit colleagues, a few family members. About what you'd expect."

The agent stopped and drew in a long breath. "What I didn't expect were the Arapaho names."

"Joseph had friends here," Father John said. It seemed a simple matter.

The agent shrugged. "Only a few people on the list are still here. Esther Tallman. Some of the Holden clan. When I talked to them, they said they hadn't heard from Father Joseph in thirty-five years. Not until he came back. Most of the others on the list left the res twenty, thirty years ago. It will take time to run them down. The addresses Father Joseph had were thirty-five years old."

Father John crossed the room and sat down in the leather chair behind his desk. He said, "Any names of people from town?"

"You know somebody named Joanne Garrow?"

"No." Father John had never heard of the woman.

"Funny thing," the agent went on. "Garrow says she hardly knew Father Joseph. He hadn't contacted her since he left here. Why do you suppose he had her name?"

Father John raised one hand and pinched the bridge of his nose. There was much about Joseph Keenan he didn't know. Much he was having difficulty trying to understand. He said, "Was Mary James on the list?"

Gianelli stared at him. "As a matter of fact, she was. But she also says Father Joseph didn't contact her. I take it you know her?"

Father John told the agent about Mary James's telephone call, about the meeting this afternoon. He mentioned the clipping he'd found in Father Joseph's Bible. "She believes her sister was murdered," he said.

Gianelli crossed one leg over the other. He swung a black loafer into the small space in front of the desk. "The woman's delusional," he said. "Every three or four months we get a letter begging us to look into her sister's murder. We send her a regular form letter, the Mary James form, we call it. Says, sorry, but unless some new evidence comes to light, we must accept the coroner's ruling. Then somebody gets murdered, and she gets busier. More letters. More phone calls. In her mind there's always some connection. She thinks we should reinvestigate her sister's death while we're investigating the latest murder. So let me guess." He waved an index finger like a baton. "She wants you to convince me there's some connection between her sister's death and Father Joseph's murder."

Father John looked away a moment. He'd counseled a couple hundred people. He'd known people with delusions. Mary James might be angry, frustrated, determined, but she was not delusional. He said, "Maybe there is a connection. Why would Joseph have kept the clipping through the years? Why would he have Mary James's name on his list?"

"I'll tell you why." Gianelli scooted to the edge of the chair. "She's been writing to him. She told me she'd been begging him to come back and help solve her sister's murder. She was like a dog that had gotten a hold of his leg. The poor man could never shake her off." The agent glanced around the study, as if he were trying to pull from the air some explanation for the woman's behavior. "Naturally I checked out her whereabouts the afternoon Father Joseph was shot. She was at her desk at the Mid-Central Bank. About a dozen people can vouch for her."

"Look, Ted." Father John kept his voice calm, logical. "Dawn James may have given Joseph some information. Maybe she was involved in something that weighed on her conscience. Let's suppose she confessed to him. After her murder, he feared for his own life and left."

Gianelli's hands flew up. "Conjectures, John. An obsessed woman's conjectures. Not enough to reopen a thirty-five-year-old murder case. We don't have the resources, not with a killer running around. And not when, most likely, you're the one the killer was after." He paused and drew in a long breath. "Look," he went on, a softer tone, "I had a talk with Sonny Red Wolf yesterday. He claims he was nowhere near Thunder Lane Monday afternoon. But someone may have seen him there."

This was news. Father John leaned back, studying the agent.

"Lucy Travise," Gianelli said, his jaw muscles beginning to flex. "White girl staying out on Thunder Lane with James Holden, Ben Holden's nephew. Vicky tried to talk the girl into telling the truth. Got Red Wolf's attention real fast."

Father John leaned forward. "What are you saying?"

"He gave her a scare, that's all. Nothing came of it."

A wave of dread washed over Father John. Was everyone he cared about in danger? Everyone whose lives touched his? Maybe he'd been the target after all, just as he'd first thought. Maybe Mary James's theory, the yellowed newspaper clipping in Joseph's Bible, the woman's name in the list — maybe none of it had anything to do with Joseph's murder.

"Soon's we locate Lucy Travise —" the agent was saying.

"What happened to her?"

"She's scared, John. Red Wolf's been harassing her, trying to get her to leave the res, just like he's been doing to other white people around here. She and James have gotten themselves lost, but, sooner or later, we'll find her. If she can place Red Wolf out on Thunder Lane at the time Father Joseph was murdered, I'll get a warrant for his arrest."

A quicksand of ifs, Father John was thinking.

In the meantime Sonny Red Wolf had tried to frighten Vicky and someone had attacked Megan. For half an instant he considered closing the mission and leaving. If he were gone, the people he cared about might be safe.

A hard thump sounded, cutting through his thoughts. The door opened, and a police officer stepped into the study, right hand looped over the handle of the revolver holstered at his waist. "We picked up a prowler out back of the house, Father," he said. "Looks like we got the man who broke in here tonight."

17

Father John walked over to the man slumped against the side of a police car, head bowed, hands cuffed in back, an officer beside him ready to discourage any idea of making a break for it. Banner and a couple of other policemen stood to one side. Robert Cutting Horse glanced up — a quick, furtive look. In the dim glow of the red and blue police lights, Father John could make out the man's tight, strained expression, the stone-dead eyes. He was sick, and he was drunk.

Suddenly Robert shook himself into an upright position and stumbled sideways. Alarm came into the officer's face. Banner reached out and grabbed the Indian's arm. "My boys found him in the field behind the residence," he said.

Gianelli stepped over. "What were you doing out there? Sonny Red Wolf send you over?"

"Sonny?" The Indian blinked. "He don't know I'm here. He don't want Indians goin' to the mission."

The chief said, "His truck is stuck in the ditch over on Raptor Road."

"Is that where you left it while you broke into the buildings here?" Gianelli persisted, his voice tight.

"Broke in? I don't know about 'broke in.' " He slumped back against the car and started coughing. The handcuffs rattled against the metal. "Tell 'em, Father," he said when the coughing stopped. A look of desperation came into the man's eyes.

"What do you want me to tell them, Robert?" Father John moved closer.

"You told me to come over here."

In an instant Father John understood. Robert had mistakenly turned onto Raptor Road, a half mile from the entrance to the mission. He'd run into the ditch and set out across the field on foot. It wasn't Robert who had broken the lock at the administration building, ransacked Father Joseph's office, found his way to the residence, attacked Megan. He was too drunk.

Father John turned to Gianelli. "I ran into Robert yesterday. He said he wanted to talk to me, so I told him to come to the mission. He's right." Partially right, he was thinking. He had told the man to come to the mission when he was sober.

Gianelli switched his gaze to the police chief. "Any weapons on him? Any sign of Father Joseph's computer?"

Banner shook his head. "Truck's clean. Nothing on his person." Then, facing the Indian, he said, "Looks like another DUI, Robert. We're gonna have to lock you up."

The muscles in the Indian's neck began to twitch. Suddenly he doubled over and started coughing again — a staccato retching, like that of an engine trying to catch.

Father John felt his own throat go dry. He

186

said, "He should be in the hospital."

"Well, we don't have the budget every time we pick up a drunk —"

"He's sick," Father John interrupted. "He's probably been drinking for days. He'll need help coming off it." He kept his own eyes on the Indian. The dry hacking filled the silence. "I know," he said. "It's going to be rough as hell."

Banner didn't respond at first. Then, a nod to the officer: "Get him over to Riverton Memorial."

The officer gave Robert a slight shove into the backseat, then hurried around and got in behind the wheel. As the police car moved away, headlights blinking into the darkness, a truck banked around Circle Drive and screeched to a stop in the space the car had just vacated.

Leonard jumped out. "You okay, Father?"

"I'm okay," Father John told him.

"Megan? She okay?" There was a pleading note in his voice.

An image flashed into Father John's mind: the warrior posted outside the village. If the enemy slipped past, he had failed. It was a mark of cowardice and bad judgment that would stalk his life. "Megan's going to be fine, Leonard," he said. "Everything's okay."

The caretaker thumped a fist on the truck's hood. "Pardon, Father, but so long as the killer's out there" — he nodded toward Seventeen-Mile Road — "things ain't okay." He took a step closer. "I talked to my boy, Arnold, and a couple

187

of my nephews. We got a plan to guard the mission."

"Leonard, it isn't necessary —" Father John began.

"Beggin' to disagree with you, Father." The Arapaho's tone was polite and humble. "We're gonna take shifts and keep watch on the place twenty-four hours a day. You're gonna look out the window in the middle of the night and know one of us is here, makin' sure nobody comes around. We see anything suspicious" — a quick look at the police chief — "we're gonna call you guys."

"Not a bad idea," Gianelli said.

"Don't try any heroic stuff." This from the chief.

Leonard's face broke into a half-surprised smile, as if he had expected he would have to put up a stronger fight. He turned away and looked out across the mission grounds stretching into darkness. "This here is our place," he said.

18

Through the ponderosas Vicky could see the Hell's Corner Dude Ranch: white canopies flashing in the sun, a crowd milling about. She eased up on the accelerator, urging the Bronco around another bend in the narrow mountain road. Branches scratched at the side windows. A line of pickups and vans stood along the right side of the road.

Vicky parked behind the white van with CHANNEL 2 on the rear doors and set out along the line of vehicles, the heels of her pumps teetering on chunks of dirt and gravel. The mournful sound of a flute mingled with the wind sighing in the branches. The air was cool. She clutched her bag in front of her suit jacket, against the wind.

The road emptied into a wide expanse of manicured lawn that struggled to hold back the oncoming ponderosas. Three large canopies stretched over tables with white cloths that flapped in the wind. Under the canopies, waiters in white coats were arranging chairs and setting out trays of food. Groups of people stood around the lawn. Sprawling on the far side was a two-story log cabin with a veranda that extended along the front. A smaller group huddled around the stairs leading to the veranda. Several men shouldered large, black cameras. As Vicky

189

started toward the cabin, she recognized most of the reporters. They had been outside of her office the last couple of days.

Suddenly Sharon David came through the front door. A man and woman — Indian people — were at her side. Arms linked, they walked across the veranda, smiling, bowing into the sun, posing for the cameras below. The actress was in a white dress with a long, flowing skirt and low, ruffled neckline. Her skin was the color of copper; her hair was pulled back and tied with a blue scarf that draped over one shoulder. The woman on the movie screens: the star of *The Sky People*.

Suddenly the actress caught Vicky's eyes. She came down the stairs and dodged past the crowd, ignoring the shouted questions, the cameras and microphones thrust in her face. Vicky went to meet her.

"I'm glad you're here." The actress took Vicky's hand. Then she waved over the couple still on the veranda. Together they started down the stairs: the man glancing about, self-consciously patting the sides of a dark suit coat that looked a couple of sizes too large; the woman nodding, smiling, dressed in a tailored green suit with gold buttons that blinked in the sun. For a moment they were lost among the reporters, and then they were free, hurrying across the lawn.

"I want you to meet my parents, Edna and Wylan Linder," Sharon said as they approached.

190

"I know Edna." Vicky struggled for a neutral tone.

Edna Linder was staring at her out of narrow, determined eyes. She seemed tense, coiled like a snake and ready to spring. A woman somewhere in her fifties, Vicky guessed, a few inches shorter than Sharon, with a round, puffy face that almost blurred the defined facial features of the Arapaho. She was a breed. Only part Arapaho.

A year ago she'd walked into Vicky's office with the same tense look about her and announced she needed a lawyer. The United States attorney was about to charge her with embezzlement. "Just let him try." Her laugh was hard and defiant. "He's gonna look like a bigger fool than he is. There's no evidence."

She was right. The U.S. attorney had only the allegation of Edna's coworker in the Tribal Fish and Game Department, but no proof that she had been pocketing license fees paid in cash. Vicky had talked the U.S. Attorney into dropping the charges. She was still trying to collect her fee. Every time Laola called about the bill, she heard a different excuse. Edna had lost her job. Wylan was out of work.

Now Wylan shifted from one foot to the other. Part Cheyenne, he was a slight man, with thin graying hair and pockmarked skin. His chest seemed hollow inside the outsized suit coat. Like a wild animal watching its captors, he cast quick, furtive glances toward the knot of reporters tightening around them, the groups of people

191

wandering over from the canopies.

"I want to thank you for finding our daughter," Edna said, defiance and contempt mingling in her expression. "Sharon's done so much for us already." A glance toward the canopies. "She's holding a feast for the whole family to celebrate her coming home. She's a very generous daughter."

"I'm afraid I can't take any credit," Vicky said.

"What do you mean? You've been helping Sharon, haven't you?" A reporter in a dark red suit with wavy blond hair and intelligent eyes pushed forward: the Channel 2 anchorwoman.

Sharon let out a little laugh. Nodding toward the reporters, she said, "You're the ones responsible. Thanks to your stories, Edna and Wylan were able to find me. I think we should all celebrate." She threw out one hand in the direction of the canopies. Long, red-tipped nails flashed in the sun. Then, turning to Edna: "Will you lead everyone to the feast?"

A satisfied smile crossed the older woman's face as she shouldered past the reporters, like a general leading the troops. Wylan started after her, and gradually, the reporters and the rest of the crowd fell in behind.

"Meet me inside," Sharon said, her eyes on the departing guests. "I'll get away as soon as I can." Slowly she started after the others.

Vicky cut across the lawn to the log cabin and let herself through the front door into a spacious living room that ran along the front. Woven

Indian rugs lay scattered over the plank floor separating areas of overstuffed couches and chairs and small tables. Massive moss-rock fireplaces stood at each end of the room, and windows framed by blue denim draperies looked out over the lawn. Sounds of voices, little bursts of laughter, floated into the quiet as if from a long distance.

Vicky stood at the edge of the window near the door. Sharon was moving among the tables under the nearest canopy, greeting people, shaking hands. Then she was coming toward the cabin. In a few seconds the door swung open and the actress joined her at the window. She laid one hand against the fold of drapes and stared out at the crowd. The long fingernails looked like splotches of blood on the blue denim.

"Well, what do you think?"

"Do you really want my opinion?"

The actress didn't respond. Letting her hand fall away, she turned to Vicky. "Edna and Wylan are as phony as these nails." She held up both hands for inspection.

Vicky stared at her. "What made you think they were legitimate?"

"I don't know." There was a long, dispirited sigh. "Edna sounded so certain. She called me the minute the newspapers came out yesterday. I don't know how she knew where to find me."

"Moccasin telegraph," Vicky said. She hoped the leak hadn't spouted in her office.

Sharon gave a little shrug. "Edna said she and

Wylan had a daughter in 1964. They weren't married then, just a couple of kids with no money. She delivered the baby at home, then took her to Casper and gave her to social services." She hesitated. A profound look of sadness and disappointment came into her eyes. "And she said something else."

Vicky waited.

"She said she always knew I would come back to her." The actress walked over and sank into one of the overstuffed chairs. "That really got me. I asked her and Wylan to come right over, and when they drove up, I raced out to meet them. You don't know how I've dreamed about meeting my own parents. We sat in this room and talked and talked. I told them to invite anybody they wanted for lunch today. I called you. I wanted to believe."

Vicky walked over and perched on the arm of another chair. "What changed your mind?"

Sharon spread her hands in her lap, studying the red nails. "I spent the night going over everything they said. They couldn't agree on when the baby was born. Edna said spring, but Wylan said August. I told them I might have been born in September, and Edna said, oh, yes, she definitely remembered. September. She had been so young, only fifteen. She must have forgotten." The actress looked at Vicky out of pleading eyes. "Forgotten when her child was born?"

The words hung between them a moment. She went on: "I told them I'd found 'Maisie' among

194

my mother's things. Edna said the social worker's name was Maisie. Wylan said that was his grandmother."

Vicky rummaged in her bag for her notepad and pen. "We can check Edna's story. We have names now. We'll get Edna's name before she was married. The intermediary who's been trying to find your records can check for a birth certificate. We can compare dates —"

"Stop." Sharon held up one hand. "There's no point." She propelled herself out of the chair and walked back to the window. "She's not my mother, Vicky," she said, staring outside again. "You see, in some way, I have always known my natural mother."

She turned slowly. Everything about her seemed sad. "It's my own fault, bringing in the press. I never should have listened to them. Publicists! They can't let any opportunity go by. I wanted to cancel the feast, but the publicists got on the phone and insisted I go through with it. 'Great photo ops,' they said. 'Star of movie about Native Americans finds own Native American parents.' It will be in every newspaper from here to Paris."

Vicky heard her own sharp intake of breath. She'd guessed the truth. This was a publicity stunt.

"You think I came here to use people." The actress spoke quickly, as if she had seen into her thoughts. "It's not true. I want to find my biological parents. The only reason I agreed to go ahead with this farce" — she tilted her head toward the window — "was to put a stop to any other claims like the Linders'. The other phonies will think someone has already gotten a hook into my bank account. But my real mother . . ." For the first time the actress's eyes welled with tears. "My real mother won't give a farthing's ass for my bank account."

Vicky dropped the pad and pen back into her bag. "I've made some inquiries, Sharon," she said. "The year you were born, a lot of babies from the reservation died. If any baby was adopted outside the tribe, it was done quietly, privately. It's possible a private adoption was arranged by a local clinic. I don't know for certain. So far it's just a hunch. Do you want me to keep looking?"

The actress turned back to the window. She was quiet a long moment. Then: "They're here somewhere, my mother and father. I know it. I'll pay you whatever it takes."

"You've paid me enough, Sharon."

"Well, you're about to earn your fee," the actress said. "Here comes Edna Linder."

There was a *clip-clop* of footsteps on the veranda. The door swung open and Edna Linder stepped inside. "There you are." She swung toward Sharon. "Everyone's asking for you."

Vicky walked over. "There will have to be tests, Edna."

"Tests?" The word came like a gigantic burp out of the gaping mouth.

"Blood tests. DNA tests that will prove you and Wylan are Sharon's parents."

The woman moved closer to Sharon. "What on earth is this woman talking about? We've gone over everything. The dates, the name of the social worker. It all fits. I guess I know my own daughter when I see her. You look just like my dead aunt Ellen. I have photos. You'll see, you're the spitting image."

A barely controlled smile started on the actress's face. "I'm sorry, Edna. You know how lawyers are. They want to dot all the i's and cross the t's, make sure everything is legal."

Edna drew her lips into a tight, determined line. Straightening her shoulders and turning to Vicky, she said, "We'll take whatever tests you want."

19

Vicky guided the Bronco along the shelf road that wound out of the foothills. Below, the rooftops and gold-splashed trees of Lander crept into the plains as far as she could see. Her thoughts were on Edna and Wylan Linder. Opportunists, grabbing the chance for a free ride. Especially Edna. Last year the woman had seized the chance to pocket what was most likely a substantial amount of cash. She'd never admitted she took the money, and Vicky had never asked. When the U.S. attorney dropped the charges, Edna walked away, probably convinced she was more clever than Vicky was. Now she'd agreed to submit to tests — what else could she say? — but neither she nor Wylan would ever take them, Vicky was certain.

And yet . . . There was also the chance they would surprise her. And the tests could prove Sharon was their daughter. Vicky gripped the steering wheel and turned onto the straight strip of asphalt that led into the southern reaches of town. She was struck by the irony. Sharon David, searching for her Arapaho parents and finding Edna and Wylan — part Arapaho, but self-centered and mean. Not like the people.

Slats of sunshine lay over Main Street as Vicky parked in front of her office. She hurried through the warmth of the sun and the cool gloom of the shade, shivering a little as she ran up the stairs and down the corridor. She pushed open the door, nearly hitting Laola, who was on the other side.

"Thought that was you comin'," the secretary said hurriedly. "I been lookin' all over for you. Called the dude ranch, and they said you'd left. He's been waitin' most the afternoon."

Ben, Vicky thought. Would he never give up, never stop calling, wanting to see her? And now he was here. She started toward the closed door to her private office.

"Can you believe it?" Laola was behind her. "Two celebrities in the same week. First Sharon David and now . . ."

Vicky stopped and turned toward the secretary. "Who's here?"

"The famous Dr. Markham." It was a whisper. "He's been waitin' all afternoon. I didn't know what to say to him! I offered to get some coffee."

Vicky reached for the doorknob.

"Oh, did I tell you Ben's been calling?"

"If he calls again," Vicky said, "say I'm tied up for the rest of the day." *The rest of my life,* she was thinking as she pushed open the door.

Across the office, in front of the window, were two men — one, close to seventy, the other still in his twenties. Both were in blue jeans, denim shirts, and hiking boots. The beginnings of a beard shadowed their faces. They might have just trekked out of the mountains. The older man came forward, hand outstretched. The easy sincerity and handsome face, the gray, fatherly eyes and pencil-thin lips, the thick mane of silver hair, like that of a fox — the television camera had caught it all.

"Ah," he said as he took her hand. She could sense the strength of the man. "You must be Vicky Holden. Jerry Markham," he went on in a tone that indicated no introduction was necessary. Vicky slipped her hand free.

Glancing at the younger man standing behind them, he said, "Allow me to introduce Randy Mitchell from Rock Springs. Best hunting guide in Wyoming. We've been elk hunting. It's bow season, you know. When I checked with my office, I learned you wanted to see me. We drove into town today to replenish supplies, so I took the chance on finding you in. I'm glad we waited." His gaze traveled over her.

"Please sit down." Vicky motioned them toward the visitor chairs and took her own chair at the desk. Clasping her hands on the blotter, she waited as they settled in: the guide in the chair on the left, leaning back, gripping the armrests. A bored, yawning look, as if this was something that had to be endured so he could get back into the mountains.

The doctor sat slightly forward, shoulders squared, elbows bent on the armrests, fingers steepled under his chin. "What led you to my office?" His voice was as smooth as falling water.

She said, "A client is searching for her natural parents."

"Ah, yes." Markham's shoulders rose. "Sharon David. I heard the news on the radio. Poor little movie star out promoting her latest movie. I'm sorry for her. Darn shame the studio is using her like that. You do your best work" — he paused, no longer talking about the actress, Vicky realized — "and next thing you know, you're a celebrity. Publicists taking control of your life. Cameras flashing in your face. Reporters shouting. Everyone wanting a piece of you."

"I'm surprised the press hasn't discovered you're here," Vicky offered.

The doctor shifted in his chair. "Every year I head up into the high country. Nothing but sheep, deer, elk, and a few bears and mountain lions. I like them all a lot better than I like those vultures with cameras. Incidentally, I'd appreciate your not tipping them off."

Vicky gave the man an assuring smile. She hoped Laola hadn't already sent the news over the moccasin telegraph. "My client hasn't had much luck," she said, bringing the subject back to Sharon David. "She believes she was born in the area in 1964. She also believes she may be Arapaho. A lot of women from the reservation used your clinic." She plunged on, not waiting for a confirmation. "It's hard to imagine any woman giving up her child that year, when so many infants died, but —"

The doctor interrupted. "What are you saying?"

Vicky regarded the man across from her. "I believe some young woman may have wanted to place her child for adoption. Perhaps she turned to you for help."

"Are you saying I had something to do with the deaths?" The man sat up straighter and dropped both hands into his lap.

Vicky kept her tone calm. "I'm trying to help my client find her natural parents."

"I warn you to be very careful," Markham went on. "I have a reputation to protect, one I've rightly earned over the years. I have no intention of allowing you to tarnish that reputation with innuendos. Must I remind you of the laws protecting people against libel and slander?"

"Wait just a minute, Doctor." Vicky leaned over the desk. "I'm looking for information, that's all. My client needs to know if there's a chance an Indian woman placed her baby in an independent adoption thirty-five years ago. Doctors and attorneys have often arranged such adoptions."

The doctor tilted back his head and stared at her through half-lidded eyes. "What exactly do you want?"

Vicky held the man's gaze. "Did you arrange an adoption for an Arapaho infant in 1964? Some woman who didn't want to go through Social Services and endure a public investigation? Didn't want the tribe to know?"

The doctor remained motionless, the look of studied control on his face. Vicky plunged on:

"Perhaps the woman's family agreed with her decision and helped her to keep her pregnancy and the adoption a secret."

Had she imagined it, or was there a flicker of remembrance in the doctor's eyes? "Perhaps you knew a couple desperately longing for a child. People from another state. You could have put them in contact with the girl. A lawyer would have handled the adoption papers. It happens every day."

"If such an adoption had transpired, I would hardly break the doctor-patient confidence and tell you about it," Markham said. "In any case, adoption records are sealed."

Vicky said, "I'm asking if it took place, Doctor. My client will know whether to continue her search here. If it did, she could furnish your office and the lawyer with waivers of confidentiality. She can place ads. With all the news stories, her natural parents may come forward and waive their right to confidentiality. You could then confirm the adoption."

Dr. Markham ran his tongue over his thin lips. "I operated the most progressive clinic of the day. I did not run an adoption agency."

Vicky sat back. "You're telling me no such adoption took place?"

Setting both hands on the armrests, Markham leveled himself to his feet. The guide jumped up, a flash of eagerness on his face. "No such adoption took place," the doctor said. "Not in my clinic. If that's all you wanted to see me about,

Randy and I will return to the peace of the mountains." He started toward the door, the guide following like a bloodhound.

Vicky watched the retreating figures. The door slammed behind them. She felt the same disquiet that she felt in the courtroom when she knew a witness was lying. Yet it was hard to believe the famous Dr. Jeremiah Markham was lying. Or Luther Benson, for that matter. What possible reason could they have for not wanting Sharon David to find her biological parents?

Laola's voice drifted through the closed door — deferential and fawning. Then the door opened, and the secretary walked over to the desk. "You got a bunch of phone calls while you was out." She held out a page of messages. "Agent Gianelli's been calling, and I tol' you Ben called, didn't I?"

Vicky glanced through the messages. Ben's name appeared three times. Ted Gianelli's twice.

"You want me to call him back?" Laola asked. Her tone was hopeful.

"Gianelli? Yes," Vicky said.

"I meant Ben."

As Laola started for the door, the phone jangled. Vicky picked it up. The agent's voice boomed over the line. "Vicky, I need your help."

"Let me guess," Vicky said. "Lucy Travise and James Holden have disappeared." It was what she had expected.

"We have a watch out across the area. No sign

of them. I think they're laying low on the res. Can you get me some word on them?"

Vicky let out a long breath. "They don't want to be found, Ted."

"The girl can link Sonny Red Wolf to the time and location of Father Joseph's murder. I need her statement, Vicky. She stays in hiding, your friend John O'Malley could find himself staring down the barrel of a rifle."

Vicky closed her eyes against the idea. "I'll try," she said.

She pressed the disconnect button. There was the sound of electronic clicks as she tapped out the number to Arapaho Ranch where Ben worked. A man answered. "Ben drove outta here an hour ago," he said to her inquiry. "Left a message for you."

"He left a message?"

"Said in case you called, he was gonna be at the Roundup Café in Lander. Said you know the place."

Vicky thanked him and hung up. She knew the place.

20

The reporters gathered around a white van in the dusk of the parking lot: four or five men, a woman, faces lifted up as Vicky came down the rear stairway. A cigarette sailed in the air and plopped on the cement, the tiny red glow lingering like an ember in a dying campfire.

The reporters surged forward, a gust of shadowy faces as she hurried across the lot, steeling herself against the blizzard of questions. "What about the Linders?" someone shouted.

"Are they Sharon's parents?" A man's voice. "What's the proof?"

Vicky darted through the shouting voices and bobbing heads, the stale odor of perspiring bodies. She reached the Bronco and slipped inside. Faces peered in the windows shouting garbled questions at the glass. A man gripped the edge of the door, preventing her from closing it. "How's Sharon like having an embezzler for a mom?"

"Charges against Edna Linder were dropped!" Vicky yelled over the barrage of questions.

A woman elbowed around the man. "Did you bring them together? How much is Sharon paying you?"

Vicky tugged at the door, wrenching it free and slamming it shut. She punched the key into the ignition. An interminable wait, and finally the engine turned over. The Bronco started moving, and the reporters peeled away, rows of faces bobbing in the windows like decoys in a shooting range. In the side mirror she watched the crowd scramble for the white van and several cars.

Jamming down the accelerator, she plunged through the intersection as the light turned red. Another glance in the mirror: the van and cars were stopped at the light. She swung into an alley, swerved left into another alley, and emerged on a side street heading south, putting more space between her and the reporters. Near the edge of town, she turned onto the pavement in front of a cluster of flat-faced, peak-roofed buildings. She parked in front of the Roundup Café, next to Ben's brown truck.

He was sitting in one of the booths along a wall of plate-glass windows. He hadn't seen her when she'd driven up, she knew by the mixture of disbelief and joy on his face as she walked past the counter toward him. Most of the other booths were occupied by families. A couple of cowboys hunched over plates of food and mugs of coffee at the counter. The rumble of conversation and clank of dishes punctuated the Willie Nelson song in the background. The air smelled of hot chili.

Ben slid out of the booth and drew himself to his full six feet. One hand gripped a white napkin. His black blazer hung easily from wide shoulders and revealed the front of his checked shirt and the black strings of his bolo tie. A silver buffalo sat at the collar. His blue jeans looked clean and stiff, molded to the muscles of his thighs and calves. He was as handsome as she remembered: hair as black as obsidian, barely brushing the collar of his blazer; dark, wide-set eyes, chiseled cheekbones, and finely shaped nose with the hook near the top. His mouth parted in a smile that showed a line of perfect white teeth.

"This is a surprise," he said. He remained standing as she tossed her bag onto the booth and slid in beside it.

"You left a message."

"Just dumb hope."

Averting his eyes, she glanced out the window. The last gray light of day hung in the branches of the trees across the street; a woman pushed a baby stroller in and out of the shadows on the sidewalk. Vicky was aware of Ben taking the seat across from her, of the calmness and certainty in his bearing — the bearing of a warrior. Men listened to Ben Holden; women fell in love with him. She was seventeen when she had come under his spell. Still learning who she was, when she had begun to define herself by him: Ben's girl, Ben's fiancée, Ben's wife, the mother of Ben's children. They had been married twelve years; but they had been divorced a year longer. He still defined a part of her.

"I've been wanting to talk to you," he said.

Vicky brought her eyes to his. "It's been pretty crazy." She knew that he knew there was another reason for not returning his calls. There was always the risk of coming under his spell, losing that part of herself she had struggled to reclaim.

The waitress appeared and set two menus on the table. Her attention was directed to Ben as she ticked off the specials. He stopped her after the chili and chicken-fried steak. "Two hamburgers and two coffees," he said, handing back the menus. Then he instructed her to bring lots of fries and not to forget the ketchup.

When the waitress had gone, he said, "Used to be our favorite meal."

Vicky remembered. She kept her expression blank and said, "The FBI agent wants to talk to Lucy Travise, the white girl living with your nephew James."

Ben gave a little nod, as if this was old news. James and his friends were always in trouble with the law. "What's it about?"

"The murder of Father Keenan," Vicky told him.

Ben shook his head. "They didn't have anything to do with that."

Vicky folded her hands on the table, wishing the waitress would deliver the coffee. "Lucy saw Sonny Red Wolf's truck on Thunder Lane about the time of the murder," she began. "I tried to talk her into going to the fed. But she and James are scared. They took off. They're hiding somewhere with the family."

209

Ben ran one hand along the sharp line of his chin, his eyes fixed on hers. "I don't want James mixed up with Sonny Red Wolf."

"Ben" — she tried to keep the anxiety out of her voice — "what if Sonny meant to kill Father John and shot the wrong priest? He could try again. The fed has to stop him."

"You care a lot about that priest, don't you?"

"I don't want to see anyone else murdered," she said hurriedly.

"Especially that priest." He paused. "I've heard the rumors."

"Rumors!" Vicky said. "What rumors?" It astounded her, the way the moccasin telegraph never delivered rumors to the people they concerned.

The waitress appeared with plates of hamburgers and fries. Then she stepped away and returned with a bottle of ketchup and two mugs of coffee, which she deposited next to the plates. "Anything else I can get you?" A cheery smile bestowed on Ben.

He shook his head without returning the smile. As she stepped away, he leaned forward and said, "Rumors are there's something between you and him."

"He's a priest, Ben." Vicky avoided his gaze and concentrated on shaking the ketchup into a little puddle next to her fries.

"He's a man."

"He's an honorable man." Vicky set the ketchup bottle down hard. It made a sharp *thwack* on the Formica table. Smells of charred meat and fresh coffee floated toward her. "This isn't about him. It's about stopping a killer. Lucy has to talk to the fed."

"I don't know where James might be hanging out," Ben said. "I just got back from L.A. a week ago."

Vicky was about to take a bite of her hamburger. She set it on the plate and stared at him.

"Kids are doing fine." He spoke quickly, as if to supply the answers to the questions she was about to ask. "Lucas'll get his degree in computer science in December. Susan likes her part-time job at a law office. Says her classes at the community college are going pretty good."

"I didn't know you went to see them," Vicky said, startled at the hurt in her tone. The kids and Ben seemed to have a secret life, one from which she was excluded.

Ben took a bite of his hamburger and began chewing slowly, reflectively. Finally he said, "I've asked Susan and Lucas to come home. Lucas can work with me up at the Arapaho Ranch. Susan, she can get a part-time job and finish up school." He looked steadily at her. "Don't tell me you don't want them home."

"I want what's best for them," Vicky said, hoping the longing for her children didn't seep into her voice. She didn't let herself think of them close by: dinners together, a movie now and then, telephone conversations that continued from day to day — a normal family life.

"What's best for them is to be here instead of in that smoggy, paved-over city. They need to be with their own people so they don't forget who they are. They need family, Vicky. They need us."

"We're not a family anymore." She stared at the untouched hamburger. She was no longer hungry.

"Well, we're all they've got." Silence hung between them. After a few moments he shoved his plate aside and leaned toward her. Slivers of light glinted in his dark eyes. "I know it's over between us, Vicky. I've had a hard time admitting that I lost you" — he shrugged — "drove you off with my drinking. I lost control at times. I'm not proud of it. Jesus! I hate thinking about it. I despise the man I used to be, the man who hit you. I don't know him. I don't want anything to do with him."

A wave of sadness and futility swept through Vicky. These were memories she did not want. "That's over," she managed.

Ben leaned toward her, his face composed halfway between regret and acceptance. "I'd like for us to be friends. Get together once in a while, for the kids' sake. I don't expect anything else." He hesitated, then hurried on: "I'm seeing somebody now. She's a real nice lady."

Vicky picked up the coffee mug and gripped it with both hands. For the first time in — how many years? — he no longer wanted her. The realization gave her a new and unfamiliar sense of freedom, as if the last tie to that other life had been cut and she was, at last, completely alone. Woman Alone.

"I hear you've been hanging out with movie stars," Ben said in a lighter tone, as if they were now casual friends.

Vicky took a long sip of the coffee before she said, "Sharon David's looking for her natural parents."

Ben gave a snort of laughter. "Some parents to find yourself saddled with. Edna and Wylan Linder."

"I suspect the blood tests will prove otherwise." Vicky felt her own tension begin to dissolve now that the conversation had shifted into a neutral zone.

Ben peered at her over the rim of his mug. "I saw in the newspaper that she was born in 1964. It's hard to believe any woman let her child go that year. A lot of babies were dying. My mother lost a son. Contaminated water, so everybody said."

"What do you mean?" A small alarm sounded somewhere in the back of her mind.

"I was seven years old, Vicky. I didn't get all the details, but it was like a darkness fell over our house, like night came and never left. Mom never talked about it, and Dad . . ." Ben stopped talking and took another sip of coffee. "That's when Dad started drinking." He glanced out the window a moment. "I always wished I'd seen my brother."

"What do you mean? Didn't you go to your brother's funeral?" In that other time, when they were married, Ben had never spoken much about his own life before she had come into it. This was a different Ben, and she knew she had to be careful.

"Sure I went to the funeral over at the mission."

"Maybe you don't remember. You were only seven."

Ben was shaking his head. "I remember everything. The priest saying the Mass, the elders painting the casket."

"Painting the casket!" Vicky stared at him, scarcely believing what she'd just heard. "Was the casket closed?"

"That's what I'm telling you, Vicky. The family never got to see the baby because the casket was sealed. The elders put the sacred paint on the lid."

Vicky sat motionless, her eyes on the blur of activity: the waitress sidling to the table and slapping down a check, Ben plucking a wallet from inside his blazer, pulling out some bills. She was numb with horror. How many other caskets were sealed that year? How many other families never saw the bodies of their babies? Why? What possible explanation could there have been for sealing the caskets?

"You okay?" Ben leaned toward her.

She stared at him a long moment, trying to compose herself and force her thoughts into some kind of order that made sense. Then she grabbed her bag and slid out of the booth. "I've got to go," she said, managing a little smile.

Ben was on his feet, reaching toward her. She turned and hurried toward the rest rooms, looking for a telephone. She had to call Laola and tell her to clear the schedule for tomorrow. She wouldn't be in the office.

21

The morning sun glanced off the gray-stone library that stood among the pines in north Lander. Vicky parked at the curb and hurried up the sidewalk past a couple of women with three young children trailing behind, books gripped in pudgy hands. She pulled open the heavy wood door and stepped into the cool, spacious interior. Rows of book stacks jutted from the side walls, and in the center, several elderly men sat at rectangular tables, bent over newspapers that rattled into the quiet. She threaded her way among the tables to the reception desk, where a young woman with dark hair and serious eyes was peering at a small computer screen. "Yes?" she said. Her eyes remained on the screen.

Vicky asked to see the local newspapers for 1964.

The woman sighed and rose from the chair, allowing her gaze to drift slowly from the screen. Stepping around the desk, she threw Vicky a sideways glance that indicated she should follow. They walked past the book stacks on the right and into a small cubicle with filing cabinets against one wall and a microfilm machine on a table against the other. She opened a cabinet drawer, extracted a small box, and tipped out a roll of film. Then she sat down at the machine and, with quick, efficient fingers, threaded the film through the spools. "There you are," she announced as she stood up.

Vicky thanked her and took the chair in front of the blinking black-and-white images. Out of the corner of her eye, she saw the librarian slip past the door. There was the soft stitch of footsteps across the reading room. Vicky turned the focus knob until the flickering light settled into the typed lines and photos of the front page of the *Gazette*, January 1, 1964. The pages began to slip by: snow piled over houses, a truck crushed against a telephone pole, school kids visiting the courthouse, boys running down a basketball court — ordinary news of ordinary days.

Halfway through the month, she found a two-inch column at the bottom of an inside page. The small headline read: RESIDENTS COMPLAIN ABOUT WATER. She glanced through the article. People living around Ethete complain to tribal council about red-colored water in faucets. Council asks county health department to investigate.

The pages move past — January, February. Finally another article appeared: initial tests confirm water is safe. Further tests to be conducted. Vicky hunched toward the screen, watching for an article on the test results. She found it in the first week of March. Tests on local water indicate possibility of small levels of contamination. Health-department officials believe problem caused from drainage of old gold mines in the mountains.

"Are you going to be long?"

Vicky took her hand off the knob and looked around. A gray-haired woman stood in the doorway, an anxious look in the large eyes behind pink-framed glasses.

"I'm afraid this may take a while," Vicky said.

"Oh, dear." The woman sighed and glanced back at the reading room, as if she expected the librarian might come to her assistance. "I'm working on my genealogy." She gave another sigh. "I guess I'll have to wait." She turned and walked to a table a few feet from the door, pulled out a chair, and sat down, facing the cubicle.

Vicky turned back to the screen, aware of the woman's eyes on her as she turned the forward knob and glanced through the moving pages. She stopped on the front page dated March 12. Large, black headlines ran across the top: RESERVATION WATER CONTAMINATED. Slowly she brought the page into sharper focus, then read through the article. Further tests conducted at county lab confirm uranium, sulfate, and molybdenum in surface soil, groundwater, and well water in area near Ethete. Source of contamination unknown, but officials of company that operated the uranium mill on the reservation in the 1950s deny responsibility. Health department assures residents that the levels of contamination do not exceed acceptable safety limits. There is no cause for alarm. Since toxicity may damage fetuses, however, pregnant women are urged to avoid piped water as a precautionary measure.

In the newspaper dated March 30, Vicky found the first newborn obituary. Eric Morning Star, son of Aly and Merwin Morning Star, died at birth. Cause of death: meningitis. She stared at the names a moment, searching her memory. The Morning Star family, a small frame house at the edge of Ethete. The light-skinned, pretty girl in her class for a time at St. Francis Mission School. She hadn't heard of them in years. *Most the people have left,* Aunt Rose had said. Vicky found the notepad and pen in her purse and jotted down the name. From the reading room came the impatient sounds of the gray-haired woman clearing her throat and chair legs squeaking against the hard floor.

Ignoring the woman staring at her through the doorway, Vicky started the pages moving again across the screen. The following week's paper reported the death of another baby, and Vicky wrote down the name. Then other obituaries began appearing every week, sometimes two in the same week. Always the same story, newborn infant died. Cause of death listed either as infectious virus or meningitis. Funeral services scheduled at St. Francis Church, Father Joseph Keenan presiding. Only the family names were different. She added the new names to the growing list. The microfilm machine whirred into the quiet.

The obituaries continued throughout the summer, along with scattered, front-page articles on the water contamination. There were veiled acknowledgments from the health department that the contaminated water might be a factor in the deaths of newborn babies. Gradually suggestions gave way to urgent warnings that pregnant women should not drink piped water.

Then, in the August 15 paper, Vicky found the article she had been looking for: an interview with Coroner David Stresky placed inside the paper next to a large advertisement for a local hardware store. The coroner stared out of a photograph, a pinched-faced, middle-aged man with dark hair flattened across the top of his head and a tie knotted at a collar too large for his skinny neck. "Contaminated water may be the source of the infectious viruses that have caused the recent deaths of several infants," the coroner was quoted as saying. "But until further tests establish without a doubt that a virus is in the water, we must proceed with caution. In the interests of public safety, the caskets must be sealed to prevent any possibility of the virus spreading through the community."

There were more obituaries through August and into September. Vicky stopped at each one and wrote down the family name. The list of names now covered two pages of the notepad. She glanced up at the square white tiles on the ceiling a moment, then brought her eyes back to the screen and the possibility of still more names. There was a sense of vacancy beyond the doorway. The old woman must have left. Vicky kept her eyes on the pages slipping by in front of her.

Something caught her attention, and she stopped the machine. A plain, serious-eyed girl with a fluff of dark hair under a starched white hat and hands primly clasped in the lap of her white nurse's uniform smiled into the camera. Above the photo was the headline LOCAL NURSE FOUND DEAD. The caption identified the woman as Dawn James, nurse at the Markham Clinic, and Vicky realized that the words *Markham Clinic* had drawn her eye. She read through the article. The twenty-four-year-old woman had been found shot to death on the banks of the Wind River. The coroner had ruled the death a suicide. Vicky stared at the photo a moment, wondering why a young nurse at the Markham Clinic had decided to take her own life.

In the newspaper two days later Vicky found Dawn James's obituary. The funeral Mass was to be held at St. Francis Church. The priest who would conduct the services was not Joseph Keenan, however, but the other priest who had been at the mission at that time. Vicky barely re-membered the man. She moved through the pages for the rest of the week and then, in the Sunday paper, she found a small article about the sister of the dead nurse, Mary James, pro-testing the coroner's ruling, claiming her sister had been murdered. The coroner and FBI agent in charge of the investigation stated that there was no evidence of homicide.

Still the pages rolled past. More obituaries for infants, and in late September Vicky found the obituary for Ben's brother. She added her own name, Holden, to the list. Now there were fifteen names. October slid by, then November. The obituaries seemed to have stopped.

In an early December issue, two-inch headlines jumped across the page. NEW WATER SYSTEM APPROVED. The article stated that the new system would bypass the contaminated groundwater and deep wells in the Ethete area. Water would be piped from reservoirs in the northern part of the reservation.

Vicky sat back, staring at the black-and-white images on the screen. Something didn't make sense. If the water was contaminated, why were only newborn babies infected? Wouldn't the mothers have also been infected? And what about other people on the reservation? And if that were true, why was it necessary to seal the caskets to protect people already exposed to the virus?

She turned the knob and watched the images slide in reverse to the first day of January. Then she began slowly moving through the pages again — looking for what? She didn't know. In February, she found a small notice about an outbreak of gastroenteritis at one of the elementary schools on the reservation. In March, another article about the high absenteeism in the schools. Doctors cautioned parents in the Ethete area to boil the drinking water. Another article two days later: residents of a new housing area complained to the tribal council about having to boil water. "Water oughta be safe in brand-new homes," one of the elders told the council.

Vicky leaned forward, reading again through the article. Then she glanced up and began rubbing her neck, trying to work out the stiffness. She'd found what she was looking for. The water had been contaminated, all right, but not by toxic chemicals. If the water had contained chemicals, boiling wouldn't have done any good. The water was contaminated by microbes, most likely from sewage, and she would bet everything she owned that the source was the new housing area outside Ethete. Where had the developer dumped the sewage? Directly into the nearby creeks, where it would eventually work its way into the drinking water? How much had the developer paid the building inspectors and health-department officials to look the other way? To blame the contamination on old gold mines and uranium mills?

When people took sick, when the babies began dying, a new water system was quietly built that bypassed the contaminated creeks. No blame was ever attached to the housing developer. There was no accountability, no chance for lawsuits. It all made sense.

And yet, and yet . . . It didn't explain the closed caskets. The families of dead babies had the right to view the remains in private, even if the caskets were closed for the funeral services. But the coroner had ordered the caskets *sealed.* Why had David Stresky taken such extreme measures? To protect people already exposed to an infectious virus? Or to prevent the families from seeing what was inside the caskets? And why had a young nurse at the Markham Clinic committed suicide? What had made her life so impossible?

Vicky turned the knob again, trying to concentrate on the pages slipping toward the end of the year. She was about to start rewinding when her eyes fell on a headline on the front page of the December 29 issue: CORONER FOUND DEAD. Embedded in the article was the same photo — dark hair flattened to one side, pinched face, skinny neck. She read quickly. David Stresky found shot to death on the banks of the Wind River. Twenty-two-caliber pistol in right hand. Wind River officials call the death a suicide.

Vicky felt her heart thump against her chest. The sound of her own breathing filled the cubicle. She rewound the film to September and reread the article on the death of Dawn James. Then she moved back to the coroner's death. The two deaths were identical. Both had been shot in the right temple with a twenty-two-caliber pistol. Both had been found on the banks of the Wind River.

Vicky turned the rewind knob to top speed, her gaze fixed on the stream of light flashing across the screen. The nurse at the clinic where the babies died, the coroner who ordered the caskets sealed — both had committed suicide. Yet a woman named Mary James believed her sister had been murdered. What if Dawn James and David Stresky had both been murdered? Suddenly the cubicle seemed hot and stuffy. Vicky felt slightly sick to her stomach with the realization that the shadowy idea hovering in her mind was not preposterous. It made sense. Dawn James and David Stresky had been murdered to protect a terrible secret, and now she understood clearly what that secret was.

22

Father John spotted the small frame house among the cottonwoods ahead, the only house he'd seen in the last several miles. The wind swept across the plains and knocked at the sides of the Escort. He let up on the accelerator. The air was wavy in the afternoon sunlight.

He'd picked Megan up from the hospital in the morning and brought her back to the mission, where he left her at the guest house with instructions to rest. They both understood that she had no intention of doing so. He had been in his office about an hour when she showed up, complaining that the walls were closing in and that she preferred to work rather than die of boredom. The morning had slipped by him: phone calls, people dropping by, and his own unsuccessful attempts to get some work done. He managed to complete the arrangements for Father Joseph's memorial Mass and the feast that would follow. Finally, after a quick lunch of tuna-fish sandwiches with Megan at the residence, he'd driven out of the mission and headed west on Seventeen-Mile Road.

Now he wheeled into the dirt yard in front of the house. Esther Tallman was pulling laundry off a line that stretched between the cottonwoods on one side. The sheets and towels billowed in the wind, like the sails of a boat slipping across the plains. He let himself out and started toward her, holding down the brim of his cowboy hat in the wind. She stuffed the last towel into a basket at her feet. Stepping past her, he picked up the basket. "Let me give you a hand!" he shouted over the wind.

He followed the old woman up the cement steps to the little stoop at the front door. She stepped inside and waited as he brought in the basket and deposited it on the floor. Then she closed the door against the noise of the wind. A hush fell over the small living room. Faint smells of detergent and stale coffee wafted through the door to the kitchen in the rear of the house. "Get you some coffee or cola?" Esther asked, heading toward the door.

He said a cola sounded good, tossed his hat onto the sofa, and sat down next to it. In a moment she returned with two cans of cola. She handed him one and took the chair next to the television. After straightening her skirt over her knees — a prim, nunlike gesture — she pulled the tab on her can, took a long drink, and fixed him with a steady gaze. "It's good to see you, Father. Don't get many visitors out this way."

He followed the old woman's lead and kept up his end of small talk: there was a cool bite to the wind; winter was coming. Finally, the exchange of pleasantries over, he set his cola can on the small table next to the sofa and leaned forward, elbows on his thighs, hands folded between his knees. "Grandmother," he said in a supplicant tone, like that of a sinner, "I'd like to know about Father Joseph."

A questioning look came into the old woman's face. "He came by here last week."

Father John nodded. "What can you tell me about when he was here before?"

"Like I tol' you, he was a real good man." The old woman's features relaxed, like a mask slipping back into place. "He come here every day while Thomas and me and the kids was havin' our bad time." The dark eyes swept the room with an expectant look, as if a dead husband and grown children might materialize. "Sat right where you're sitting. Had the sense not to say anything. Just grieved with us, real quiet, and tried to take some of the pain off us. That was when we lost the boy. He was our last baby. We'd thought we was too old to be havin' any more, then we found out another baby was on the way. Well" — she paused, gathering the memories — "Thomas was like that stallion we had out in the pasture, prancing 'round, proud as all get out."

The old woman took in a long breath and continued: "Guess that's what made it so hard when the baby got that meningitis. Doctor took it real hard, too. There was tears in his eyes when he come into my room that mornin' and told me our baby was dead."

Father John nodded slowly and gave the woman a smile of sympathy. "Where was the baby born?"

"Over there in Lander at that real nice clinic. We thought that was where I oughta go, me bein' older and all."

"The Markham Clinic?"

"How'd you know? Dr. Markham's been gone a long time. He's real famous now."

"Do you remember Dawn James, the nurse who worked for him?"

"Dark-haired girl, small, with strong, comforting hands." The woman gave a quick nod. "Seemed pretty smart. Knew what she was doin'. She was a real good nurse. I felt bad when I read about her shooting herself down by the river. Guess she just couldn't take it — workin' around all the babies that died. There was a lot that year."

Father John waited a moment before he asked how many babies had died.

The old woman threw her head back and stared at the ceiling. "Twelve, fifteen. All lost because of that bad water. The doctor said don't drink the water. But where was we supposed to get good water? There wasn't fancy water for sale, those days. A lot of women was lucky. Maybe they was able to do like the doctor said. Their babies was fine. It was hard seein' those chubby babies on the res and watchin' them grow up."

"What else happened, Grandmother?" Father John heard the persistence in his voice. "What did you hear about Dawn James and Father Joseph? Did anything happen that they would have wanted to keep secret?"

The woman's expression dissolved into puzzlement. "What're you gettin' at, Father?"

"I don't know exactly," he admitted. He didn't want to explain how Dawn James's sister was convinced the woman had been murdered. "It must have been a sad time for Father Joseph. I can't understand why he wanted to come back."

"That's easy, Father. He never forgot us. He wanted to see how all us folks that lost our babies was makin' out."

"Who else did he visit?"

She listed the names of several families he didn't know. Then she said, "A couple families are all dead now. Some others left the res. Went off to Denver or Cheyenne or Casper or someplace that didn't remind 'em of what they lost. Lucas Holden — that's Ben's father — died some years back. Cyrus Elk's been dying up at Riverton Hospital."

Father John swallowed hard. He'd intended to ask Father Joseph to stop by the hospital and see the old man. The request would have been unnecessary. If Joseph had been visiting the families still on the res, he'd probably visited Cyrus.

Father John thanked the woman for the gift of information. Then he picked up his hat and got to his feet. Motioning her to stay in her chair, he let himself out. He didn't know much more than when he'd come, other than that it seemed Dr. Markham and Dawn James were good at what they did.

23

It was late afternoon when Father John turned in to the mission. As he came around Circle Drive, he spotted the Bronco angled in front of the administration building. He parked beside it, scarcely believing Vicky was there. She must have learned something about Joseph's murder — a legitimate reason to return. He was immeasurably glad. There was so much he wanted to talk over with her.

As he let himself out, a pickup slowed around the drive and pulled up alongside him. Leonard leaned out the window. "You lookin' for Vicky, I seen her walkin' that way." He waved at the alley between the administration building and the church.

Father John started down the narrow alley. Cottonwood leaves littered the ground and snapped under his boots. Branches swayed overhead in the breeze, a flash of golds and coppers against the blue sky. Vicky was walking ahead, wearing blue jeans and denim jacket, the black bag dangling from one shoulder. Walks-On trotted on his three legs at her side. Suddenly the dog turned and ran toward him. He reached down and patted his head as they walked along.

Vicky had turned around and was waiting. "I've got to talk to you in private, John," she said when he reached her. The dark eyes flashed with intensity. "Can we walk down to the river?"

He set one hand lightly on her arm and guided her back in the direction she'd been heading. Whatever she wanted to talk about was important. He could feel the tension in her. It didn't surprise him that she wanted to walk to the Little Wind River, where the Arapahos had camped more than a hundred years ago when they had first come to the reservation. It was a sacred space.

They started down a path that wound through stands of cottonwoods and a tangle of red-gold underbrush that spread like smoldering fire beneath the trees. The last of the day's sunshine dappled the path ahead where Walks-On trotted, tail wagging, his coat a shimmer of gold.

When they reached the riverbank, Vicky stopped and faced him. Her expression was one of barely controlled fury. "What do you know about the black market for infants?" she asked, the tone hard and tense.

"What are you talking about?"

She turned away, as if to gather her thoughts, and stared out across the river at the endless stretch of the gold-drenched plains. The sound of lapping water mingled with the shush of the wind. Finally she looked back. "I believe there was a black market operating here in 1964."

He was quiet. A black market for babies? The year fifteen infants died? The same year Father Joseph had been pastor of the mission? He took her arm again and led her to a fallen tree trunk.

Vicky dropped down on the nubby surface, and he sat next to her. Walks-On stretched at their feet. "Tell me what you've found."

"The infants were buried in sealed caskets," she said. "I checked with Aunt Rose and called three elders. They all said the elders performed the funeral rituals — the sacred painting and cedar smudging — on the caskets, not the bodies. The families never saw the dead babies. I spent the morning at the library checking the newspapers. The caskets were sealed."

"Sealed!" Father John said. It was incredible. Beyond imagining. How could such a thing be? From his own experiences — how many funeral services? — the family determined whether the casket would be opened or closed. "The families had the right to see the bodies," he said.

"The right?" Vicky's eyes widened in surprise. "You can talk about rights, John. You're a white man. Thirty-five years ago the people didn't know they had any rights. The coroner said the caskets had to be sealed. He was the authority — a white authority. No one would have questioned him."

Father John glanced toward the river, his mind searching for some logical, rational explanation. "Maybe the coroner ordered the caskets sealed to protect the people," he said. "The water was polluted. It must have carried some infectious virus. Esther Tallman told me her infant died of meningitis."

Vicky got to her feet and started carving out a

small circle in front of him. "All the babies supposedly died of meningitis or some other infectious disease," she said. "I found the obituaries in the newspapers." She stopped pacing, dug a piece of folded paper out of her jeans pocket, and handed it to him.

Father John unfolded the paper and glanced through the names. Fifteen infants. Tallman, Holden, Red Feather, other families he knew. Still others he had never heard of. He looked up at Vicky. She had started pacing again. She always paced, he knew, when she was angry or upset.

"The water was polluted all right," she was saying. "There were several articles about it in the newspapers. The county health department sent out a couple of investigators and did some tests. They concluded the contamination came from the old gold mines in the mountains or from the uranium processing mill that had been here in the fifties. A handy explanation that no one questioned back then. The company that owned the mill denied that possibility, of course."

Vicky stopped pacing and locked eyes with him. "The water wasn't contaminated by chemicals. It was contaminated by raw sewage from a housing development near Ethete." She glanced away a moment. "The county officials had to know. They looked the other way."

Suddenly Vicky resumed pacing, creating a path between a stand of trees and the fallen trunk. "Don't you see, John? Jeremiah Markham took advantage of the contamination. There's always been a black market for healthy, white-looking babies. Couples that can't adopt any other way, desperate for a child, for a family. Babies are sold for fifty, a hundred thousand dollars today. How much did they bring thirty-five years ago? Fifteen, twenty thousand? A fortune. For that kind of money, there have always been people willing to supply the babies. Doctors like Jeremiah Markham, running private clinics. Lawyers willing to produce false birth certificates and relinquishment papers and other documents to satisfy the courts. Whole organizations devoted to acquiring healthy babies and placing them through independent adoptions with well-heeled couples."

Father John was quiet a moment. "What makes you so sure it happened here?"

"It happened, John." Vicky tossed her head in impatience. "There's no other explanation for the sealed caskets. People were already exposed to the virus. And if the mothers had been exposed, they would have developed antibodies that would have protected the new babies. It's highly unlikely the newborns would have died.

"The polluted water played right into Markham's hands." Vicky stopped circling and stepped toward him. "It was an opportunity he couldn't pass up. People were frightened. They didn't know what was in their water. It was almost a year before pipes were laid to bring water from a reservoir north of Ethete. But until then, the health department simply issued a warning. People boiled their drinking water. They drove to other parts of the reservation to fill bottles of unpolluted water. Still they couldn't be sure the water was safe. So when Markham claimed the babies had contacted some infectious disease, no one questioned him. He listed viral infection or meningitis as the cause of death on the death certificates."

Now Father John was on his feet. He took hold of her shoulders, stopping her as she circled. "There were death certificates?" Her theory was collapsing under the weight of facts.

"Jeremiah Markham is no fool, John." Vicky gave a hard laugh. "He came to my office yesterday afternoon."

"He's here?"

Another laugh. "He says he's bow-hunting in the mountains. He had a guide with him from Rock Springs." She shrugged and glanced away. "Markham is very smooth. Just the type of man to make certain everything looked legal. All the proper forms were filed with Vital Records. No loose ends. He needed help, of course. The coroner must have been involved. One David Stresky. He ordered the caskets sealed. I found his obituary in the papers. He shot himself in December that year. He must have been involved in taking the babies. There was no other reason for him to order the caskets sealed. The nurse who worked for Markham also shot herself. I think she was involved, too. They both knew what was going on."

Pulling free from his grasp, she started pacing again. "There had to be a lawyer in the scam. Somebody to prepare false birth certificates and relinquishment papers. My guess is that Markham was tied to a shyster somewhere who was involved with the black-market ring."

Father John turned and walked the few feet to the river. For a moment he watched the water eddy and swirl at the willows along the bank. Walks-On shuffled over and sniffed at his hand. He ignored the dog. He was thinking about Dawn James. Was she involved? Had she suffered a pang of conscience and taken her own life? Or were both she and the coroner murdered?

He looked back at Vicky. She had sat down on the tree trunk, posture stiff with anger, eyes shadowed in exhaustion. Slowly, logically, he told her what he had learned about Dawn James, about her sister's insistence that she had been murdered, about his own theory that the nurse had confided some secret to Father Joseph.

Vicky propelled herself to her feet. "You're saying Father Joseph knew?" Her tone was one of rage. "He knew what Markham and his crowd were doing? He knew they were taking the babies? And he didn't do anything about it?"

Father John held her eyes a moment. "Whatever Dawn James told him, it was in the confessional."

"He knew!" Vicky gave a shout of pain. "He could have stopped it!"

"I don't know when he knew. Maybe not until just before Dawn James was killed on September twenty-fifth. He left the following day."

"It went on after that, John. There were other babies. Ben's own brother. How could Father Joseph have kept it secret!"

Father John glanced away, his thoughts on the young priest thirty-five years ago, the whispered sins in a small cubicle, the ages-old seal of the confessional, and the crushing burden of secrecy. Bringing his eyes to hers, he said, "Joseph came back, Vicky. He lived with the secret for years and he came back to tell the truth."

Vicky didn't say anything. She walked over to the river. The sun had dropped behind the mountains, and streaks of orange and red spread through the sky. The trees were tinged with orange. Finally, her voice low, barely a whisper, she said, "Not all the babies that Markham delivered supposedly died. Aunt Rose said a lot of babies survived. It was only the lighter-skinned babies that Markham wanted. They bring the highest price on the black market. He didn't know which infants he would take until he saw them. Sharon David's amended birth certificate lists her as white. All the Holdens are light-skinned."

Father John could hear the sound of her breathing, controlled and angry. "We have no proof, Vicky," he said. "It's only a theory. No court is going to order graves exhumed to see if the caskets are empty without evidence, especially when there are death certificates. And the families —" He shook his head, remembering the shadow of pain in Esther Tallman's eyes. "Just the idea of having the graves dug up would be horrible."

"I've thought about that." Vicky turned around. The fury was still in her eyes. "There's another way. Markham's business manager still lives in Lander. Her name is Joanne Garrow. She's an old woman, bitter, mistrustful. I went to see her, and she ordered me off her property."

Father John flinched at the idea of someone ordering Vicky away. He realized the woman's name was also on Joseph's list.

"You could talk to her." There was a note of insistence in Vicky's tone. "You're a priest. She's been carrying a horrible burden for a very long time. She might welcome the chance to free herself."

It was possible, Father John knew. Thirty-five years ago a nurse had brought her burden to Father Joseph. And Joseph had brought his burden here. There were times when guilt grew too heavy to carry. He said, "I'll call and arrange to see her."

They started back through the cottonwoods. Walks-On ran ahead, disappearing around a bend. The breeze was steady, and a chill invaded the air. "Tell me about Megan," she said.

A new sense of uneasiness moved through

him. This was not a subject he had thought of talking over with her. "Megan's an architect, lives in Manhattan, twenty-five years old."

"Who is she?"

"My niece," he said quickly. When Vicky didn't say anything, he asked, "What does the moccasin telegraph say?" He wasn't sure he wanted the answer.

"She's just like you. Red hair and white skin and freckles. Nods her head when somebody's talking." He saw her glance up at him. "Like you're doing now. Rumor is she could be more than your niece."

He felt chilled. This was what he had feared. The Arapahos would think the Jesuits had scraped the bottom of the barrel and sent the poorest kind of man to them — an alcoholic, a man who had abandoned his own child. Were they not worthy of better?

He felt the pressure of Vicky's arm on his. They stopped walking and he turned toward her. There was always a faint smell of sage about her, and he smelled it now.

"Listen to me, John," she said. "I know what bothers you. You want to be the best priest imaginable. You want to be perfect. Is it so bad that the people know you're human? Is that so bad? Aren't priests allowed to be human?"

"I was in love with her mother once," he found himself saying. Confessing. That he had made love to her was a sin he had confessed long ago. He had believed himself forgiven. But now . . . "I

240

don't know whether Megan is mine," he said. "When I went into the seminary, her mother married my brother."

Vicky nodded slowly. Her expression became blank, her eyes unreadable, and he had the sense that she was now seeing someone else, a stranger she might have just met for the first time. "I see," she said. Nodding. Nodding.

They started back down the path toward the mission. He felt as if an invisible barrier had dropped between them, and it was beyond his power to push it away.

24

"I spoke with Mom today," Megan said.

Father John set down his mug of coffee and gave the young woman sitting across from him at the kitchen table his full attention. In the white glare of the ceiling light, her eyes took on a violet cast. All through dinner — ham and scalloped potatoes, a feast — he'd been only half listening to his niece. She'd talked on about growing up. The tomboy of the family, playing volleyball and softball, falling out of trees. Other trips to other emergency rooms. He'd prodded her with questions. Kept her talking while his own mind was on what Vicky had told him at the river. The lost children.

Now, as if she knew she finally had his attention and she could take her time, Megan sat back, eyes watchful, studying his reaction.

After a while — one, two, three seconds — she said, "Mom's never going to tell me the truth. She doesn't want to face the truth. She figured out why I'm here but refused to talk about it. She talked about the weather, the latest news on my brothers and sisters. Everything but what matters."

"Megan," he began, "there are tests that could determine the truth. If you wish . . ."

"I know." She waved a slender white hand through the air between them. Turning her head sideways, she peered for a long moment at the darkness beyond the window. The old house groaned and shifted in the silence. There was a faraway sound of the clock ticking on the mantel in the living room.

Finally she brought her eyes back. "Last night, when you walked into the emergency room, I thought you were Dad. He was always there when I needed him. Only he wouldn't have left me alone in the hospital. He would have sat all night outside my door. He's nuts, your brother."

"He loves you, Megan."

"It would kill him, you know."

He knew. He finished off the coffee, got out of the chair, and refilled his mug. Then he topped off Megan's mug and sat back down. "You know what I think, Megan?" he began — a gambit. "I think you already know the truth."

She slid her chair back. The legs made a loud scraping noise on the vinyl floor. "You're wrong, Uncle John. It's not that easy. You can't just pretend the truth is what ought to be." She shook her head and gave a little laugh. It was mirthless. "You and Mom are just alike. Neither of you wants to face the truth about yourselves."

"What do you mean?" he said, surprised at the harshness in his voice. They both knew what she was talking about.

"That woman. I saw her on television. She's the lawyer trying to find Sharon David's parents." Another mirthless laugh. "Seems I'm not the only one trying to find out who I am."

"Vicky Holden is a friend," he said.

"I saw the look in her eyes when she came into the office asking for you, wanting to know when you'd be back. I saw the two of you walking together — the way she was leaning toward you, looking up at you."

"We work together on different things." He started to enumerate the legitimate reasons for them to be together, then stopped. There was no need for explanations.

"I think you're in love with her, but you won't face the truth."

Father John pushed his chair back and got to his feet. Leaning down, he said, "Your imagination's in overdrive, Megan."

"You could leave the priesthood." She rose slowly.

"I'm a priest, Megan." He kept his eyes on her. "I'm trying to remain faithful to my vows and do my job. Just like your mom and dad. They kept their vows; they did their job. I'm trying to be like them."

For the briefest moment something new came into her expression — a look of wonderment, he thought.

"Come on," he said. "You'd better get some rest. I'll walk you over to the guest house."

In the quiet of his study, Father John picked up the phone and punched in the number for Joanne Garrow. He'd tried to reach the woman earlier, but no one answered. Now he listened to the intermittent ringing. Still no answer. He glanced at his watch. Almost eight-thirty. In fifteen minutes he would try again.

He stared at the piles of messages and letters still awaiting his attention. His mind was full of what Vicky had told him. It explained the murder of a young nurse. It explained the murder of Father Joseph: the man who had kept the secret and had come back to expose the truth.

Suddenly Father John understood what the intruder had been looking for in Joseph's things. Joseph had some kind of proof. Something to connect Markham to the lost babies, maybe even to Dawn James's murder. A letter, perhaps. Notes on the counseling sessions he may have had with the nurse.

Father John rose from the chair, crossed the study, and stood at the window. His own reflection moved in front of him, agitated, searching. And then he knew. It wasn't a document. Gianelli would have found a document in Joseph's things or in his computer files. Joseph's killer had taken the opera tapes in the Toyota. When he found out they were opera tapes, he had come to the mission, ransacked the office, and gone to Joseph's bedroom to search for a tape. Whatever proof Joseph had was on a tape.

He glimpsed his own reflection, the look of comprehension crossing his face. He knew what was on the tape. Joseph had gone to see the one person still in the area who knew about the stolen infants: Joanne Garrow. And somehow he had taped the conversation. What did he say to the woman? That the truth about the stolen babies had to be told? That he would break the seal of the confessional? What did she say that had incriminated the clinic, that had made Markham so determined to find the tape?

Father John strode across the study and sat down in his chair. There was the possibility — a slim thread of hope — that Vicky was right and Joanne Garrow might be ready to let go of her burden. As he reached for the phone to try her number again, a jangling noise broke through the quiet. It startled him. He stared at the ringing phone. Another emergency? Another dying woman? He did not want to go out tonight. Reluctantly he reached for the receiver.

"John." A woman's voice, low, little more than a whisper, with a throatier quality than he remembered from phone conversations twenty-five years ago. "Mike said you called."

He felt his breath sharp in his lungs. "How are you, Eileen?"

She ignored his question. "What has Megan told you?"

Father John waited a moment, searching for the right words. "Your daughter is searching for the truth about her parents," he said.

"Megan knows the truth." The voice rose, harsh and edged with impatience. "She refuses to believe me. She'll believe you, John. Just tell her."

"Tell her what?"

"That Mike is her father, of course. Tell her that, and she'll believe you."

"Megan believes she was a full-term baby," he said.

The voice came over the line like a cry. "Why is she doing this? Why is she causing all this confusion and pain? What is the point?"

"The point is the truth," he said. "Was she full-term?"

He heard her emit a long sigh. There was a loud knock, as if she had set a glass onto a hard surface. "I've explained all this to her. She was almost full-term."

Almost. The word hung before him, as if it had taken a physical shape. "Eileen." He spoke slowly. "Megan deserves to know the whole truth. I have the right to know."

The line went silent — the hollowness of eternity. Then the sobs came, long and shuddering, barely muffled, and over the sobs, the sound of his own heart beating. After a while she said, "What do you want from me, John? What do you expect me to tell my daughter? That the day after you left me, I fell into bed with your brother, a man I hardly knew? Is that what you want me to tell her? That is not how she was brought up. That is not the way we have taught her to live. What will she think of us, her own parents?"

Father John exhaled the long breath that had been caught in his chest. His whole being seemed to gather together, reform itself in familiar ways, his sense of himself coming again

247

into focus. The line was quiet again. He said, "Eileen, your daughter will think you're human." Vicky had said the same thing to him a few hours ago, he realized. "Is that so bad, Eileen? To be human?"

The sobbing started again, softer. After a moment she said, "I'll call her tomorrow." Another silence, then: "Mike is a good husband and father. I love him."

"I know," he said.

After he hung up, Father John sat at the desk, trying to sort through the emotions flowing through him, a tide of relief and emptiness, joy for Mike and Megan and sadness for himself. Megan was not his own. That was the truth, and the truth was hard, with sharp edges that cut and scraped at his heart. A drink would smooth the edges, he knew, and he wondered for an instant if that was why he would always want a drink, to make the truth easier to take.

He picked up the phone and punched in the number for Joanne Garrow. Still no answer. In forty minutes he could be in Lander. Surely the woman would be home by then.

Outside the breeze was cool, a warning of winter coming from the north. Next to the Escort stood a dark pickup. Two young men sat in the cab, black cowboy hats pushed up on their heads: Arnold Bizzel and one of his cousins. The door snapped open as Father John approached. "I have to go out for a while," he said. "Megan's

248

alone at the guest house."

"Don't worry, Father," Arnold said. "Me and Tom'll stay right here. Nobody's gonna get close to the mission tonight."

25

Thirty minutes later Father John parked in front of a two-story red-brick house a couple of blocks west of Main Street in Lander. The house was dark except for the faint gray light glowing in the front window. A sedan sat in the driveway. Joanne Garrow was home.

He hurried up the sidewalk and mounted the stairs to the porch that jutted from the front of the house. There was the muffled sound of chimes inside as he pressed the doorbell. He waited for the shush of footsteps, the crack of the door opening, but there was only the soft rustle of the wind and, in the distance, the hum of tires on asphalt and the sound of a baby crying. He tried the doorbell again and waited several moments.

He was about to turn away, wondering whether to wait awhile in the Escort when something drew his attention: the gray light flickering across the porch floor — the light of a television. He stepped toward the window and glanced past the edge of the drapes. Light spilled from a television against the far wall of the living room, but there were no images on the screen. Only a smudge of light that cast silver shadows over the sofa and chairs and sparkled in the crystal figurines on the small tables. A woman sat in one of the chairs, head tilted back, arms flopped over the sides, legs sprung out. The heels of her black shoes dug into the Oriental carpet. A dark mass spread over the front of her white blouse.

Father John darted back to the door and tried the knob. Locked. Then he ran down the porch steps and around the side of the house. The backyard lay in quiet shadow, a thousand stars blinking overhead. The back door was also locked. Retracing his steps, he hurried across the lawn to the house next door. As he came up the porch steps, he heard the muffled television voices inside. He leaned into the doorbell.

There were sounds of movement inside, and the door swung open. A large, burly man in blue jeans and T-shirt stood in the opening, backlit by the shimmering lights of the television. "Yeah?" he said.

Father John introduced himself and said the woman next door had been hurt. He asked the man to call 911.

"That crazy old lady," the man said. "What she do, fall down the stairs?"

"I think she's been shot."

"Shot!" The door snapped back. "Come on in, Father. Phone's over there, you wanna call the police." He motioned past the woman sunk in one of the two recliners in front of the television. She held a remote in one hand; the television had gone mute, leaving a fullness of quiet.

Father John stepped over to the phone that sat on a small counter. Beyond the counter was the shadowed space of the kitchen. He punched in the numbers and waited, pressing the phone hard against his ear, counting the number of rings. "Come on, come on," he said, mostly to himself.

"I told you, Walter." The woman's voice cut over the ringing noise. "That wasn't any engine backfiring. That was a gunshot. I should've called the police right then, only you said —"

"Be quiet," the man barked as the 911 operator came on the line.

Father John gave his name and told the operator what he'd found. Then he said he'd wait for the police.

He leaned against the side of the Escort, jacket zippered against the cold snap of the breeze. From the distance came the wail of sirens that gradually grew into a wall of sound rushing toward him. Then the sound abruptly cut off, leaving a ringing in his ears. Two police cars and an ambulance swung into the curb, blue and red lights on the cars flashing over the sidewalk and lawn. Father John walked over as doors flung open and officers and attendants spilled out. A man in a dark sport jacket approached. "You Father O'Malley?"

Father John nodded.

"Give us a couple minutes." It was an order. Then the officers started up the sidewalk toward the house, the attendants following. A flashlight beam played across the front door as one of the officers bent over the lock. In an instant the door opened, and the men filed inside.

People began spilling out of the houses across the street and down the block, gathering in shadowy clusters, heads craned toward the two-story house. A couple of men sidled up and asked what happened. Father John said he wasn't sure, and they moved away. The buzz of voices filtered around him and mixed with the sounds of the breeze.

After several minutes the plainclothes officer emerged from the house and came down the sidewalk, through the blue and red lights. "You know the victim, Father?"

Father John shook his head. He wasn't even sure the woman was Joanne Garrow. "Who is she?" he asked.

"One of the ambulance attendants knows her. Name is Joanne Garrow."

Father John told the officer he'd come here to talk with the woman, that he'd tried to telephone her earlier and hadn't gotten an answer.

The officer withdrew a small notebook from his jacket pocket. Then he produced a ballpoint. "So you don't know the lady, and you drove over here tonight for a visit?" Thin dark eyebrows came together. "Now why is that, Father?"

Father John started to explain. A priest, his assistant at St. Francis Mission, had been murdered a few days ago on the reservation.

"FBI case." The officer interrupted. He was jotting something in the notebook.

Father John went on: it was possible Joanne

Garrow had known the priest when he was at the mission thirty-five years ago. He'd wanted to ask her about him.

The officer stopped writing and looked up. He blinked into the flashing lights. "You saying there might be some connection to the priest's murder?"

Father John glanced away a moment. The sidewalk was crowded with groups of people. Still other groups formed in the street and, in the shadows, he could see more people hurrying down the block. "I have no idea," he said. He and Vicky had a theory, that was all. They'd hoped that Jeremiah Markham's business manager would confirm the theory, but now the business manager was dead.

"Chances are it's a big coincidence," the officer said. "Priest shot on the res. Old woman shot at home. My bet is there's not gonna be a piece of jewelry or stick of silver or camera in that house. Whoever surprised her probably threw it into a pillowcase and ran out the door after he shot her." He snapped the notebook shut. "We'll call you if we need anything else."

He was dismissed, he realized. He started toward the pickup, then turned back. Nodding toward the house next door, he said, "The neighbors may have heard the shot."

The officer had already started up the sidewalk. "We'll tend to our business, Father," he called over his shoulder.

Father John slid onto the seat of the Escort

and turned the ignition switch. The engine flickered to life, and he pulled into the street, guiding the car past the knots of bystanders. Two people from the Markham Clinic were dead. The nurse who had confided in Father Joseph thirty-five years ago, and now the business manager. He decided it was time that he and Vicky took their theory to Gianelli.

26

The evening air rushed past the half-open windows and filled the Bronco with a sharp, refreshing coolness. Outside the dark expanse of plains melted into the black, star-spangled sky. As Vicky left the sounds of Lander behind — the wailing of a siren, the hum of traffic curving off the highway — and drove deeper into the reservation, she began to feel calmer, more in tune with herself.

She'd found it hard to concentrate when she arrived home. She'd checked in with Laola and gotten her messages. A couple of clients inquiring about pending cases, people wanting appointments. Edna Linder had called with some excuse about why she and Wylan couldn't make the appointment for the blood test tomorrow. Vicky wasn't surprised.

She had jotted down notes as the secretary talked, then hung up and paced the living room, her thoughts consumed with the stolen infants. What John O'Malley told her about the nurse and Father Joseph confirmed her theory. Now she understood why, despite the publicity about Sharon David, no one other than the Linders had come forward. Sharon's real parents thought their daughter was dead.

Why hadn't she suspected earlier that the infants born at the Markham Clinic might have been stolen? There had always been a black market for healthy, white-looking infants. Always well-meaning couples turned down by legitimate adoption agencies because of age or some infirmity or disease. Always monsters like Jeremiah Markham ready to traffic in any commodity that brought money — drugs, human body parts, infants.

She continued pacing — the front door, the desk, the sofa. It was still just a theory. There were no witnesses, no evidence. If she could find Sharon David's parents, she could prove the theory. She had the names of families that had lost infants, but most had left the reservation. They could have remarried, changed their names. They could be dead. It would take time to find them. And in that time anyone who knew about the stolen infants could be in danger. The coroner and nurse were dead; Father Joseph was dead. But Joanne Garrow was still alive.

Vicky had stopped pacing and stared into the shadows of the dining room, which opened off the living room. Garrow was a frightened woman, maybe even remorseful. John O'Malley might convince her to tell the truth before Markham realized she had any remorse.

John O'Malley. The thought of him hovered at the edge of her thoughts, like a shadow that drifted away as she approached, eluding her grasp. He had told her about himself this afternoon, and the words had been like a hard knife of reality cutting through her. A man who would not give up the priesthood for the woman he loved — a woman who may have been carrying his child — why had she ever thought . . . ? Why had she ever dared to hope such a man would turn away from the priesthood for her? She'd been a fool. She had missed the chance to put her own life back together, to repair the brokenness in her own family.

Suddenly Vicky had realized there was someone who might be able to help prove her theory. Ben. If she could get Ben to agree to the exhumation of his brother's grave, she could take the theory to Gianelli, along with the means of proving it. Gianelli might stand a chance of getting a court to order the exhumation if the family didn't object. She'd decided to drive out to the Arapaho Ranch and have a talk with her ex-husband.

Now she swung north, burrowing deeper into the reservation, the stars a bright carpet of lights overhead. At the base of the Owl Creek Mountains she turned onto a wide dirt road and passed the Arapaho Ranch bunkhouse, a sprawling log cabin with light streaming through the windows and pickups and 4x4s lined up in front. About a mile farther she bore right and started the climb into the foothills. Ponderosas crowded the sides of the road, dark sentinels outside her windows.

As she came around a bend, she saw the flickering lights, like fireflies darting among the trees. She rounded another bend and stopped in front of the foreman's cabin. Ben's truck was parked a few feet away. The cabin door opened, and her ex-husband stood in a well of light. Stepping outside, he started toward her. "Vicky!" he said, his tone fresh with surprise.

Vicky got out and leaned against the Bronco, scrunching the soft leather of her bag against her chest. In the slant of light from the cabin door, she saw the questions in his eyes. The odor of aftershave and the musty smell of his wool shirt drifted toward her. "I'd like to talk to you," she managed.

"It's a little awkward," he said. A glance toward the cabin.

Vicky felt a sharp sting of embarrassment. He'd told her there was someone else. "I'm sorry," she stammered. "I should have called first."

"It's okay." He stretched out his hand, and the touch of his fingers on the ridge of her shoulder sent an electrical current coursing through the emptiness inside her. She felt weak with an old, half-remembered desire and startled by the force of its power. She had to stop herself from darting into the Bronco and driving away. She stood in place, savoring the warmth of his hand emanating through her jacket.

He said, "You drove all the way out here tonight to see me." It was a statement. "Is that true? Because if you tell me it's true, that woman in there" — he nodded toward the cabin — "is going to leave."

He leaned closer. "I want to hear you say it, Vicky."

"I need you, Ben," she said.

Vicky waited in the Bronco. After about five minutes the door to the cabin flung open. A woman stepped out and marched around the side. In a moment a puff of exhaust burst past the corner and red taillights blinked into the darkness. A sedan began backing out, then started down the road. Ben walked toward the Bronco. He opened the door, took her hand, and led her into the cabin.

The odor of fresh coffee filled the small room. In one corner was the kitchen: sink, stove, refrigerator, rectangular table, and two chairs. Across the room, the bed covered with the star quilt Ben's mother had given them for their wedding. A fire crackled in the stone fireplace on the wall close to the bed.

Vicky sank into one of the chairs at the table and waited while Ben poured a couple mugs of coffee.

"I found James and his white girlfriend for you," he said, placing the mugs on the table and taking the chair across from her. His dark eyes reflected the firelight.

"Where were they?"

"Hiding out at a cousin's ranch. Scared of Sonny Red Wolf. I took them to the fed's office this afternoon to make sure they got there. The girl gave a statement about seeing Sonny's white truck on Thunder Lane about the time of the priest's murder."

Vicky took a sip of the hot coffee. She could be

wrong. Maybe Father Joseph's murder had nothing to do with Markham's clinic. Maybe her theory was some half-baked notion that Gianelli and the other white authorities would dismiss as preposterous. Yet John O'Malley hadn't dismissed it.

Ben said, "Does he mean that much to you?"

Vicky kept her eyes to his. "Who?" she asked. She knew who he meant.

"The priest you're worried could get killed."

"No." She stopped herself from adding, *Not anymore.* The room was quiet, except for the snap of the fire, the muffled sounds of the wind outside. She was debating whether to tell him about her theory. An hour ago it had seemed so logical: enlist Ben's help in proving her theory had merit. She had been certain of the truth as she'd read through the newspapers today. And when she'd learned of the birth and death certificates, she'd been convinced that Jeremiah Markham had left nothing to chance.

But Sonny Red Wolf had been seen on Thunder Lane. What if her theory was wrong? What if the infants had died? She had driven out here to ask Ben to agree to exhume his brother's grave, to relive the pain of the past. In the waves of warmth from the fireplace, she felt a cold shiver run across her shoulders.

"What is it, Vicky?" Ben reached across the table, as if he were reaching for her hand, then stopped. "What brought you out here?"

In his eyes she saw a reflection of her own

searching, questioning. He had a right to know. Even if it was only a slim possibility that his brother might be alive, only a theory, he had the right to know. "I've something to tell you, Ben," she said finally. Then she began explaining what she'd found: the sealed caskets, fifteen dead babies in one year, all born at the Markham Clinic, the possible murder of the nurse and the coroner, the murder of Father Joseph. As she talked, she felt him grow stiller, leaning back against the chair, moving away from her into someplace inside himself. He remained quiet for a long while after she'd stopped talking, his eyes fixed on some point across the room.

"I don't want to have the grave dug up," he said, finding her gaze again. "Mom's old and sick. I don't want her to get her hopes up that her son is alive somewhere. Not until we know for certain that this happened."

Immediately Vicky regretted having told him. She had raised his hopes, given him the possibility that his brother was alive, and if her theory turned out not to be true, he would lose his brother again. The air seemed cooler; the fire had died back. Ben asked if Sharon David was one of the infants.

"I think so," she said. "But there's so little to go on. She found a piece of paper in her mother's things with some notations she thinks are about her birth. It has the initials 'WRR.' She thinks that could refer to the reservation. There are numbers that could be her birth date, and the name Maisie." Suddenly Vicky realized who had written the note that had stayed with the infant girl, tucked among a tiny shirt, a blanket, piles of diapers: the person who had delivered the baby to Markham's contacts — a nurse, Dawn James.

"Maisie." Ben repeated the word. "Don't know anybody by that name."

"There was also a small drawing of a bird," Vicky said. "I checked the obituaries on the babies. No families with bird names. No Crows or Hawks or Eagles. No Redbirds or Yellowbirds."

"Ummm." Ben made the sound he always made, she remembered, when he was trying to recall something. He took a draw of coffee. Then: "Used to be some Indians lived down the road from us. One of their babies died same time as" — he hesitated — "my brother. Mom used to visit the woman. I went along sometimes. I remember them crying together in the living room. After a while the people moved away. Went to Casper, I think. Their name was Mason. But their Indian name, if I remember right, was something like Little Bird."

Vicky held her breath. Mason was one of the names on the list. In her mind she saw the tiny figure of a bird. "Was the woman named Maisie?"

Ben shook his head. "I think it was Marie."

"Marie!" Vicky leaned over the table. "The name could have been misspelled. My God, Ben. Sharon's mother could be Marie Little Bird."

Now Ben reached over and took her hand. "You might be able to find the Little Bird family in Casper. If they turn out to be her people, well, we'll know it happened. Then I'll talk to Mom about the grave. I'm sorry, Vicky. It's the best I can do."

"It's okay." Vicky nodded. He'd already helped her more than she had guessed he could.

"It was so hard on Mom, losing the baby." He tightened his grip on her hand, and she felt the warmth of him spreading through her body, chasing back the coldness. Something inside her began to melt: the reserve, the determination.

"Hard on all of us," he was saying. "I don't want Mom to go through it again unless there's a real chance my brother's alive."

"We never talked about these things before," Vicky heard herself saying.

"There were lots of times I wanted to tell you what I was thinking and feeling." He gave his head a hard shake. "I guess I didn't know how."

Vicky allowed her hand to stay in his a long moment. Then she pulled away and got slowly to her feet. She walked around his chair, set her hands on his shoulders, and leaned over him, kissing the top of his head, the warm curve of his neck. "Oh, Ben," she said. "There's so much we didn't know about each other."

They made love on the bed pushed against the far wall, under the star quilt. Afterward Vicky huddled close to him, the palm of her hand resting on the smooth, light brown skin of his chest. Outside the wind rose and fell, an eerie, disjointed chorus. There was the occasional *tap-tap* sound of a branch against a window. An occasional ember crackled in the fireplace.

Vicky listened as Ben talked about his life since she'd left, about his longing for her. The past — the years of their marriage — remained a silent presence between them. She knew that sooner or later they would have to confront that time. But not now. Not tonight.

The soft daylight filtering through the ponderosas glowed in the window when Vicky awoke. The bed beside her was empty, and she realized the swishing noise she had thought was the wind had been the sound of the shower. There was a strong odor of freshly brewed coffee, a small fire burning in the grate. She got up and pulled on an old woolen robe thrown over a chair, tying the belt tightly at her waist. Ben was gone. On the table she found a note in the familiar, generous handwriting: *I love you. Come back to me.*

From outside came the growl of an engine turning over. She stepped to the window and watched the brown truck move through the ponderosas, the metal trim catching the sun until finally the truck disappeared from view. Still she stayed at the window, thinking of other times when she had watched Ben's truck drive away. She had been someone else then, not the woman she was now, not a lawyer with an office in Lander and clients waiting to see her. That other woman's days had been planned for her: caring for the children; looking in on her own parents and on Ben's; helping the other women prepare the feasts for the tribal celebrations.

It had been a busy little life that she had assumed would go on until she was a grandmother, sitting back at the feasts, waited on by the younger women. She had given scant thought to the wider world — a quick glance at the morning papers, a TV newscast — until she had found herself thrust into it: *hisei ci' nihi*, woman alone. And now, here she was in Ben's life again, where she had sworn she would never be. What a mess she had made of things. She had seen the future she had hoped for with another man slip away, and so she had tried to reclaim the past. As if the past could ever be reclaimed.

"It will take some time, Ben," she said out loud to the empty cabin. Her voice punctuated the quiet. "I'm going to need some time."

She walked over to the phone mounted next to the kitchen cabinet, dialed directory assistance, and asked for the number of a Mason in Casper. Within a couple of seconds she was dialing the number for Russ Mason. She gripped the receiver. One ring, two, three.

Finally, a voice. "Hello?"

She asked to speak to Mr. Mason.

"Dad's at work." The voice might have belonged to a girl somewhere between adolescence and maturity.

"How can I reach him?"

Vicky heard the hesitation. "I guess you can call Capco." Then, the number.

Capco. Vicky knew the company. They collected oil from storage tanks on the reservation and delivered it to refineries in other areas. If Russ Mason was a driver, he could be anywhere between the res and Cheyenne or Denver.

Vicky thanked the girl, hit the disconnect bar, and dialed the company's number. A woman answered, and Vicky asked again to speak to Russ Mason. He was out in the field, the woman said.

"I'm an attorney," Vicky said into the line. "There's a very important matter I must speak to him about." She hesitated, then added: "It's an emergency. Where can I reach him?"

Vicky could hear the indrawn breaths, the considering. Finally the woman said, "He handles the storage tanks over by Winkleman Dome."

27

Vicky drove south past the buttes that erupted out of the plains on both sides of the road. Winchester Butte. Bighorn Butte. She crossed the flat expanse of the Bighorn draw, still moving south, squinting into the sun that broke the windshield into a rainbow of colors. The Winkleman Dome oil pumps came into view ahead, black sculptures rising out of the earth.

As she neared the pumping area, the shape of a large white truck loomed ahead, shimmering in the sun like a mirage. She pulled to one side and jumped out, waving her hands overhead, the wind whipping out her skirt and snapping at her jacket. She set one hand on her forehead to keep her hair out of her eyes. The tank truck drew close, lumbering through the wavy air, and slid to a stop, tires kicking out little pieces of gravel. A large man — an Indian — in a cowboy hat leaned across the seat toward the open passenger window. "Trouble, lady?"

"Are you Russ Mason?" Vicky approached the driver's side.

"Wish I was, if you're lookin' for him."

"Where I can find him?"

The man pushed his hat back and seemed to ponder the windshield. "Seen him earlier. Probably finished up around here and headed up to Maverick Spring Dome."

Vicky groaned silently. She had passed the area an hour ago. Thanking the man, she started for the Bronco.

"Hey, wait a minute," the driver called.

She swung around. He was staring in the rear-view mirror. She followed his gaze to the truck coming over a rise in the road. "You might be gettin' lucky. That could be old Russ comin' now."

Vicky gave the man a wave. The gears ground heavily into place, and the truck started past her, gaining speed. Gravel spattered her leg, forcing her back toward the Bronco. She hugged her jacket in the wind as the other truck drew close. Then she walked back into the road and waved at the driver.

The truck stopped — a jerky motion that sent the hood bucking up and down. "I'm looking for Russ Mason," she called, walking to the driver's side.

"Who wants him?" The man leaned over the arm crooked on the door ledge and fixed her with dark, narrow eyes. He was somewhere in his sixties, she guessed, with a long, sun-etched face and gray hair that showed below the rim of a black cowboy hat. He had a prominent nose and cheekbones — the sculptured features of her people. In a crowd, she would have picked him out as Arapaho.

She gave him her name and asked again if he was Russ Mason.

"Maybe." His tone had a sharp edge. "Depends on what you want."

"I'm an attorney. I'm trying to help a client who's searching for her natural parents." She was stammering, groping for the words to explain why she was standing in the wind on an empty road, waving down his truck.

The Indian threw back his head and gave a snort of disbelief. "You that lawyer lady I seen on TV. You're workin' for that movie star, what's her name . . ." His eyes glanced around the cab.

"Sharon David."

"Yeah, that's the one. I seen in the papers she found her real parents."

Vicky shook her head. A gust pushed her sideways. She shouted into the wind: "They're not her parents! She was born into the Little Bird family."

The man reared back, as if he'd touched an exposed wire. "What're you talkin' about?"

"Sharon has a few clues to her identity," Vicky said hurriedly. The wind burst around them. "She has the drawing of a tiny bird."

The thin cheeks puffed out, and the man exhaled a long breath. "That don't make her a Little Bird. We don't give away our babies. Not this family. Me and the wife raised six kids. Still raisin' a couple of 'em."

Vicky saw his hand moving to the gear knob, and she laid one hand on the door next to his arm to prevent the truck from pulling away. "Sharon is one of the people," she said. "I'm certain of it. She may not have been given up for adoption. She may have been taken from her real parents."

The Indian leaned into the window space, the dark eyes narrowing into accusation. "What'dya mean? Kidnapped?"

Vicky gave a little nod. She didn't want to alarm the man. She didn't want to start a rumor on the moccasin telegraph that would send the reservation into a panic, a rumor that might not be true.

She said, "Is there anyone in your family named Maisie or Marie?"

The door snapped open — a wind-amplified thud — and the Indian slid out, planting heavy boots onto the road. "You better tell me what you're gettin' at, lady," he said in a tone of barely controlled anger. He was looming over her, a powerful man with broad shoulders inside a brown corduroy jacket and white-knuckled fists hanging at his sides.

Vicky fought the urge to back away. "I told you, I'm trying to help Sharon David find where she belongs."

"What do you know about Marie?"

Vicky kept her voice steady. "Only that Sharon found a name that could be Marie on a scrap of paper among her adoptive parents' things."

The man said nothing. He stared down the empty road a moment, then brought the narrow eyes back to hers. She saw the moisture brimming at the corners. He raised one fist and ran a knuckle along the ridges of both cheeks. "Marie was my first wife." His voice was so soft she had to lean toward him to pluck the words from the wind.

"Where can I find her?"

"You can't." A gust cracked between them, and he seemed to stagger back, grabbing the door handle to steady himself. "Marie's been dead a long time."

"I'm sorry," Vicky muttered.

"So the Marie on that woman's paper can't be my Marie." Opening the door, he set one boot on the running board, ready to launch himself into the seat.

Vicky grabbed the man's sleeve. The corduroy was warm and smooth. "Mr. Mason," she said, "I'm sorry to bring back painful memories, but I must ask you something. It's important to a woman who is very lost and alone. Did Marie ever lose a child?"

The man wrenched his arm from her grasp. The boot slid from the running board and stomped onto the ground. "You sayin' this movie star thinks she was our baby?" He bent close; the sour smell of his breath floated toward her in the whirl of the wind. "Well, tell her for me to get out of here and go back where she belongs. What business she got comin' 'round here and upsettin' folks? She don't belong with the people. What kind of woman shows up and starts claimin' she's somebody's dead child?

272

What kind of woman does that?"

"She was born at the Markham Clinic in 1964," Vicky said.

The Indian was staring at her. "Nineteen sixty-four?"

"September fourteenth."

"Oh, God." The Indian sank back against the door, crumbling downward, folding onto the running board. Vicky set her hand on his shoulder to steady the fall. "Our baby girl was born in the middle of September," he said. "In that fancy clinic in Lander. Supposed to be safe, but that doctor couldn't save the baby. Said her brain got some infection. Said there wasn't nothin' he could do. She was a real pretty little thing. She looked real healthy."

"When did you see her?"

"Right after she was born," the man said. "Before the doctor said she was real sick and he was gonna put her in isolation. Couple hours later he comes into Marie's room and says our baby's dead."

Vicky's jaw clenched. She blinked back the tears blurring the figure of the man slumped before her. "It's possible," she began, then hesitated. His eyes searched hers a long moment. "It's possible your child did not die. It's possible Sharon David is your daughter."

The Indian hunched over and dropped his head into his hands. His shoulders shook. Low, gravelly sobs punctuated the sound of the wind. After a moment the sobbing stopped, and he glanced up. "Marie always said our little baby was alive. She just knew it. But I didn't pay it no mind because Marie got so strange after the baby died. She was never the same, staying locked up in the house all day, not wantin' to go anywhere. Couple nice ladies used to come visit. One of 'em had her own baby die. I thought, maybe, we move to Casper, where there's more people around, she'd come out of it. But I come home from work one day and found her out in the garage. She'd took an old sheet and hung it over the rafters and was danglin' there."

Vicky sat down next to the man and placed one hand on top of his. It was trembling. The wind muffled his quiet sobs.

28

St. Francis Church was filled with people packed shoulder to shoulder in the pews. As Father John came down the center aisle wearing the white vestments of mourning, he heard the barely concealed coughs and nervous clearing of throats. Leonard walked ahead, holding out the Mass book. The Indian stepped up into the sanctuary and set the book on the large drum that served as the altar. Then he moved back, and Father John took his position at the altar, facing the congregation: elders and grandmothers, young couples with youngsters squirming in the pews. Megan sat in a back row, head bowed. To the right of the altar, the singers and drummers were bent over a small drum. Sunlight streamed rays of reds, blues, and golds through the stained-glass windows.

Father John began the Mass. "Dear Lord," he prayed, "we ask You in Your kindness and mercy to remember the soul of Joseph Keenan and grant him the peace and joy You have promised awaits those who serve You faithfully on this earth." There was the soft murmuring of amens, the rhythmic beat of the drum, the voices raised in chants. He glanced at the rows of bowed heads and prayed silently for the lost children, the men and women they had become, and their families.

At the consecration, he lifted up the small

plate filled with pieces of unleavened bread. Behold the Body of Christ. This was the heart of the Mass, of his being: the witnessing of God in the world.

He finished distributing Communion — placing the small pieces of bread in cupped hands, saying the words: "This is the body of Christ." Over the sound of people settling back into the pews came the flash of excited voices and a scuffling noise at the entrance. Father John looked up from the prayer book. Heads craned toward the door, toward Sonny Red Wolf striding down the aisle, an usher scurrying behind. "No seats in front." The usher's voice was loud in alarm. "You need to stay back."

But the Indian kept coming, the look of pure hate on his face. Was this how it was to be? Father John thought. How his life would end? Like that of Archbishop Romero, murdered at the altar? He stood motionless, watching the barrel-chested man coming closer to the sanctuary.

"Father O'Malley!" Sonny Red Wolf stopped below the altar. The usher stood at his elbow, embarrassment and fear mingling in his eyes.

"We demand that you take your white man's religion and leave our land." There was a stir in the congregation, the scratchy sound of people shifting in the pews.

"We don't want you white people here. We been like a bunch of sheep, gettin' led away from our own Indian religion and our own ways. Now

I'm here to lead the people back. I say to you, Father O'Malley, you must go."

At the edge of his vision, Father John saw the slender figure of the elder, Will Standing Bear, slide out of a front pew. He walked past Sonny and stepped up to the altar next to Father John. Suddenly the sound of his voice boomed across the church. He spoke Arapaho, the words strange and barely familiar. Father John realized that the elder was speaking in the formal style. It was the style the chiefs in the Old Time had used to speak to the people on important matters.

Except for the roar of the elder's voice, the church was quiet. Father John caught enough words to realize that the elder was asking Sonny Red Wolf if he could speak Arapaho. There was a pause. Sonny stared up at the altar with blank, uncomprehending eyes. Then Will Standing Bear switched to an angry tone, scolding the younger man for daring to speak for the people when he could not speak the people's language. The scolding went on as the elder gestured toward the other elders in the front, saying that Sonny had shown disrespect for them. It was not the Arapaho Way.

He finished speaking, but remained at the altar. A low rumble of laughter started through the church. It gathered strength, growing into a satisfied hilarity. Father John realized the grandmothers were laughing at Sonny Red Wolf. The grandmothers! Usually it was the grandmothers who protected and encouraged the younger men. They never laughed at them.

Sonny threw a glance over one shoulder, then the other. A mixture of anger and confusion came into his face, like a slow-burning fire. He swung around and started down the aisle. The front door slammed behind him into the sounds of laughter.

Will Standing Bear turned to Father John. *Wo'ukohe'i.*

Father John understood the meaning: *We welcome you here.*

Father John made his way among the people eating sandwiches and drinking coffee at the tables set up in the gym at Eagle Hall. Over against the far wall, a line of people wended past a long table, helping themselves to the roast beef and potato salad, the cakes and cookies the Ladies' Sodality had prepared. He greeted the grandmothers and elders, patting shoulders and shaking hands. Voices were hushed in remembrance of the priest who had once been among them.

No one mentioned Sonny Red Wolf, and Father John knew that the news of the man's shaming was probably already on the moccasin telegraph. Any hope he may have had of getting elected to the tribal council had ended this morning.

Father John glanced about the gym. He hadn't seen Megan since the Mass. A little knot of worry tightened inside him. Maybe she wasn't feeling well. He let a few minutes pass — still no sign of her. He slipped out of the gym. Gianelli had said he'd come by later. The agent might have arrived early and was interviewing Megan. He wouldn't learn anything. Father John knew she still had no memory of the attack.

The wind swooped over the grounds, raising little clouds of dirt and gravel as Father John walked down the alley. He passed groups of people on their way to the memorial feast — a quick wave and greeting. Pickups and cars stood bumper-to-bumper along Circle Drive. He could see other pickups turning off Seventeen-Mile Road as he mounted the steps to the administration building.

The building seemed vacant and deserted: the empty corridor, his office with papers sprawled across the desk. There were muffled sounds of voices and motors outside. He walked to Joseph's office. It looked as if Megan had just stepped away, leaving the spiral notebook opened on the desk, a ballpoint on top, the chair pulled out.

A loud thump sounded outside, and Father John stepped over to the window. Leonard and Arnold were unloading folding chairs from the bed of a pickup and taking them into Eagle Hall. Groups of people stood around talking. Kids were running about, dodging and tagging one another. Squeals of laughter seemed to come from far away.

Father John felt himself begin to relax. What was he worried about? The caretaker and his son were keeping an eye on the mission. A couple hundred people were roaming about. Megan was somewhere. He just hadn't seen her. In the few days she'd been at the mission, he had come to feel like a father hovering over a helpless child. She was not a child, he knew, and he was not her father. Still, he wondered where she was.

He retraced his steps through the building. Outside he headed back down the alley, annoyed at the illogical urgency building inside him. As he reached Eagle Hall, Leonard stepped through the door.

"Have you seen Megan?" Father John asked.

The Indian gave him a hard stare. "I seen her at Mass."

"What about since then?"

Leonard shook his head. "You want me to look for her?" His voice echoed the worry Father John was feeling.

"Yes," he said. "Check the guest house. I'll see if she's at the residence." Megan could be in the kitchen giving Elena and the other women a hand with the food. He turned back in to the alley, picking up his pace across the grounds. As he came up the steps, Elena stepped past the screened door carrying a large can of coffee.

"Is Megan here?" he asked.

"Megan?" Something new came into the old woman's eyes — surprise, alarm? "Haven't seen her all morning." The phone started ringing

280

inside, and the housekeeper gave a hurried glance over one shoulder, as if she couldn't decide whether to abandon the question of Megan's whereabouts for the screeching phone.

There was the sound of running footsteps on Circle Drive, and Father John swung around. Leonard started up the sidewalk, chest heaving, arms swinging. "Nobody at the guest house," he said. "Arnold says he seen her this morning in front of the administration building" — a nod toward the yellow stucco building. "Says she and some white guy was standing by a tan Jeep. My boy figured some friend of hers drove up this way for a visit. There was five-plate tags on the Jeep."

Father John felt his breath stop in his throat. The Rock Springs area had license plates that began with the number five. Vicky had said Markham's guide was from Rock Springs.

He hurtled past the door and into the entry. Elena was at the hall table, holding out the receiver. "Man says he's got to talk to you."

Father John reached past the woman for the disconnect button. "It's about Megan," Elena said.

He could hear his heart beating as he took the receiver and set it against his ear. "Who is this?"

"My identity is of no importance, Father O'Malley." The man's voice on the other end of the line was self-assured and definite, the voice of someone used to the microphone and an audience. "You have something I want, and I have

281

something you want. It is a matter of a simple exchange."

"Listen to me," Father John said. "I know who you are, Markham. I'm warning you. If you harm her, if you so much as touch her . . ."

Elena gave a small, stifled cry beside him, and he turned his back to the woman, as if to protect her, jamming the receiver harder against his ear. Leonard was standing inside the door, one fist gripped in the other.

"Please, Father O'Malley." The silky, civilized tone again. "You will follow my instructions, and your niece will be returned safely. Please believe me when I say I have no need for her."

"What do you want?"

"There was an audiotape in the possession of Father Keenan. I must have that tape."

He had guessed right. Joseph had made some kind of tape. But there was no tape, no recorder, among the man's things or in his car. Father John had no idea where he might have hidden them.

"You will bring me the tape, and I will return your niece to you. I believe you will understand the importance of this transaction when I say the tape is as valuable your niece's life."

"Where are you?"

"You have the tape?"

Father John drew in a breath. "I have the tape."

"Good. You will come immediately to Dickinson Park." He gave the directions slowly: west out of Fort Washakie, a series of turns to the outfitter's cabin. "Need I tell you that if you inform the authorities, Father, your niece will die. Such a waste. She is a very pretty young woman. You must understand, it will not be my choice."

There was a click, and Father John slammed down the receiver.

"Is Megan okay?" Elena asked, a little sob in her voice.

He brushed past the housekeeper and went into the study. Leonard followed. "You gonna call the police?"

"I'm going to Dickinson Park after her." He lifted a small box of tapes from the bookshelf behind his desk and started through them. Puccini, Verdi, Berlioz, Mozart. Rummaging. Rummaging. Finally he found the tape he wanted — one on which he had copied his favorite arias. He flipped open the plastic container and removed the card on which he'd listed the titles, then snapped the container shut and slipped it into his jacket pocket. A plain tape. Anything could be on it. He started toward the door.

"Shouldn't you call the police, Father?" Leonard stepped back into the hall as Father John walked past. Out of the corner of his eye, he saw Elena rooted by the phone table, gripping the coffee tin, one hand over her mouth.

He pushed open the screen door, then turned back, struggling to keep his thoughts rational, logical. "Give me a fifteen-minute head start, then call Gianelli. Tell him Markham and another man took Megan to Dickinson Park."

29

The wheels of the Escort screamed into the wind as Father John drove around Circle Drive, past the line of pickups, the people milling about. The side mirror framed Elena and Leonard on the stoop in front of the residence, Arnold walking purposefully up the sidewalk.

As Father John turned into the straightaway, the Bronco headed down the center of the road toward him. He hit the brake pedal, and Vicky wheeled in alongside him. She rolled down her window. "I've found the evidence, John." The excitement in her voice carried through the wind.

"He took Megan!" Father John shouted.

A sudden look of understanding flashed across Vicky's face. "Markham!"

Father John kept his boot on the brake pedal. The sedan was shaking around him, like a bull waiting to burst out of the corral. "She's at an outfitter's cabin in Dickinson Park. I'm going after her."

In an instant Vicky was out of the Bronco and around the Escort. The passenger door flew open, and wind swooped inside. "I'm coming with you," she said, sliding onto the seat.

"Wait at the residence."

Vicky kept her face straight ahead. "Just drive. I know a shortcut."

He clamped down on the accelerator, and the Escort leaped forward, rocking down the straightaway past the school, past the stop sign, and left onto Seventeen-Mile Road. Except for a pickup glinting in the sun ahead, the road was clear, and he pushed the pedal harder into the floor.

"They killed Joanne Garrow," Vicky said, another kind of excitement in her voice. "I saw the news on TV."

Father John didn't respond. He knew that she knew they would also kill Megan. Outside the wind kept up a steady banging noise over the hum of the tires on asphalt.

"What happened?" Vicky asked.

Father John held the Escort steady. The wild grasses and scrub brush blurred past. "I don't know for sure. Markham took advantage of the fact that there were a lot of people at the mission this morning. He sent his guide, the guy from Rock Springs. He must have had a gun on her; Megan wouldn't have gone otherwise. Markham called five minutes ago. He wants the tape Joseph made." He glanced at the woman beside him. "Joseph must have gone to see Joanne Garrow and taped the conversation. He probably tried to persuade her to tell the truth. He must have told her he intended to go to the authorities."

"But he couldn't prove any of it," Vicky said. "The police would check the birth and death certificates. Everything would appear normal.

So he had to tape the conversation. Then he must have told her he had the tape. Garrow got nervous and called Markham." She exhaled a long breath. "Where's the tape?"

He slid the plastic box from his pocket and handed it to her. "I've got to make Markham think this is what he's after."

"What's this? The best of opera?"

He glanced over at her. She was lifting the flap, pulling out the small plastic tape.

"How long do you think that's going to fool a man like Markham?"

"Long enough to get Megan away."

Vicky set the tape into his hand, and he stuffed it back into his jacket pocket.

Vicky said, "We have other evidence, John. I found Sharon David's father. His name is Russ Mason. He doesn't want to meet her until the tests confirm that she's his daughter. Then he'll give Gianelli a statement that he was told his baby had died." She talked on about how she'd found the man, how other families might be united through the publicity about Sharon, how Ben might someday find his brother. Ben, Ben, Ben, punctuating her words.

Father John slowed through Fort Washakie and started the climb into the foothills.

"Take the dirt road ahead," she said after a long while. "We'll drive up the back way."

He turned onto the road, still climbing. The hood angled upward. Ahead the road spilled into a meadow of wild grasses ringed with willows and ponderosas. He could see a small log cabin near the trees.

He pulled in at the side of the road about a hundred feet from the meadow. "Wait here," he instructed, cutting the motor. He left the key in the ignition.

"You're going to walk into that meadow?" Vicky placed one hand on his arm, as if to hold him in the car. "You'll be exposed. He'll shoot you."

"Not until he gets this." Father John tapped his pocket and shot her an assuring smile as he got out. Leaning past the door, he said, "If I'm not back in ten minutes, get out of here as fast as you can."

He shut the door quietly and started down the road. When he reached the meadow, he cut along the line of trees. There was a cold bite to the wind that whooshed across the open meadow and slammed his jacket against his chest. He worked his way toward the front of the cabin, then set off through the wild grasses. Parked next to the cabin was a tan Jeep and a green sedan. The cabin looked vacant: stone steps leading to a small porch with shaved-log poles that supported the sloped roof. "Markham!" he shouted.

The front door moved slowly inward. Father John stopped about twenty feet from the steps. A thin man in jeans, wearing a red blanket jacket and black-and-white cowboy boots stepped onto the porch. A white Stetson shaded a smooth-looking face: the jaw jutting forward in an angle of contempt, the eyes dark under the hat brim, and the pinched, scissor-cut mouth.

"Where is she, Markham?" Father John called.

The thin mouth broke into what passed for a smile. "I can assure you, your niece is perfectly fine." He started down the steps. "You have the tape, I trust."

"I brought it, but you won't get it until Megan's in the car." Father John nodded toward the trees.

"I'm afraid you are not calling the shots, Father O'Malley. Give me the tape." He was in the meadow, moving closer, holding out a thin, well-manicured hand.

Father John said, "The tape can send you to prison for the rest of your life, Markham. I have the only copy." The wind gusted around them, like steam bursting from a locomotive. "It's yours as soon as you let Megan go."

The doctor was shaking his head, coming closer. Father John could see the steel glint in his eyes. "You're a stubborn man, O'Malley. I could order Randy to shoot you right now." He gave a nod toward the cabin.

"But then you wouldn't know where I put the tape. You could spend a lot of time looking for it in this meadow, and then you might not find it. But sooner or later someone else would find it."

The doctor stopped. The thin lips drew inward, the eyes narrowed in a conscious assessment. He turned and walked back toward the cabin. "Bring her out!" he shouted.

In an instant Megan stumbled past the door, looking like a thin, scared child, Father John thought, in a white blouse and tan slacks, clumps of red hair falling about her face. Behind her was a young man with a thick neck and wide shoulders inside a bulky denim jacket. One hand pushed a pistol into Megan's ribs; the other jerked her upward, maneuvering her across the porch and down the steps to Markham. Then they started forward into the wind, the doctor gripping the brim of his Stetson.

"Don't believe anything they say, Uncle John!" Megan cried out. "They're going to kill us both. I heard them talking." She gave a sharp yank and pulled free. The guide lunged at her, snapping an arm around her chest and jamming the gun to the side of her head.

"Let her go," Father John said as he moved toward them, fists clenched.

Markham stepped in front of Megan. He lifted one hand and grasped the brim of his hat. "Now, Father . . ." A projected shout, as if he were addressing a crowd. "We are both reasonable men. You see that the girl is alive and well. But you haven't told me where the tape is. How do I know you brought it?"

Father John pulled the plastic box from his pocket and held it up. It rattled in the breeze. "Let her go!" he shouted.

"You can't expect me to do that until I've confirmed you've brought the correct tape." Markham tilted his head toward the parked vehicles. "I must ask you to step over to the Jeep, Father O'Malley. It has a very good tape player."

"Come on, Markham," Father John said — grasping, stalling. Out of the corner of his eye, he glimpsed something in the trees — a movement. *Stay away, Vicky!* He kept his gaze on the doctor. "Do you think I'm fool enough to bring you the wrong tape? This is what you want." He waved the plastic box and plunged on, taking a chance. "Everything Joanne Garrow told Father Keenan." He saw the flash of affirmation in the doctor's eyes, followed by a series of blinks. "She admitted everything. How you took healthy, light-skinned infants and told the mothers their babies had died. How you sold the infants on the black market."

"My God!" Megan struggled to turn toward the doctor.

"Shut up!" the guide shouted, jerking her back.

"Then you murdered your nurse and the coroner, didn't you, Markham? What happened? Did they have enough? Did they tell you they didn't want any more part in stealing the babies?"

The doctor flinched; he looked paler. "If that is what Garrow said on the tape, she was lying. I am not responsible for murder. I have never killed anyone, Father O'Malley. Nor did I condone murder then or now. Unfortunately my associate thought such actions were necessary. My own actions were the best for the infants." The doctor drew in a long, considered breath. "Surely you know the problems the infants were spared, the poverty and alcoholism. They were very fortunate. I can assure you they were placed with the finest families. Given opportunities they would never have had on the reservation. I'm sure today they are productive, happy people."

"They are lost," Father John said. "They are like the birds that flew away and never found their way back."

The doctor gave a brittle laugh. "You've been on the reservation long enough to know what I say is true, Father."

"How much were the babies worth?" Father John said, his throat tight with anger and alarm. The figure in the trees at the edge of his vision was slowly advancing.

A look of mock surprise came into Markham's eyes. "Do you think it was about money?"

"Of course it was about money, Markham. You wanted a clinic in a big city like Los Angeles. You had big plans, big dreams. But your theories were controversial. Thirty-five years ago the banks probably laughed at you, isn't that right? So you found a way to accumulate a large amount of cash very fast."

Markham reared back, and for a moment Father John thought the man would lunge toward him. His muscles tensed in readiness.

"You don't know what you're talking about." The man's voice cracked, and Father John caught the hint of desperation in his tone. "I have devoted my entire career to the well-being of infants. I have always done the best for them that was in my power. You've lost touch with the wider world, Father O'Malley. That is the world I sent the infants into for their own good. But people like you refuse to understand. That is why I must have the tape." He held out a hand and came forward. "Give it to me."

"Here it is." Father John snapped his arm back and pitched the tape into the air, spinning it over the doctor's head, like the curveballs he'd once sailed across home plate. The guide let go of Megan's arm and grabbed at the wind as the tape spun away.

"Run, Megan!" Father John shouted, but she was already dodging, running — a white blur — as he lunged past the doctor. He swung his leg back and brought it forward with all of his strength, kicking at the pistol in the guide's hand. There was a sharp crack, like a tree snapping in lightning, followed by a howl of anguish. The black pistol flipped up and hung in the wind before dropping into the grass. Like watching a film in slow motion, Father John saw the guide folding to the ground, clasping his hand to his chest and rolling in the grass; Markham bending forward with Megan clutching his back, nails raking his face; Vicky running, running, and throwing herself onto the grass.

Suddenly Megan fell back, and the doctor swung around, a fist raised over her. Father John slammed into the man, knocking him sideways as Vicky started screaming, "Stop! Stop!"

She was kneeling on one knee, working herself upright, the pistol in one hand, the other hand steadying her grip. The gun was pointed at Jeremiah Markham, who stared up at her from the ground, eyes wide in disbelief. Little trickles of blood had started from the red scratches across his cheeks.

"Put the gun down," he said in a shaky voice. "There is no need for this kind of violence. We've made our deal. You can leave. I have the tape." He glanced nervously toward the place where the tape had landed. The other man was rolling and moaning a few feet away.

Vicky kept the gun on the man. "You monster. I could kill you myself." Her voice was thick with fury.

Father John moved to her side. Reaching out, he ran his hand along the curve of her arm to her hand. It trembled under his own. Slowly he slipped the gun away.

"Stay down," he ordered the doctor. Still keeping the gun on the man, Father John motioned to Megan and Vicky. "Go to the car." He waited until they had run past the cabin and were out of sight before he began moving backward after them. "I don't want to have to shoot you or your friend," he said. "Stay where you are until we get out of here."

When he reached the corner of the cabin, he jammed the gun into his jacket pocket and started running across the patch of meadow toward the trees. Megan and Vicky were ahead. He caught up, and they turned onto the dirt road. A man stood in front of the Escort, swaying from side to side. He had on blue jeans and a tan jacket. In one hand was a rifle. Father John grabbed the women and pulled them to a stop.

The man slowly raised the rifle and aimed it at them.

30

"Luther Benson!" Vicky's voice rang into the wind. Father John shoved Vicky and Megan into the cluster of willows as the shot exploded in the air and reverberated against the trees. He pushed the women ahead, running, stumbling, crashing through branches that sliced at his hands and tore at his jacket. Megan went down on one knee, and he lifted her up, pushing her after Vicky toward a stand of ponderosas. The wind hissed around them. Then another crash, like thunder. There was the sharp splintering of wood, the sound of Megan screaming: "He's going to kill us!"

Father John spotted some fallen trees and a thicket of scrub brush ahead. Still gripping Megan's arm, he caught up with Vicky and, taking her hand, guided both women to the thicket. Then he stepped ahead and lifted a clump of branches. Wordlessly the women scrambled inside. Just as he dropped the branches, a loud clap split the air. Then: the quiet of the forest, the whoosh of the wind through the ponderosas.

He stayed low, trying to get his bearings. Markham and the guide were in the meadow beyond the stand of trees to the west; Luther Benson, on the road to the east. "Stay here," he said into the thicket.

Vicky pushed back a branch and grabbed his

arm. "You don't know Luther. He's lived here all his life. He's an expert hunter. He'll see you."

He's a drunk, Father John wanted to say. He had seen the unsteadiness of the man, the sideways lurch as he'd raised the rifle.

Father John shook himself free of Vicky's grasp. Bending over, he ran among the trees, moving to the southeast. He thought he heard the sound of sirens in the distance, but the sound faded in and out, like that of sirens in a dream. Through the trees he caught intermittent flashes of Luther Benson's tan jacket. Keeping the man in view, Father John worked his way behind him. The leaves rustled beneath his boots, and suddenly the lawyer swung around. He lifted the rifle.

Father John remained still, his breath hard in his chest. After a moment the man turned and resumed his unsteady walk along the edge of the trees. Father John stepped when Luther stepped, stopped when he stopped — a pas de deux — as he pushed through the branches. He was within ten feet, staring at the man's back. He slipped the pistol from his pocket.

Suddenly Luther raised the rifle. Another crack broke the air, as if the clouds had collided, and in that instant Father John sprinted into the road and jammed the pistol through the tan jacket and into the man's spine. "Drop the rifle!" he shouted into his ear.

The man stood motionless. Slowly he let the rifle drop to his side.

"I take it you're that Indian priest."

"Set the rifle on the ground." Father John pushed the pistol harder against the man's back. The odor of whiskey drifted between them.

"I don't think you're gonna shoot me," Luther said. "I don't think you or any other priest's got the guts."

"Don't bet on it." Father John drew out the words. In his mind was the image of Vicky and Megan huddled in the thicket. He would do what he had to do to protect them. He kept one eye on the road ahead, half expecting Markham and the guide to appear.

"You're just like that other fool priest." The lawyer's voice was raspy — the voice of alcohol and cigarettes, of dim nights in smoke-filled bars. The rifle jerked at his side. "Why couldn't you let things be? What happened is over and done with. People gone on with their lives. Why did that old fool have to come back and stir it all up?"

Father John drew in a sharp breath. He understood. "You're the man who shot Father Joseph," he said, his voice tight with anger. "You killed a helpless man."

"Helpless!" the lawyer barked. He tilted his head sideways and spat a large chunk of phlegm into the wind. Specks of moisture prickled Father John's face. It smelled of whiskey.

"You got that wrong!" Benson yelled. "That priest was gonna blow everything to hell. Couldn't live with it any longer, he said. What

298

the hell did he have to worry about? He wasn't in on anything. Just happened the little nurse went and got religion and thought she was goin' to hell if she didn't confess all her sins. Well, I sent her to hell all right. Just too bad I didn't do it sooner, before she unloaded on the priest." He gave a quick shrug. "What's it matter? I told Markham. The priest's wettin' his pants, he's so scared. He's gonna beat the hell out of here. That's exactly what he did."

He stopped. Father John could see the muscles in the sides of his neck bulging. "I told Markham, quit worrying. That priest's got that confessional-seal thing. He's never gonna spill his guts. For thirty-five years I was right. Then, what d'ya know, here comes Keenan, back to the reservation. Pays a visit to Garrow and tells her she's gotta come clean." He threw his head back and gave a hard, tight laugh. "The man was crafty. I'll give him that. He was a crafty old buzzard. He had a tape recorder on him. So he gets her to talkin', and all the time he's tapin' away. Then he lowers the boom. Says he's gonna take the tape to the police. That she doesn't have any choice but to tell the truth. Well, he was wrong."

"You killed the woman," Father John said. At the edge of his vision he saw a flicker of movement in the willows next to the road, like a sudden burst of wind. "Why, Benson? Did Joanne Garrow start to get nervous? Did she want to tell the truth? Did she come to you and say it was time to tell the truth? Is that what the coroner did thirty-five years ago? Get nervous and want to tell the truth? Is that why you killed him?"

"Oh, Jesus." The man shook his head. "You don't understand anything. I couldn't have him and the nurse shootin' off their mouths and ruinin' the reputation of Benson and Benson in these parts. We were the most important law firm around. Everybody respected the firm. Dad was still alive then. I wasn't gonna let them destroy everything he'd worked for, so I took care of them." He stopped for a moment. Then he said, "Why do you care, anyway? You're not getting out of here alive. Markham and Randy are up there." He tilted his head toward the meadow. "You're not going to shoot us. You're not going to shoot any of us."

Suddenly he lurched forward and swung around. Father John saw the tremor in the man's hand as he lifted the rifle and the blurred, dazed look in his eyes. "Shoot-out time at the O.K. Corral, O'Malley," he said. "Let's see who's gonna shoot first."

Father John stared into the black tunnel of the rifle barrel, his finger brushing the pistol's trigger — a tiny, cold piece of metal that could snuff out a man's life, a murderer's life. He was sure of one thing: he could pull the trigger faster than the half-drunk man in front of him. And his shot would be more accurate.

In the distance, floating through the trees, came the sound of sirens, definite and real. He had faced down drunks before, but never one with a gun. Still, if he could keep the man talking a few more minutes . . . He let his hand fall, pointing the pistol to the ground. "You hear that, Benson? The police are on the way. You can't shoot me and get out of here before they arrive. They'll block you off. They know everything."

"They don't have any proof." The rifle drifted sideways in the wind.

"They have the tape."

"You're lying!" The yell burst like the cry of a wounded animal. Benson hunched over the rifle.

Father John stared into the barrel, a circle of blackness. Then, out of the corner of his eyes, he saw the figure of a man careen out of the willows. The man slammed into the lawyer, knocking him off his feet and sending the rifle scuttling across the road. Father John dove for it, gripping the smooth, cold metal barrel. As he got to his feet, he saw Leonard kneeling on the man's stomach, pounding a fist into his face.

Father John rammed the pistol into his pocket and grabbed the caretaker's shoulder. "Enough," he said, pulling the Indian back.

Leonard got to his feet. His breath came hard and fast. His face was dark with anger. "Arnold and me knew you was gonna need some help," he said, gasping. "We come up the main road. Heard the shooting, so we parked the pickup. Arnold grabbed a tire iron, and we started through the trees. He seen those other two guys about to get into the Jeep out in the meadow. He says one of 'em was the guy that took Megan, so he went after 'em. I came after the sound of gun-shots."

The sirens were closer now, a shrill wail into the wind. The sound of tires crunching gravel and engines straining uphill came from the road behind. Leonard grinned. "Hope you don't mind, Father. Soon's you left the mission, I called Agent Gianelli and Chief Banner."

Father John waited at the Escort. Vicky stood beside him, hunched inside his jacket. He had taken it off and placed it around her shoulders against the chill of the wind. Megan had slipped into the backseat. The door was slightly ajar. No one spoke. A string of police cars stood at the side of the road, blue and red lights flashing against the trees, radio static sputtering. Gianelli's 4x4 stood in front of the line. Several policemen had headed into the meadow. Others were milling about. Every once in a while one stooped over, scooped up something, and held it out, examining it. A bullet. A cartridge.

Markham and the guide sat in the backseat of the nearest police car. Luther Benson had been hustled into the back of another car. Father John tilted his face into the wind. It smelled of dry leaves and dust. The sun had disappeared beyond the treetops, and there was the bite of fall in the air. He glanced at Vicky. "It's over," he said.

He heard her gasp. "It will never be over."

Gianelli and Banner broke from the policemen and started up the road toward them, twin expressions of grimness on their faces. As they approached, the rear door pushed open, and Megan stepped out. Gianelli faced her. "I just put the best-known doctor in the country and one of the local luminaries under arrest for kidnapping and possible assault. There better not be any misunderstandings."

Father John slipped an arm around his niece. "You forgot murder and conspiracy," he told the agent. "Check Luther Benson's rifle. You've got the man who killed Father Joseph and Joanne Garrow."

"What I don't have is the motive." The agent looked from Father John to Vicky. "Okay, let's hear that theory of yours."

Vicky began talking. She explained about the clinic, the stolen babies, the elaborate black-market operation Markham had set up, the nurse and coroner who had ended up dead, and Sharon David, one of the stolen infants, whose father Vicky had found. The agent never took his eyes off her. Banner moved in closer, arms folded, eyes rigid in anger. As Vicky talked, Father John could feel Megan begin to shiver, as if a winter storm had blown through.

When Vicky finished, Father John told the agent about Father Joseph: how he had returned to St. Francis and gone to see Garrow, how he had taped the conversation, how Markham had

303

contacted Luther, who lured Father Joseph out to Thunder Lane and shot him. Then Markham probably panicked and sent his hunting guide to the mission to find the tape, and the guide had attacked Megan.

Gianelli slipped one hand into his jacket pocket and withdrew a plastic audiotape box. "This the tape you're talking about."

Vicky let out a little laugh. "You're an opera fan, Gianelli. You'll like that tape."

The agent lowered his head and looked up, shifting his gaze from Father John to Vicky. "You came out here to get Megan with a phony tape? You could've all been killed. When are you gonna . . ." He let the thought trail off and took in a long breath. "Okay, okay. Somewhere on that mission, Father Joseph hid the real tape. Not in his office. Not in his bedroom, and probably not where somebody else would've seen it or accidentally picked it up. So you tell me, John, where are we going to find it?"

"If I knew the answer —" Father John stopped. He did know the answer. Father Joseph had left the tape where no one would find it, except, possibly, another priest.

31

"Wait here," Father John said.

The small group stood in front of the church — Vicky and Megan, Gianelli, Banner, and Leonard and Arnold. Shadowy figures in the fading gray light. He walked up the steps and let himself through the heavy wooden doors. The church was dark. A tiny red light flickered in front of the tepee-shaped tabernacle on a table in the sanctuary.

He flipped the switch inside the door. Soft white light flooded down the aisle and lapped across the pews as he turned toward the door on the right. A bronze-colored sign in the center said RECONCILIATION ROOM. He opened the door and flipped another switch.

In the middle of the closet-sized room were two chairs, side by side. Between them, a wooden grate with armrests on both sides. He had spent hours in this room, sitting in the chair on the far side of the grate, leaning on the armrest, listening to the fears and pain, the regrets and sorrows, the firm amendments to sin no more.

He glanced around the room: the cream-colored stucco walls, the crucifix hanging above his chair, the painting of Jesus with black hair and the sharpened features of the Arapaho — a forgiving Jesus, arms outstretched toward the people. He walked around the chairs, checking the legs, the stand on which the grate was balanced. No sign of a tape.

He sat down on the priest's side and leaned toward the grate. The church was perfectly still. A faint smell of cedar lingered in the air. He ran his hand along the top of the armrest, then underneath. Nothing but smooth, vacant wood. Then his fingers touched the hard lump jammed against the stand beneath the armrest. He slid out of the chair and down onto one knee. Gray duct tape held a small plastic box against the stand. Taped next to the box was a pocket-sized recorder.

He pulled the duct tape back slowly and slipped out the plastic box. Then the recorder. Holding them in one hand, he got to his feet and retraced his steps, snapping off the lights as he went. Outside he handed the box and recorder to Gianelli. "Here's your proof beyond a reasonable doubt," he said.

Gianelli's Jeep led the parade of vehicles around Circle Drive: the chief's police car, Leonard's pickup. Megan turned away silently and started down the alley toward the guest house, leaving Father John and Vicky standing in front of the church. He took her arm, and they started across the grounds to her Bronco out on the straight stretch of road where she had left it.

"The media will have a feeding frenzy," she said. "Movie star stolen from parents as infant finds Indian father after thirty-five years. No publicity department could have dreamed up a better public relations campaign." She stopped and turned to him. In the shadows, he saw the light dancing in her eyes. "There are others like Sharon, looking at themselves in the mirror, wondering where they belong. Maybe they'll find their way home." They started walking again. "Like the birds," she said quietly.

They reached the Bronco, and he opened her door. The keys still dangled from the ignition, a flash of silver in the gathering darkness. She slid inside, and holding the door, he leaned toward her.

"Vicky," he began, reluctant to let her go, searching for the words that would allow her to return, that would ensure they could still be friends. "I wish it hadn't happened. I wish Father Joseph . . ."

She reached out and touched his hand. "I know," she said.

32

A rectangle of light from the lamp fell over the study, framing the desk and wingback chairs, a patch of carpet. The residence creaked into the night. Father John read again through the names Vicky had given him. Esther and Thomas Tallman. Rayleen and Lucas Holden. Betty and Cyrus Elk. Marie and Russ Mason . . . The list covered the page. A litany of loss. The next weeks would be filled with prayer services and counseling sessions for families riven again by the pain of thirty-five years ago.

The moccasin telegraph had beaten the nightly television news with the story: famous doctor and well-known local attorney arrested on charges of kidnapping, interference with parental custody, endangerment of a child, conspiracy. Murder charges were pending. Hunting guide held on charges of kidnapping, burglary, assault with a deadly weapon, conspiracy.

The phone had hardly stopped ringing. Voices hushed with shock. Could the unspeakable be true? He promised to let people know the minute he had any more news. He promised to schedule a special Mass where everyone could come together to grieve and pray for courage. He'd refilled his coffee mug two, three, four times — he'd lost count — trying to bolster his own courage.

Another jangle into the quiet. Reluctantly he reached for the receiver.

"John?"

He knew the Provincial's voice. "How are you, Bill?" he said.

"I expected you to be on a plane to Boston." The voice was sharp with impatience.

"Yes, well, there's been a new development. The FBI and police have arrested Joseph's murderer."

"I'm watching CNN, John. I'm listening to a reporter standing in front of the Lander courthouse talking about how a mission priest led the authorities to an alleged murderer and operator of a black-market baby ring. What is going on out there?"

"Trust me, Bill. It's over. The mission will soon be back to normal."

"Trust you? Trust you?" the Provincial's voice boomed through the line.

Father John moved the receiver a couple of inches away. "Remember, Bill, you don't have anyone else who wants this job."

He hung up, folded the list of names, and set it in the center drawer. Just as he was about to switch off the light, a soft knock sounded, and Megan slipped past the door, into the scrim of light. She perched on one of the wingback chairs. She had tied her hair back, but a couple of red curls corkscrewed around her face. The blue eyes were filled with pain.

"You okay?" he asked.

She gave a little nod. "Not really. I keep thinking about that jerk outside the church this morning. How he came up behind me and rammed something hard in my back and said, 'Just walk real ladylike to the tan Jeep over there.' I was shaking all over, I was so scared."

She had told him the same story earlier. It had produced the same stab of guilt that he felt now. "Megan," he said, allowing her name to float in the air a moment, like a melody. "I'm so sorry about everything that has happened to you here."

"It wasn't your fault." She shook her head. "Besides, you came after me today. You know, Uncle John, that was a very dumb thing to do. You could have gotten killed. It was just what my Dad would've done."

She catapulted to her feet and walked to the window, beyond the light. Turning back, she said, "I didn't tell you that I called Mom this morning before Mass. I told her if she didn't tell me the truth, I would never go home again. She said I didn't have to threaten her, that she'd already decided to tell me. So . . ." She paused. "Now I know what happened."

Father John didn't say anything. The silence drifted into the shadows. After a moment she walked back and stood in front of the desk. "Promise me you won't tell Dad that I ever doubted . . ." She stopped. Her eyes glowed feverish in the light. "Promise me you'll keep this a secret. I don't want to hurt him."

He nodded. "A good secret to keep."

She exhaled a long breath. "I'm going home for a while before I go back to New York. I'm leaving tomorrow, right after the court hearing for Markham and the others. But I'll be back to testify at the trials."

Father John got up, walked around the desk, and took her hand. He would miss this niece of his, this part of himself. "When you come back, the guest house will be yours. It will probably be quiet around here."

"Quiet," she repeated. "Well, that will take some getting used to."

33

"He's not going to come," Sharon David said.

"He'll be here." Vicky glanced at the profile of the woman next to her in the Bronco: large, black sunglasses balanced on the bridge of her nose, blue scarf wrapped turban-style around her head. A movie star.

Outside the window the pale yellow sun arched into a morning sky of clear-rinsed blue. Vicky had picked up the actress at the dude ranch at a quarter to six — more than an hour ago. They had driven to Ethete and turned down the dirt road to the Sun Dance grounds. Clumps of scrub brush dotted the grounds, and dried leaves scuttled in the breeze. This was where Russ had said he wanted to meet his daughter — a sacred place.

There was no sign of reporters. No cameras or microphones, no shouted questions. After Markham's arrest last week, hordes of reporters had descended over the area. They camped outside the courthouse and swarmed over the reservation. They set up a permanent post outside the dude ranch and outside her office.

She had become adept at dodging microphones and ignoring cameras. Her own face stared at her from television screens and the front pages of newspapers, along with photos of Sharon David darting into the ranch house,

Gianelli caught midway up the stairs of the courthouse, and John O'Malley hurrying across the mission grounds.

"I wouldn't blame him if he didn't come."

"He'll come," Vicky said. Then: "Why do you say that?"

"What happened changed his life. It changed mine. I don't blame him for not wanting to try to remake the past. It's impossible, you know."

Vicky nodded. She did know.

"Nothing can make it all right," the actress went on. "I lost the chance to grow up here with my own mother and father, my own family, my own people. My father lost his daughter. And more. He lost his wife. Nothing can change that. It doesn't matter what happens to the famous Jeremiah Markham and the others."

"You're wrong, Sharon," Vicky said. "It does matter. Markham will spend the rest of his life in prison, where he belongs." She didn't say that he would probably be sent to a medium-security federal prison. The doctor was willing to explain everything in exchange for such a sentence. He was already leading Gianelli and the U.S. attorney through the tangled web of a black-market that extended from the clinic in Lander to Denver, Seattle, San Francisco, and Los Angeles — the cities where he had sent Dawn James to deliver the tiny infants. And the doctor was willing to testify against Luther Benson, who would probably also spend the rest of his life in prison. No doubt the doctor would also testify against his hunting guide, who had been charged with kidnapping, assault, breaking and entering, and theft.

"Let's go, Vicky," Sharon said. "My father doesn't want anything to do with me, and I can't blame him."

"That's not true." Vicky let her window down a few inches. The cool morning air washed inside, restoring her own confidence. She glanced at her silver wristwatch. It was past seven. "He's your father. He'll be here." Yesterday Vicky had received the laboratory report on DNA tests that proved Sharon David was the daughter of Russ Mason.

"Let's go." The actress shrank against the door, behind the dark glasses, the swirl of blue silk around her hair. "I've been looking for my parents for a long time. When I came here, I knew I had come home. I had found the missing part of myself. I was one of the people. It will have to be enough." She groped for the door handle. "If you don't start the car, I'll get out and walk."

Vicky turned the key dangling from the ignition, sensing the reluctance in her fingers. The engine came to life, and the Bronco started forward across the bare dirt, bouncing over washboard ruts. The leaves crackled like fire beneath the tires. A gust of wind washed over the hood and roof as she wheeled toward Ethete Road.

A brown truck was slowing on the road. It

turned and started toward them. Russ Mason was behind the wheel. The silver band on his cowboy hat sparkled in the sun.

Vicky rocked to a stop. Over the shush of the breeze, she heard the gasps of the woman next to her. The truck slid to a stop a few feet away. Russ got out and stood for a moment at the opened door — head high, shoulders back, like a warrior. He had on a black cowboy hat, a white shirt with a silver bolo tie dangling in front, and sharply creased blue jeans stacked over black cowboy boots. Raising his right hand, he tipped his hat toward the woman on the passenger side.

Sharon yanked off her sunglasses and tossed them onto the dashboard. They clanked against the windshield. Then, dipping her head, she began unwinding the blue scarf. She tossed it over the glasses, where it rippled like water in the sun. She ran her fingers through her black hair, letting it fall free around her shoulders, and pressed her palms against her cheeks a moment. Her hands were unadorned, the nails clear.

Drawing in a long breath, she got out and closed the door. Vicky watched as Russ stretched out his arms and Sharon David stepped into them.

After a moment they started walking away. In the rearview mirror, Vicky caught them moving toward the Sun Dance area, arm in arm, heads bent together — nodding, nodding.

She stepped on the accelerator and drove

around the truck. In the breeze drifting past her window came a faraway murmur of voices and the tinkling of laughter as high and light as the whistle of an eagle bone.

34

Father John said the prayers of the Mass slowly. He offered the prayers for the people and for Cyrus Elk. Yesterday Father John had stopped in at the hospital. The old man was unconscious, but Father John had talked to him anyway. He'd told him that the son he had thought he'd lost thirty-five years ago was alive somewhere. Cyrus had seemed to relax, his expression became calmer, his sleep quieter. Father John wasn't surprised when the call came later from Cyrus's granddaughter saying the old man had passed away.

The congregation joined in the prayers, a reverent murmuring that filled the church. Leonard stood at his elbow, the musicians huddled around the drum beating out the rhythms of the hymns, voices high-pitched and mournful. When he walked to the lectern, a cloud of quiet fell over the pews. He had spent last evening working on the sermon, coaxing out of himself the words he wanted to say. Later on today, two graves would be exhumed in St. Francis Cemetery.

Now he pushed his notes aside and clasped his hands, looking out over the upturned faces. "You are a people who have suffered much," he began. "There were times in the past when your children were taken from you. Now they have been taken again from you."

He stopped. His eyes roamed the congregation. Sitting in a front pew were the Mason family: Sharon David, Russ, a middle-aged woman, and two teenaged girls who looked a lot like the movie star. Vicky sat in a back pew. Beside her, shoulders erect, head angled slightly in suspended judgment, was Ben Holden. The narrowed black eyes in the handsome face, watching him.

Father John went on: "May God have mercy on those who were a party to this injustice. May God have mercy on those who knew and did nothing."

A hush fell over the church, as if breath itself had been stopped. He saw Vicky's eyes close, her head drop. He said, "Please try to remember that the Shining Man Above does not forget you. In your pain, please try to remember His love for you."

As Father John stepped back, Will Standing Bear rose from the front pew and walked to the lectern. He cleared his throat — a low growl into the microphone, echoing across the church. "We have heard the words you say to us, Father. We take them to our hearts, and they comfort us. Now we must think what we are to do for the future. We believe our children are alive. We believe they will return someday, just like Sharon David has come home to the people."

He was quiet a moment, drawing in a long breath. "We're gonna start a registry." The words boomed through the church; people moved in the pews, reaching out, clasping hands. "Arapaho families and people that have been adopted can put their names on the registry. We're gonna try to get families matched up. We're not gonna stop workin' till all our children out there" — he waved toward the stained glass windows and the world beyond — "find their way home."

The elder brought the snake of the microphone closer. "I'm askin' Father John here to keep our registry at St. Francis. Everybody's gonna know exactly where it is. Won't be no confusion. The registry'll be in the same place, don't matter how long it takes for families to get matched up." The old man glanced back at Father John. "I'm askin' you, Father, to do this for the people."

Father John kept his gaze on the elder: the black eyes as deep as pools, the leathery face. He searched for the words. "Thank you for your trust," he managed.

Father John waited with Esther Tallman a few feet from the open grave. It was marked by a small wooden cross with the words GEORGE REDWING TALLMAN, BELOVED SON. Gathered close by was the Tallman clan — Esther's children and grandchildren, nieces and nephews. Their pickups and trucks lined the narrow road circling the perimeter of St. Francis Cemetery. A warm wind swept across the bare-dirt cemetery, rattling the plastic flowers and tossing little spirals of dust into the air. It whipped at the back of Father John's windbreaker.

Banner and Gianelli stood at the edge of the opened grave, their eyes on the man shoveling dirt into a growing pile at their feet. Close by were a couple of U.S. attorneys, the local lawyer representing Benson, and two lawyers in blue suits and tasseled loafers, gray with dust, who had flown in from Los Angeles to represent Markham.

Suddenly Gianelli turned away and walked over. "It's just what we expected," the agent said. His voice was nearly lost in the swoosh of the wind. "Nothing in that coffin except a few rocks."

Banner joined the agent. The police chief's face was flushed, his eyes angry. Turning from side to side, like a chief in the Old Time addressing the people, he said, "We got the evidence to put those bastards into hell."

Father John slipped an arm around Esther's shoulder. She was trembling. "All these years I been thinkin' of my boy like he was livin' somewhere else." She spoke so quietly, he had to bend his head to hear what she was saying. "Every day I wonder, what's he gonna do today? Maybe he's gonna take a trip to some place far away. Maybe he's gonna see the world. Or maybe he's gonna ride his pony out on the plains. Every day I think he's doin' something different." She straightened her shoulders and raised her chin. Peering at some point on the horizon, she said, "He's thirty-five years old now. He's tall and handsome like his father." She gave a little sob.

The other members of the clan started forward, arms reaching for the old woman. Father John stepped back as the family embraced her, enclosed her in their circle. He watched a moment, then started along the rows of graves toward the center of the cemetery, where another man was shoveling dirt. The Holden grave was also being exhumed. "We can establish a pattern by exhuming two graves," Gianelli had explained earlier. There was the steady, monotonous scrape of a metal shovel against the hard-packed dirt.

Across the cemetery, Father John could see a line of pickups snaking along the road, a brown truck in the lead. It passed the parked vehicles of the Tallman clan and stopped. The driver's door snapped open, and Ben Holden got out, tall and confident looking in dark blazer and tan cowboy hat. He strode around the truck and pulled open the passenger door. His eyes never left the woman inside.

Father John stood still, barely aware of the pickups moving along the road and obscuring his view for half seconds. He watched Vicky slide out of the truck and wait as Ben closed the door behind her. She was looking up at Ben, telling him something, and he leaned toward her. There was an air of expectancy and solicitude about him, like that of a lover.

It was as it should be, Father John thought. She had the right to some happiness. She had the right to reclaim her own family, to reclaim the man who had once been her husband and who still wanted her. Of course Ben wanted her.

Father John pulled his gaze away and stared across the cemetery at the expanse of plains that ran into the horizon and melted into the everlasting blue sky. The days and weeks and months ahead would be filled with work, he told himself. There would be counseling sessions, prayer services and special Masses, the registry to get up and running. There would be no time for his thoughts to drift into what ifs or maybes. The people here needed him; he had obligations and he would honor them. They would consume him.

A gust of wind caught at his windbreaker. He pulled up the zipper and started again toward the grave. The attorneys had already positioned themselves close to the edge. Members of the Holden clan were also making their way along the rows of graves and, out of the corner of his eye, Father John saw Gianelli hurrying over. From behind came the scuffing sound of footsteps, and then the blue flash of Banner's uniform at his side.

"The Holden clan's here." The chief sounded out of breath.

"I know."

"Vicky's come with 'em."

"I know."

"Moccasin telegraph says Ben and Vicky might be gettin' back together."

"I know."

They stopped. In the other man's eyes, Father John saw the quiet look of understanding. He rested a hand on the chief's shoulder and said, "Thanks, Banner." Then he turned and went to meet the Holden clan.